OTHER HALVES

OTHER HALVES

Nick Alexander

BLACK & WHITE PUBLISHING

First published 2014
by Black & White Publishing Ltd
29 Ocean Drive, Edinburgh EH6 6JL

1 3 5 7 9 10 8 6 4 2   13 14 15 16

ISBN: 978 1 84502 764 3

ALBA | CHRUTHACHAIL

A CIP catalogue record for this book is available from the British Library.

Typeset by Iolaire Typesetting, Newtonmore
Printed and bound by Grafica Veneta S. p. A., Italy

ACKNOWLEDGEMENTS

Thanks to Rosemary for being my touchstone, and to Allan, Giovanni, Vince, David, Paul, Sarah and Jenny for all your help with the text. Thanks to Marinella for your help and support, and to Black & White for making this book a reality. Thanks to my "framily" for being there and to my readers for all their enthusiasm – you make it all worthwhile. Finally, thanks to Lolo for all the cuddles he supplied while this was being written. It made the time spent writing this book so much nicer.

ONE

Hannah

I was in the middle of a family holiday in France when I walked out on my marriage. Some would say that I could have chosen my moment better, but the appearance at our holiday villa of the man I had fallen in love with in my twenties – a man who unfortunately happened to be my fiancé's brother – not only provided the opportunity, but opened the floodgates on a tsunami of revelations that revealed my marriage to be built upon nothing more substantial than a sea of untruths.

My husband, Cliff, had been revealed as a compulsive liar – to keep us apart, he had told me that James had died, when in fact he had simply been living in Australia – and my feelings for James were rekindled with the same intensity as fifteen years earlier.

But though one could explain my walking out of that door in terms of these events – my attraction to James and my betrayal by Cliff – in hindsight, I think that would be somewhat missing the point.

What really happened that day was that my bubble of steely self-control burst. A muscle that I had been exercising, stretched to its limit in order to keep myself centred in the middle of my life, gave way. The desire to break free, to live something new, to change not this, not that, but *everything* about my life became, in an instant, irresistible.

Perhaps it *was* what people call a "midlife crisis". Some buy sports cars, others have affairs, and perhaps it was a similar thing going on here, only in my case, it didn't build slowly enough for me to identify small safety valves that might enable me to get by. In my case, the water suddenly boiled and blew the top right off the pressure cooker.

I blamed Cliff, of course, for making a lie of our marriage, and I thanked James for returning and providing a catalyst and a suitable destination, but the truth is, I think, that both were almost innocent bystanders in a much larger process grounded not in events but in some internal body-clock. I truly believe now that the explosion would have happened anyway; it was just a matter of time.

So, one minute I was sitting on the bed feeling trapped in my marriage and confused about my feelings, and the next I was walking away from the house with a bag over my shoulder – my husband protesting behind me.

I don't know what Cliff was thinking as he watched me walk away, but I expect he thought I had gone mad. Perhaps I had, a little.

As Cliff didn't know that James was staying in the little auberge down the road, it certainly must have seemed crazy of me to head off on foot without any apparent destination.

When I got to the auberge, I asked Jean-Jacques, the barman, if he could put me through to James Parker's room.

"Il est parti," he said, which I somehow managed to understand: James had already left.

I surprised myself by thinking, *"Oh, OK then."*

One part of me watched the other react calmly, and was surprised at the lack of emotion. That was the moment I first suspected that this was bigger than Cliff or James – that this was about escape.

I ordered a glass of wine and, because all the seats outside were wet from the recent rainstorm, I sat in a window seat and watched steam rising from the ground. I thought, "*So, no James.*"

I felt unexpectedly calm and strangely wise. It was such an unusual feeling that I thought, as I sipped my wine, that I might be having some kind of nervous breakdown.

It was a surprise, and I wondered if all the melodrama hadn't perhaps been because I needed to be alone. As a wife and a mother, day after day, you forget to notice just how stifling, how suffocating motherhood and marriage can feel. After the drama of the day, a glass of wine, alone, in an empty bar felt like everything I had ever wanted. It crossed my mind that this might be a momentary need, that perhaps I would want, in an hour or so, to return to the villa to carry on as if nothing had happened.

Jean-Jacques brought me a plate of nibbles and said something that I didn't understand.

"I'm sorry," I reminded him. "I don't speak French."

"Ah . . ." he said. "Will you be stay 'ere? In the 'otel?"

Exactly as he said these words, the door to the hotel lobby opened, James reappeared, and my heart did a little somersault.

At first he didn't see me, and I didn't say a word – I just watched him and thought about my feelings.

Jean-Jacques returned to the desk and retrieved James' room key from a board. Jean-Jacques glanced in my direction and so James turned and saw me sitting with my bag and my glass of wine. He broke into a smile – a lopsided, confused smile – and said, "Hannah?" and my heart fluttered again. So my feelings for him were real, after all.

"Hannah!" he said again, distractedly taking the key that Jean-Jacques was proffering and crossing the room to where I sat. "What are you doing here?" he asked, crouching down beside me.

"I . . ." I stammered.

James raised his eyebrows expectantly.

"I think I've left him."

James nodded. "Wow," he said.

"I thought you'd gone. I thought I'd missed you."

"Nah, I just went to get some food. I didn't think you were coming."

"Yes," I replied. "I know."

"Are you . . . ?"

"Yes?"

"I don't know," James said, looking hopeful and scared at the same time. "Are you . . . here for me? Or just . . ."

"I'm not sure," I said, aware that I was sounding less enthusiastic than I intended. "I think so."

James nodded slowly. "D'you want me to go?"

I shook my head. "God, no!" I said. "I'm just . . . I feel a bit strange. It's all been a bit much."

James glanced at the barman, then back at me. "Do you want to go up to the room?" he asked.

I sipped my wine and stared outside for a moment before I replied, a little robotically, "No, actually, I think I'd like you to take me somewhere else."

James nodded thoughtfully.

"Can we do that? Can we go somewhere away from here?" I asked, with increasing urgency. "Can we just get out of here

4

and go stay somewhere else?" I suddenly needed to be as far from Cliff as possible.

James nodded. "Sure," he said, standing and offering me a hand. "Sure we can."

The hotel in Antibes was beautiful. It was set on the ramparts behind the old town, overlooking the sea.

We had barely spoken during the drive there, just sitting side by side in a weird, numbed silence, but James seemed OK about this. He seemed to understand that the day had been monumental, and that it was perhaps normal that this hadn't been a passionate falling into each other's arms.

The receptionist asked, "A twin room or a double?" and I replied without thinking, "A double." I think that was the moment both of us realised that this was really going to happen.

The receptionist took our names down and assumed that we were married. I was – stupidly – surprised to find that James and I shared the same surname. It hadn't crossed my mind that his being Cliff's brother would make hotel check-ins that much easier. And then we followed the porter up to the room.

Our room had the most stunning sea view, and the afternoon sun was low enough to be flooding through the windows.

While James tipped the porter, I opened the French doors, then stood on the tiny balcony and sniffed at the air. It seemed like the freshest, purest, most oxygenated air I had ever breathed.

James came and stood behind me, so close that I could feel his breath on my neck, and after a moment, I reached for his hands and pulled his arms around me.

He nuzzled my neck and my spine tingled and he said, "I'm so glad you're here."

And like some other, younger, more confident woman I barely remembered from way back, I said, "Yes, I know," and I turned to kiss him.

My newfound confidence lasted precisely until I had to undress in front of him; after all, it had been fifteen years since I had shown myself to anyone other than Cliff. This time around, I was closer to forty than twenty. Plus I had had a baby in the intervening years.

I had never been that sure how attractive Cliff had found me, and though I now realised that this sense of doubt might not have been entirely of my own making, I still felt incredibly uneasy about my body.

I broke free from James' embrace just long enough to pull the blinds and switch the lights off. Daylight was still filtering around the edges, but it was certainly an improvement. If James did notice my stretch marks or cellulite, it certainly didn't put him off his stride and that reassured me sufficiently that I was able to relax – just enough – to enjoy sleeping with him.

We stayed in that hotel for five nights, eating in little local seafood restaurants, wandering the streets of the old town and making love in the semi-shade of our room.

Though occasionally I would think of Cliff and my vision would tint red with rage or blue with guilt, I mainly managed to push every other aspect of my situation from my mind, and for five days and five nights, I let myself live in the moment. I felt a little crazy, but that craziness felt heavenly.

Jill, my sister, phoned a couple of times from the villa, and I reassured her that I was fine, thanked her for looking after my son, Luke, and headed her off when she tried to tell me anything about Cliff. Whatever it was, I didn't want to hear it. Whatever it was, I couldn't *bear* to hear it.

In Antibes, we visited the Picasso museum, which had beautiful floor tiles but little else of note – "It's a bit shit really, isn't it?" was James' comment – and another day we drove along the coast around the stunning shallows of Cap d'Antibes past the millionaires' residences, on to the golden beaches of Golfe-Juan and then Juan-les-Pins, and then Cannes, where, sitting on a sandy beach with James' arms around me, I wept for the mess that, unexpectedly, my life had become.

"It'll all be OK, Hannah," James said, but I didn't believe him. I couldn't see any way that could possibly be true.

Opposite the beach in Cannes we could see two small islands that looked gorgeous, so the next day we returned and took the small ferry out to the larger of them. Here, we wandered around the island, pausing to kiss, or picnic, or sit on the beach and stare back at the mainland, where everything seemed, from this calm haven, so unreasonably chaotic. Armed with pots of lavender honey bought from the monks, and over a rougher sea – the wind had got up – we travelled back, eating in a gorgeous but outrageously expensive restaurant in Le Suquet, before driving back to Antibes.

James was gorgeous throughout: a little abrupt at times, a little vulgar at others, but thoughtful and kind and, above all, undemanding. I think he understood that for our time together to be anything but horrific, reality had to be suspended. And that required avoiding whole areas of discussion, specifically anything pertaining to the future or the past.

At the end of the holiday, I bought a plane ticket so that I could fly home with James.

The horrid security personnel at the airport confiscated my pots of honey – apparently they were potentially explosive – and, ridiculously, I worried that, as they were the only thing I had bought with James to take home, this was somehow a bad omen.

It wasn't until we were actually seated side by side on that EasyJet flight that James asked me, rather nervously, "So what happens now?"

"I don't know," I told him. I purposely hadn't projected any further than passport control.

"Do you just go back to Cliff?" James asked.

I shook my head. "I don't think I can," I said.

"Do you like me?" he asked.

I laughed. "Can't you tell that?"

James nodded. "Well, I can hang around, or I can head back to Oz," he said, once the safety demonstrations were over.

I nodded. "Then hang around."

"Yes?"

"Definitely."

"Will you go back to the house?"

"Luke's there," I said, simply. "So, yes, initially at least . . . God, James. I don't know . . ."

"I could just find somewhere to stay then. Somewhere not too far from you. I can stay for a while. Ryan, my manager, is running the farm."

I covered my eyes with my palms, trying to think, then dropped them and said, "Yes. Then please stay."

"And then we just, what?" James asked. "See how things pan out?"

I nodded. "I don't know how else to play it," I said. "I'm sorry."

James nodded. "Suits me fine," he said. "I'm cool with that."

It's strange that those are the only words we exchanged on the subject – I think that it all seemed too vast to think about, the links between everything and everything else too criss-crossed and confusing even to be considered.

I had never been a big *let's-sit-and-talk-about-this* kind of person anyway, and I now realised that this part of my relationship with Cliff – the stilted communication that we had always experienced – had probably been more my doing than his, and would probably follow me wherever I went and whoever I was with.

On arriving home, I braced myself all the same for hysterical arguments with Cliff, but they didn't transpire either.

Cliff knew, through Jill, that I had spent the week with James, and by the time I got to the house he had moved to the spare room. It wasn't the first time in fifteen years that he had slept in the spare room, so Luke, though unusually surly, simply assumed, I think, that we were going through a rough patch.

For a few weeks we lived this strange, brittle silence of non-communication, gliding around each other without any unnecessary word being uttered. It was horrible, tense, unbearable, almost . . . but as the days went by it became more and more obvious, to me at least, that there was no going back.

Things with James, though unscheduled, continued in a relatively easy manner. Considering the horrifically stressful circumstances surrounding us, the fact that we never had a single argument struck me as astounding. He was undemanding and easy to get on with – a model partner. When I looked at him, I felt myself melt with desire, and whenever he was elsewhere, I missed him. My feelings for James were growing stronger by the day and my marriage to Cliff was revealed to be a sham. It was over, and I attempted to make Cliff realise this in the only way I knew how: through my actions.

TWO

Cliff

I had moved into the spare room because I was angry. I knew that I had been guilty of various transgressions, but that didn't stop me being outraged that Hannah had abandoned us in the middle of a family holiday. It seemed to me that she could, for Luke's sake, at least have waited until we got home.

So I was too angry to speak to Hannah when she arrived from the airport, and way too angry to share a bed with her. And yet I think she took my abandoning the marital bed as some kind of capitulation. She exuded a certain kind of glee, as if perhaps she had won the first round in a war of attrition.

After two weeks of general frigidity around the home and of Hannah discreetly leaving the house to see James, he shockingly stayed over. He crept in late at night once we had all gone to bed, but I heard him all the same – I wasn't sleeping well.

In the morning, I sat on the edge of the single bed and stared at the pile of boxes in the corner of the room. When I heard the front door close, I stood and quietly opened the bedroom door. Leaning over the bannister, I listened carefully. I could hear Hannah talking to Luke in the kitchen, the rhythmic hum of the washing machine, and outside, the nervous whinnying of a starter motor. I let myself breathe and headed for the bathroom.

Once I had showered, shaved and braved the master bedroom long enough to recover a clean suit for work, I headed downstairs. Luke glanced up at me and shot me a grin. "Morning," I said, ruffling his hair as I passed en route to the kettle.

"Morning Dad." Luke spoke through a mouthful of breakfast cereal. "Are you taking me this morning?"

"I think so," I told him, glancing back at Hannah, engrossed, when I had arrived, in a copy of *Elle*, now already standing and leaving the room.

"You are," she said from the doorway, without turning back to look at me.

I pinched the bridge of my nose and sighed and wondered how much longer I could stand the tension. I forcibly reminded myself that despite my constant desire for fight or flight, nothing was actually happening here. I was not physically in danger. There had been no violence. We hadn't even argued since France. But all the same, the crackling static of unspoken anger filling the house was hard to bear. And James staying in the house was beyond unbearable.

The kettle clicked off and I poured water onto a teabag, grabbed a bowl and a spoon and joined Luke at the table.

"Whatcha doing?" I asked.

Luke stopped peering at his phone and glanced up at me. He had a Rice Krispie stuck to his bottom lip. It looked like some mediaeval pox. "Um?" he asked. "Oh, texting Billy. He wants to know if I can go round after school."

"You'll have to ask your mother," I told him.

"She said to ask you. She says you're picking me up."

I rolled my eyes. "Then yes. I can get you on the way home. About seven?"

Luke nodded vaguely. He was busy texting again.

Watching Luke from the corner of my eye, I wondered for the hundredth time how much he understood about what was going on here. I wondered if he cared, worried, was losing any sleep over it. He seemed the same as ever: a happy-go-lucky eleven-year-old sliding slowly but surely into adolescence. I was impressed by his resilience.

Luke snorted and slipped his phone into his pocket. "Billy's such a dork," he said, now pushing his bowl away and standing.

"Bowl. Dishwasher," I prompted, and Luke groaned with the physical effort of interrupting his movement, turning back to the table, and lifting the – apparently incredibly heavy – breakfast bowl from the table.

Less than ten seconds after Luke had left the kitchen, Hannah appeared in the doorway.

It's not that we weren't speaking to each other, it's just that we were speaking the minimum number of words required to get through each day in a vaguely functional manner. And we no longer spoke to each other in front of Luke. I assumed that this rule, implicitly imposed by Hannah but respected by both of us, was in case the next conversation was the one – the moment where everything spun out of control. It was a constant possibility with potentially thermonuclear consequences.

"Luke tells me that I'm doing both school runs today," I said as flatly as I could manage.

"That's right," Hannah replied, her features as rigid as my voice. The lack of expression expressed her mood quite succinctly. It said, "Don't mess with me." Her face had carried the same message every morning since we got back from our disastrous summer holiday.

"I just thought you might ask," I said. "I have to work late today. I'm behind with the Telma account."

"He can go to Billy's after school," Hannah replied. "He wants to anyway."

"I know."

"Then there isn't a problem, is there?" she muttered, now staring at her feet.

"No," I said. "But you don't work Wednesdays, so I would have thought . . ."

Hannah raised her gaze and stared me in the eye. She sighed, silently, but I heard it; I felt it. "I'm busy," she said.

"You're seeing *him*, I suppose?"

Hannah raised one eyebrow briefly, but didn't reply.

"He stayed the night," I said.

Hannah glanced out of the side door, then looked back at me. "Is that a statement or a question, Cliff?" she asked.

I turned my attention to the advertisement on the back of the box of Rice Krispies. Because Hannah was right – it was neither a question nor a statement. It was a reproach. And reproach wasn't going to take me anywhere I wanted to go today.

* * *

I never expected this would happen. I honestly had never imagined that Hannah and I would reach this point. Maybe I just didn't want to imagine it, because "this point" was frankly terrifying.

Hannah had been the only woman in my life, you see. She was the only woman I was ever in love with, the only woman I had ever fancied. She was the only woman I had ever slept

13

with, indeed the only woman I had ever *wanted* to sleep with. And perhaps, most of all, she was the only woman who had ever made me feel like I might, myself, be attractive, manly, loveable.

But here we were: it was falling apart. More probably, it had already fallen apart. My brain was now starting to accept the idea that we might go our separate ways. And with hindsight, this ending had been inevitable from the very beginning. Because with hindsight, she had always been in love with someone else. Though I had lied and schemed and dissimulated to keep them apart, I was never going to manage it – not for an entire lifetime.

If I had known, if I had had the benefit of hindsight, or foresight, or whatever it would have been called back then, would I have done anything differently? That is the question.

Even if I had believed that Hannah would have a life of happiness with a worm like James, would I have let her head off with him? The only honest answer is, "no".

Because though it had all, now, so clearly fallen apart, that didn't undo what we had had together. Hannah, and Luke were still the best things that had ever happened to me. And even with hindsight, I knew, if I were being honest, that I had never been brave enough to give that up. Or not voluntarily, at any rate.

It was nearly seven-thirty by the time I got to Billy's place, a tatty council house lost in a sea of other identical houses. Only the junk in each front garden and the colour of each door differentiated one house from the other.

As I was glancing at a washing machine, dumped, rusting on the front lawn, Luke's friend, Billy, opened the front door, turned and ran upstairs, shouting, "Luke, he's heeeeyaaaaa!"

Brenda, Billy's mother, appeared in the doorway to the lounge. She walked towards me, smiling slightly, then paused six feet away and leaned against the wall. She nodded gently, and said, "Cliff."

"Brenda," I replied.

She smiled at me, then, under pretence of watching for Luke's appearance, averted her gaze and faced the stairs instead.

"Has he been good?" I asked.

Brenda glanced back at me and nodded. "Fine," she said. "I haven't heard a peep out of them." She blinked slowly, then asked, "So, how is everything?" and because she maintained eye contact just a second too long, I realised that she knew, or at least that she thought she knew *something*. Her regard, her tight-lipped smile, the silent sigh, it all added up to compassion passed generously from one disillusioned adult to another.

"Fine," I replied. "You know . . ."

Brenda sighed again and nodded as if to say that, yes, she really *did* know, and then thankfully, Luke surged into view, swinging on the bannister and then galloping down the stairs taking them three at a time.

"Thanks Bren'," he said, now pushing past me and on down the path towards the car.

I smiled and shrugged at Brenda, an unspoken apology for my son, and she did the slow blink again, somehow expressing that in the midst of everything else that was going on in her life, or my life, or perhaps life in general, the abruptness of a goodbye from an eleven-year-old was neither here nor there.

I raised one hand and waved vaguely, then pulling the door closed on the vision of Brenda leaning – perhaps flirtatiously, perhaps not – against the door jamb, and thinking about the surprising depth of conversation we had just managed to mime, turned to follow my son towards the Mégane. As I drove away, I asked Luke, as ever fiddling with his phone, "So is Brenda a single mum?" I had never thought much about Brenda before.

"Uh-huh," Luke said.

"Uh-huh yes, or uh-huh no?"

"Yeah. Keith's in Birmingham or something."

"For work, or . . . ?"

"Uh-huh."

"Temporarily?"

"No. They split up, like, ages ago. He stopped paying something. That's why she had to cancel the washing machine."

"The mortgage?"

A frown.

"Child support payments?"

"Yeah, maybe."

"So they don't have a washing machine anymore?"

When Luke didn't answer, I glanced across at him and saw his frown lit by the pale glow from his iPhone. "Luke?"

"Didn't you see it?" Luke asked, incredulous now. Adolescence, it seems, makes incredulity an easily attainable state of mind.

"The dead one, on the lawn?"

"Well, *yeah*!"

"But that doesn't work," I said.

"The delivery guys were gonna take it. But she cancelled the new one so . . ."

"And they don't have a car to take it to the tip or whatever?"

From the corner of my vision, I could see that Luke was shaking his head.

16

"So how does she do the washing?"

Luke shrugged.

"God, Luke. Could you be any less communicative? Honestly, it's like getting blood out of a stone."

"I don't get why you're so interested in Brenda's washing machine."

"It's called conversation."

"OK. Whatever."

"So does she work?"

"Yeah. In Asda or something."

I imagined poor single Brenda, working mother of two, dragging bin bags of washing to the launderette. How would she get there? Was it walking distance? Or did she have to take it on the bus? I wondered if I could buy her a washing machine. What would that cost? Two hundred quid? But no, that would be weird, wouldn't it? She would see it as weird. You're not allowed to get that involved in other people's lives. My own may have been complicated, but at least we weren't short of money. At least we didn't have that to worry about.

When Luke and I got home, we found James and Hannah sitting at the kitchen table: a first. Luke headed straight to his room, wisely leaving the three of us alone.

"Hi Cliff," James said. His voice sounded a little smug, but I was aware that I might have been projecting that.

I didn't look at James' face to check; in fact I didn't look at him once. "I think I'll go change," I announced to no one in particular. I then glanced at Hannah just to make clear, in case James thought I had been addressing him, that it was Hannah that I had been talking to. She had her head supported by one hand, her elbow on the table, and looked angry, or perhaps just miserable. I wondered if they had had a row. I hoped so, and it crossed my mind that this probably made me a bad person.

Upstairs I shucked my suit, pulled on cords and a sweatshirt, then sat on the bed that used to be our bed. I glanced at the sheets and thought about who had rumpled them. I watched from the front window and soon I saw James leave.

Back in the kitchen, I found Hannah leaning against the worktop, looking ferocious. "You could at least be civil to him," she said.

"Civil?" I asked, heading for the kettle, more as a distraction than from any real desire for tea.

"Yes, there's no need to be rude."

"I didn't say a word."

"Well, quite. You could say 'hello'. You could say 'goodbye'."

I suppressed a sigh, swallowed hard, then replied, quietly, "Actually, I *couldn't*. If I start to speak to James I'm not sure that what would come out would be hello or goodbye."

"It's like having two adolescents in the house," Hannah said.

I forced a tight smile and, struggling to think of some witty remark that might defuse the situation, I turned to face her. But she was already leaving the room, abandoning this piece of territory to me, for now.

"There's some pasta bake in the oven," she offered, over one shoulder. "If you're hungry."

"Thank you."

"It's just leftovers," Hannah said, "it was going spare, so . . ."

I peered inside the oven at the leftover remains of Hannah's and James' meal, and thought about her pointed explanation that this was a leftover, a spare, not a specific act of generosity created with me in mind.

I was living in the spare room and eating leftover pasta cooked by my wife for my brother. That's where my life was at. Like a champion chess master, James was, move by lethal move, clearing the board. And I wasn't sure I had the stamina, or even the desire, to fight it. But then I had never been good at standing up to James.

*   *   *

I know you're supposed to love your family. And I'm sure that it's written somewhere that this rule applies doubly to those who have a single sibling. But the sad truth is that James was always a nightmare. And I really do mean always.

I was just over two when James was born, so it seems almost impossible that I can remember the event, but I'm sure that I do. I'm sure I recall a couple of years of calm contentment, of being the apple of my parents' eyes. And I'm sure I can remember a strange sensation of void entering my life once attention-grabbing James appeared on the scene.

I have a specific vision, either remembered or since created, of holding onto the edge of his pram and listening to my mother coo and purr at him as he dribbled and pissed, and wishing, even then, that he would somehow disappear. I definitely remember coming out of a shop, hand in hand with my mother, and being disappointed that his pram was still there, feeling distraught that no one had run off with him.

I had been a trouble-free baby and was a quiet bookish child, whereas James, right from the beginning, was a ball of energy, a bundle of nerves, and far too soon, an inexplicably solid mass of muscle.

By five, James was breaking my toys and managing to

manipulate circumstances so that I was the one who would get into trouble for it.

By seven, he was the same height as I was, and could pin me to the ground and dribble in my eye.

At eleven, his power over me was such that all he had to do was ask for anything and I would concede rather than have him launch into one of his reigns of terror. James' reigns of terror (his own term) were sometimes psychological – he would organise things so that I would be punished by my parents for something I hadn't done – or, more often physical. He would trap me in the tennis court and whack me over the head with the racket, or pin me to the floor and pinch me until I bruised, or put worms or spiders in my bed, or stick an insult on my back so that everyone at school laughed at me. His imagination was endless. I soon learned to just admit defeat rather than discover what the next terror would involve.

By thirteen, I was doing his homework for him, and by fifteen, I was lying to my parents to cover for his night-time excursions out of the bedroom window. He was sleeping with Ruth Peterson by then – already having sex with a girl two years his senior, a girl from my own class.

I had grown up with, grown into, all of this, and though horrific, I just took it for granted. This was my sorry lot and there was nothing I could do about it. Certainly my parents never seemed to see anything James did as unreasonable. In fact, their only response was to tell me to stand up for myself, which was absurd. I swear that from eleven onwards, even my father would have struggled to physically dominate James. But he never tried, because the type of brawny, sporty arrogance that James demonstrated was something that made my father feel proud. Quite the opposite to having a weakling son who was good at simultaneous equations, which, I think, made him feel inferior and undereducated instead.

It wasn't until I was in sixth-form college that it first crossed my mind that I didn't necessarily have to let James ruin my life anymore. As my new girlfriend, Susan, my first *ever* girlfriend, walked off down the street with James, I had a Eureka moment. I thought, "Enough."

So surviving James was a challenge. But loving him was nigh on impossible.

* * *

The next morning, I was awakened at four by a vague rhythmic beat – the sound of a couple somewhere having sex. It could have been coming from the neighbours' house, but it wasn't. It was the sound of my wife being screwed by my brother. The sound was muffled, and discreet, but I could hear it all the same. Even with a pillow over my head I could hear it. I thought for a moment that I was going to throw up.

At seven, I heard James creep downstairs and out of the front door. Neither Luke nor perhaps I myself were supposed to realise "officially" that James was staying over. But I knew Luke wasn't fooled. I had been bracing myself for the moment when he would pop the question.

"Can you pick up some bog roll on your way home?" Hannah asked as I reached the bottom of the stairs. She was in the process of pulling on her coat.

"Bog roll?"

"Yes, toilet roll. We're out. And I won't be coming straight home this evening, so you'll need to pick Luke up as well."

I wondered if Hannah had forgotten, or was intentionally pretending to have forgotten. Whichever it was, I decided not to let her get away with it. "Today's my birthday," I said. "You know that, right?"

Hannah didn't flinch. This was clearly no surprise to her. "You're allowed to buy bog roll even on your birthday," she said, exercising her new bitch persona with panache.

I stared her in the eye for a moment, watching the emotions: hatred, love, regret, determination ... They were swirling around behind her pupils, vying for dominance. "Where's Luke right now?" I asked. My left hand was trembling.

Hannah nodded behind her. "He's gone to get Peter. I'm taking them both this morning."

"Right. Well ... Good. I ..."

"Yes?"

I coughed. "I don't think I can do this much longer, Han'." I said.

She exhaled slowly and, momentarily, sympathy became the overriding emotion I could see. Then she steeled herself, hardened herself again – I watched it happen. "Then don't," she said when she finally spoke.

"Don't?"

"Don't do it any longer."

"Meaning?"

"I'm all out of energy too, Cliff. So if you feel you're ready to move out, then maybe you should go for it."

"Move out?"

Hannah nodded. "Sure. Rent a flat or something. Have the bachelor life you never had or whatever it is you want."

"You know what I want," I said, hesitating between tears and anger.

Hannah's regard softened again. It was like watching her

play good-cop, bad-cop single-handedly. "Look, Cliff," she said. "This isn't healthy. And it isn't going anywhere. We both know that. So why not just move on?"

I swallowed hard. "You do seem to be assuming that I'm the one to move out."

Hannah nodded. "Well yes."

"James has a place," I pointed out. "If you want to be with him so much, then wh—"

"It's small," Hannah interrupted. "And temporary. There's no way the three of us could live there."

A huge lump formed in my throat. "The three of you?"

"Yes. And you wouldn't want Luke to have to move, would you?" Hannah asked, glancing over her shoulder to check that he wasn't back yet. "This is enough upheaval for an eleven-year-old as it is, don't you think?"

"So you're also assuming that Luke will want to live with you?"

"I'm assuming that he won't have the choice," Hannah replied quickly, and from the fifteen years we had been married, I could tell that Hannah had rehearsed this conversation in her head – she had it all worked out. "Unless you're intending to start taking him to school and picking him up, and cooking and cleaning," she continued. "Unless you're going to start buying his clothes and doing his washing."

"I already do half of that, and you know it."

"But you'd need to do all of it. And you can't, not with your job."

"Nor can you," I said. "Which is why you've just asked . . . sorry, *told* me to pick him up tonight."

"Well . . . that's only because James isn't here," Hannah

23

said. "So for now, I have to go out to see him. Once he's here it won't be a problem anymore."

I snorted angrily. "Do you really think I'd let James move in here?"

"Again," Hannah said flatly. "I don't think you'll have much say in the matter. Not once you've moved out."

"So you get Luke and the house, and I . . ."

"Don't get me wrong, Cliff. I'm assuming we'd have joint custody. You'd have him most weekends, maybe two out of three, and some of the holidays. Don't pretend that wouldn't work better for you than trying to look after him during the week when you're flat out. You know what you're like."

At that instant, Luke appeared beyond the frosted glass of the front door, soon joined by a second blurred form, presumably Peter.

"Look," Hannah said quietly, all good-cop again. "Think about it. Think about what you really want. And think about what's best for Luke. But something has to give. Because you're right. These last few weeks have been dreadful."

"And you're not going to change your mind?" I heard my own voice wobble, and hated myself for expressing such weakness at a time like this.

Hannah smiled sadly and shook her head. "No, Cliff. I'm not going to change my mind. So you might as well get on with it. OK, look, I've gotta go."

The second Hannah opened the door, Luke said, "Peter's got a lizard!" The buoyant optimism of his voice jarred against the deathly ambiance of the hallway. "It's awesome."

As the door closed and the three figures retreated down the path, fading into impressionistic blurs, he continued, "Can I get a lizard?"

"No," I heard Hannah say. "You can't."

I felt dizzy. I reached out to steady myself on the bannisters, then lowered myself down so that I was sitting on the stairs.

What I wanted. What was best for Luke. The answer to both of these questions was easy. The status quo. Or rather, the status quo that we had before James barged back into our lives.

But clearly, that was now out of reach. "Get on with it," Hannah had said, and beyond the fear, and the shame, and the sadness, I felt an unexpected glimmer of relief, as if a pressure valve had been located. I hadn't opened it yet, but even knowing that it was there seemed reassuring. And though I was a little ashamed of the fact, I had to admit to myself that I also felt the vaguest tinge of excitement. Because I too had practised this conversation. I too had run through every possible way this conversation might go, including the exact way it had just unfolded. So if I was a little traumatised that this had finally come to pass, I wasn't entirely unprepared.

I sat for a few minutes in the silent house gathering my thoughts, then pulled my phone from my pocket and called my work colleague Bill.

"Hey Cliff," Bill answered. "What's up? You got car troubles?"

"No," I replied, my voice a constrained croak. I cleared my throat and tried again. "No! No, not at all. Look. Bill, I was just wondering . . ."

"Yes?"

"Did you ever find someone for that flat of yours, or is it still available to rent?"

*   *   *

That night, as we drove home, Luke stared silently at the screen of his phone. When, at a set of traffic lights, I glanced over, I saw that it was switched off. "Everything OK, Champ?" I asked, reaching out to squeeze his knee.

"Um?"

"Are you OK? You seem distracted."

Luke shrugged. "Just tired," he said. "We had cross-country running. I hate it."

"I get that. I hated cross-country too. But everything's OK?"

"Yeah, course," Luke said, then, "So, are you and Mum splitting up?"

Deciding I needed to be able to look at his face to have this particular conversation, I scanned the horizon and pulled onto the forecourt of a pub.

"What are we doing here?" Luke asked.

"Nothing. Just talking."

"Right. So you *are* splitting up then."

I pulled on the handbrake, switched off the ignition and turned to face him. "Has Mum said something?"

Luke shook his head. "Nope," he said. "But she's weirding me out. And James keeps creeping in and out." A shadow crossed his face. "Shit. Sorry."

"For what?"

"For saying."

"About James?"

"Yeah. Did you know?"

"Of course I know," I told him.

"Oh, OK then."

"Look. This isn't how . . . I mean . . ." I stumbled. "I thought we'd sit you down, your mother and I . . . when the time was right to have this conversation." Luke's wrinkled nose implied that he couldn't think of anything worse. "But I can't see any point in denying it," I continued. "So yes, I guess we are. Splitting up, that is."

Luke nodded. "Don't you like her any more?"

"If only it were that simple. I like her lots, Luke. I still love her, in fact. But you know, we've been together ever such a long time. Since before you were born."

"Well, *yeah*," Luke said sarcastically.

"So now she wants something different," I continued, forgiving and ignoring the attitude.

"Like what?"

"I don't know."

"Like James?"

"Yes. Yes, I suppose so. Like James," I croaked. *From the mouths of babes . . .*

"So will it be just you and me?"

"When?"

"Will they get their own place?"

"Ah. Um, well . . . I'm not sure that's what will happen, Luke. My guess is that I'll get a flat in the centre of the town somewhere so I don't have to drive to work, and your mother and James will stay in the house."

"And me?"

"Well it would be . . . I mean, you'd obviously have your say, but—"

"I want to come with you," Luke said, matter-of-factly, and my heart swelled with love and pride and gratitude.

"Thanks, but . . ."

"God, you don't expect me to stay with *them*, do you?" Luke said. "Mum's weird all the time, and James keeps doing that paedo thing."

27

"Paedo thing? What paedo thing?"

Luke rolled his eyes. "Not *really*. But you know, he does that, '*Hello, Luke my boy. Why don't you come tell your uncle James what you've been up to today?*' thing." Luke imitated James' smooth Australian accent with stunning accuracy. "It's creepy."

"Yeah. I can see your point. But I don't think you should be calling him a paedo. That's pretty serious. That could get out of hand."

"Sure. OK."

"And I'm sure he's just trying to be friends."

"I don't want to be his friend."

"Anyway," I said, feeling vaguely smug that at least Luke hadn't fallen under James' charm, "what usually happens is joint custody. So you'd spend the school week at home – at the house, I mean. And most weekends you'd be at my place so we could do cool stuff together. How does that sound?" I couldn't believe that I was discussing this life trauma in such a matter-of-fact way.

Luke nodded, staring through me as he visualised this. "So I'd have two bedrooms, one at home and one in town?"

I nodded. "Looks that way."

"Could I choose my own stuff? Furniture and all that?"

"I don't see why not."

"Yay!" Luke said.

"So are we OK?"

"Yeah."

Wow, I thought. *That was easy.* But as I reached for the ignition keys, Luke said, "Dad?"

"Yes?"

"When I have my own bedroom, at your place . . ."

28

"Yes?"

"Can I have a lizard?"

I laughed. "Maybe."

"Really? Can I?"

"Probably, Luke. You can probably have a lizard. But don't tell your mother."

"Bad."

"Bad?"

"Yeah. You know. Like, *bad*."

"Meaning 'good'?"

"Doh."

"Meaning 'yes'?" I asked, glancing in the rear-view mirror and pulling out.

"I might get a snake instead," Luke said. "That would be sick."

"I don't think I agreed to a snake. In fact, I don't think that I even agreed to a lizard yet. I said 'maybe'."

"You said *'probably'*."

"You're right, I did."

"They actually sell snakes and lizards in the same shop," Luke explained, managing to sound utterly reasonable whilst transparently pushing his luck. "So we can look at them and choose together if you want."

* * *

Once the decision had been taken, there seemed to be no point dragging things out. The flat was empty and I could afford it. The house was a war zone and my stress levels were through the roof – I had started to feel actual chest pains whenever I was forced, by circumstance, to speak to

Hannah, and when James was around, my eyesight tinted red with rage.

The following Saturday, I boxed up an initial batch of belongings and loaded up the car.

As I carried the final box outside, Hannah's Polo swung into view. She pulled up behind the Mégane, blocking the drive.

"I need to leave in a minute," I told her as she cracked open the door.

"Oh, course . . . sorry," Hannah said, reseating herself, and restarting the engine.

Once the car was parked back on the street, she returned and peered in through the window of the Mégane, then straightened and pressed her hand into the small of her back as if she had perhaps carried these boxes herself. "So how's it going?" she asked. "Everything OK?"

I stared at my wife for a moment and when she smiled questioningly, I wondered if, even now, reconciliation might be possible. "This still isn't what I want, Hannah. You know that."

"No," Hannah said, chewing the inside of her cheek and exhaling slowly, as if deflating. She reached out and touched, barely, my shoulder. It was the first physical contact between us since France.

"It isn't," I insisted, encouraged by the gesture.

"No, well . . ." she said, pulling her hand away and turning to head indoors.

"Hannah!" I called after her, but she raised one hand in a stop sign, and said, "Just . . . don't."

I leaned back against the car and looked up at the pale October sky. I could sense tears not far away, but Hannah was right. If this was to be performed with any dignity, then we needed to remain stolid, icy, controlled.

Jolted into action by the arrival of another car in the close – thankfully not James, but I was aware that it could happen at any minute – I ran one hand over my face, exhaled laboriously, and followed Hannah inside for my coat.

I was overcome by a thought that this was some terrible mistake, not romantically, but strategically. It suddenly seemed to me that despite Hannah's assurances that we would not become *those* divorcees, and her agreement that who was to get what and who would live where would all be negotiated reasonably at some future point, I felt in that instant convinced that abandoning – or accepting being forced out of – the family home was a terrible, terrible mistake.

So that I could obtain some final reassurance, I waited at the bottom of the stairs until Hannah returned from the bathroom.

"Hannah," I said. "You promise that we will, you know, deal with all of this prop—" But at the sight of her brandishing my toothbrush, my voice failed me.

"You forgot this," she said, descending the stairs with a hard, fake smile.

I hadn't forgotten my toothbrush at all. I had simply been unable to force my hand to lift it from the rack. It was one emotional wrench too many.

When I failed to take the toothbrush from her grasp, Hannah dropped it into the pen pocket of my jacket. I glanced down at it and then, still unable to speak, nodded, took my coat from the peg and turned to leave.

"Make sure that Luke's back by seven, will you?" she asked as I walked away.

Alone in the car, I stared back at my house. At my *old* house. Fifteen years we had been living there. I glimpsed Hannah looking out at me from behind the shimmering reflection of the autumnal maple tree in the front garden. She crossed her arms, then uncrossed them again and turned back inside. She looked hard. She looked icy.

"God this is tough," I muttered to no one in particular as I started the engine and reversed to the road.

As I pulled away from the kerb, I saw a white Fiesta – identical to the one James had been renting – and had a brief fantasy about accelerating to full speed and ploughing headfirst into it.

As I passed the car, I was unable to resist glancing in, even though I knew that seeing James rushing in to take my place could only hurt. The driver was, in fact, an elderly woman. She was gripping the wheel, sitting forward, her nose almost squashed to the windscreen.

When I got to the flat, Luke was waiting outside, his pushbike chained to a tree. I pulled up onto the pavement and switched on the hazard lights.

"I've been here for ages," he said, exaggerating.

"Sorry," I told him. "It's rush hour. The traffic was bad."

"Can I have a key so I don't have to wait outside next time?"

"Of course," I said. I loved the idea that Luke had asked for a key. I wanted, at that instant, to sweep him up in my arms and hug him to thank him for wanting a key. But I knew Luke wasn't big on hugs. "I'll get another one cut tomorrow," I told him.

"So can I stay here tonight?" he asked as I popped the hatch.

"You know you can't."

Luke pulled his *it-was-worth-a-try* face and looked inside the car. "Wow," he said at the sight of the stacked boxes.

"So, you just stay here and make sure no one nicks anything," I explained. "I'll carry the boxes in."

At the top of the stairs, I balanced a box on my knee and fiddled with the lock, then lifted the box again and pushed into the flat.

It was a beautiful space – a mini loft in a converted kiln building, right in the centre of Farnham. The supplied furniture was sparse but tasteful: brightly coloured modern stuff that looked like it might have been from Ikea, but which, knowing Bill, was far more expensive.

I dumped the box on the desk and looked around the room, taking in the vast leather sofa, the huge TV screen, the sliding doors and the balcony, and tried to imagine myself living there. It was very much a single man's flat and I couldn't picture myself there, because I still didn't feel single.

"Has my room got a bed?" It was Luke's voice from just behind me.

"Luke!" I shouted, spinning to face the door. "You're supposed to be watching my bloody stuff. My laptop's in . . . Jesus!" I ran past him and jogged down the stairs.

Outside, the car was untampered with. As I piled three boxes up and linked my arms around them, Luke returned. "The flat's amazeballs, Dad," he said, and my annoyance evaporated.

"You think?"

"Yeah. It's awesome. Can I bring the PlayStation here and put it on the big telly?"

"We'll see," I said. "Now, this time, can you just *stay here* while I take these in?"

"Sure," Luke said. "I only wanted to see."

*

By seven the boxes were piled along one wall, the car was relocated behind the building and I was anticipating, with not-a-little-fear, the moment that Luke would leave.

At seven-o-five, my phone rang. "Is he still there?" Hannah asked without preamble.

"Yeah, he's just leaving."

"Tell him to leave *now*."

"Yes."

"I told you, I want him home for dinner."

"You could phone him yourself," I pointed out, thinking as I did so that this was risking a new level of conflict between us. Moving out was changing the way we related, already allowing me to take greater risks. But the line had gone dead. "You're gonna have to get going," I told Luke.

He nodded and stood wearily.

"Hug?"

Luke pulled a face.

"Please?"

Luke rolled his eyes but stepped towards me and allowed himself, rigidly, to be hugged.

I squeezed him tight, breathed in the smell of him. "We can go get a bed tomorrow, OK?" I said as I released him.

"I wish I could stay here," Luke said as he headed for the door. "You're so lucky."

I watched the front door close with a sinking feeling and thought, *am I?* I performed a slow, numb lap of the new space, peering into each room, my hard shoes echoing on the tiled floors. I thought of animals, pacing the limits of their cages, and felt vaguely similar.

I returned to the lounge and sat on the arm of the sofa. I was hungry, but I had no food in. Ordering a pizza crossed

34

my mind, but I couldn't imagine anything more depressing than eating alone in front of the television. I tried to remember the last time I had been alone for any period of time. It must have been fifteen years before, when Hannah and I had split up the first time around. That had all been James' doing too.

I considered my options. I could get something delivered. I could go sit in a restaurant, alone; in a pub, maybe. Or perhaps I simply wouldn't eat. That would be a new experience. I wondered how hungry I would get if I didn't eat at all. I might not sleep from hunger, but then I probably wouldn't sleep anyway. I glanced at the boxes and wondered in which one I had packed the sheets and then if it would really matter if I didn't bother finding them. I could turn the heating up a notch and sleep on the sofa in my clothes . . . Who would know? That thought, of no one knowing, and no one caring, produced a numbing wave of sadness.

Hearing a noise coming from outside, I crossed to the window and looked down at the street where I saw Luke, not unchaining, but chaining his pushbike.

When he re-entered the building, I crossed to the front door and opened it. He was standing on the doorstep grinning sheepishly.

"Yes?"

"Mum says it's OK," he said.

"I'm sorry?"

"Mum says I can stay over tonight so we can go do the bed thing tomorrow morning."

Tears of relief pressed at the back of my eyes. I pulled my phone from my pocket. "I'm gonna phone her to check, you know that, right?"

Luke shrugged. "Jeez, I'm not *lying*."

Hannah answered immediately. "Yes?"

"Hi, um, Luke says you told him it's OK for him to stay?"

"Yes," she said. "That's right."

"Oh, OK then."

"Just have him home by two. We're going out tomorrow afternoon, so we need him back by two."

"Sure," I muttered, trying to digest Hannah's use of the word "we".

"Night Cliff."

"Night Han'."

I lowered the phone and pulled a face at it. "What did you say to her?"

Luke shrugged.

"Oh, come on," I said. "You must have said something. She never changes her mind. About anything. Ever."

Luke shrugged again, but this time explained. "I said you were a bit mizz," he admitted. "I said you needed the company. 'Cos it's your first night and everything." He stared at his feet both embarrassed and a little proud of the lie and I slipped into my first genuine smile for days.

"That's OK, right?" Luke asked, confused by something in my reaction. "I can sleep on the sofa. I don't mind."

I shook my head and choked up a little as I said, "Sure. That's fine. I *was* feeling a bit miserable actually."

"Can we order pizza then?"

"Sure. Or we could just walk up and get one. The pizza place is just up the road now."

Luke nodded. "OK," he said. "Can we get the one with the spicy sausage on it again? I liked that."

THREE

Hannah

The second Cliff's loaded car pulled away, tears burst from my eyes. I hadn't realised that it was going to happen, and only even acknowledged that it *was* happening when I noticed that my cheek was wet. I slumped onto the sofa and puzzled at this new development. I tried to take a deep breath, but my chest felt too tight. And then I thought, *he's gone,* and let out a cry – half sob, half wail. Once I had started I couldn't stop crying, and soon tears were dripping off my chin, soaking the neck of my blouse. At times I could barely breathe for sobbing, and I was still at it when James got home half an hour later.

"What's wrong, Han'?" he asked, ripping off his coat and rushing to my side.

"He's gone," I said, simply.

"But that's good, isn't it?" James asked, genuinely confused. "That's what you wanted."

I shrugged and nodded and started to weep all over again.

Eventually the tears ran out, leaving me feeling exhausted, as if every emotion had been squeezed from my body along with the tears. James asked me again why I had been so upset, and I told him that I didn't know, but that wasn't the truth. The reality was too complex, too multifaceted, too contradictory to be explained. Or perhaps I was just too tired to attempt it.

37

I was feeling so many things at once, and they didn't necessarily fit together in any meaningful way.

I was relieved that Cliff had gone, that was the first thing. The atmosphere in the house had been intolerable, and this had largely been my fault. I had wanted him away from me, but I wanted him to *decide* to go. So I had made his home life as uncomfortable as I possibly could. Every act, from not helping him find his keys (a regular drama) to leaving him leftovers from my meals with James had been, if not quite calculated, at the very least conscious. But these acts had been excruciating for me, perhaps almost as tough on my emotions as they had been on Cliff, and I had frequently vacillated, often considered capitulating. If there had been any other reasonable outcome to capitulate to, then I probably would have done so, but I could only envisage one future and that was with James.

So when Cliff left, the war of nerves was over, and I felt an overwhelming sense of relief at that.

I felt heartbroken, too. I had always been a true believer, perhaps one of the few remaining true believers in marriage left on the planet, and overturning that belief system, adjusting my worldview to the inevitability of divorce, felt like a catastrophic collapse of self. It seemed, suddenly, as if the last fifteen years had been lost, a pointless parenthesis of wasted days. As many of those years were extremely happy, and because the fruit of that marriage – Luke, our son – remained the best thing that ever happened to me, this was clearly illogical and melodramatic thinking but, all the same, it was how I felt.

I felt guilty, as well. Horribly, numbingly guilty that I had so consciously manipulated Cliff out of the family home. Because although his own acts could have been said to justify any behaviour on my part, although he had been revealed as a

38

liar and a manipulator of monstrous proportions, I understood why. I had been there right at the beginning of our relationship and whatever else might have been going on, I knew that the love had been real. I knew too that my seduction by his brother, just days before our wedding, had been, if impossible to resist from my point of view, entirely unreasonable from Cliff's, and that somehow *anything* that he might do from that point on was in some way normal. Perhaps you simply can't spend fifteen years with someone without becoming just a little *of them*, but for whatever reason, I understood Cliff. I comprehended everything that he had done. I *got* it.

Cliff, by revealing himself a liar, provided a solution that I could cling to to justify my actions, to smooth the way, but to myself, I had to admit that he wasn't the only cause. Deep down, I had to admit that I had simply never loved him properly, that I had never felt about him the way I felt about, say, James. So I felt horrifically guilty for using his weaknesses against him.

Finally, I felt sick with excitement, in a way that I hadn't since I was a teenager. I had spotted something I wanted: a way to change *everything*, and with single-minded selfish ambition, I had decided to pursue it, *no matter what*.

And now, here we were. James and I were finally alone in the house, Cliff was living elsewhere, and I could see that from here on in, James and I were free to do pretty much anything we wanted. I felt intoxicated with the sudden breadth of possibility.

"I don't know what I'm feeling," I told James, when he asked me again. "It's complicated. A mix of stuff."

"But you're happy?" he asked, pushing wet hair from my eyes with a stroke of his finger.

I nodded. "Get me a drink, would you? I think I need a whisky."

"I can do better than that," he said, and he turned and produced a bottle of champagne from his backpack. "I thought we might be celebrating tonight so I got this just in case."

It struck me in that instant that there was something heartless, something callous in his ability to celebrate, to *plan* to celebrate such a total victory over his own brother, and in truth I wasn't in the mood to celebrate with champagne at all – I needed whisky to calm my nerves. But I acquiesced. "Lovely," I said. "Get some glasses and I'll go fix my face. I must look like a road crash."

"You look lovely," James lied. "And you're mine."

That first evening with the house to ourselves felt so strange.

I watched James wandering around studying photos from family holidays, or picking up ornaments that had been gifts, and realised just how stacked the house was with memories of my life with Cliff . . . Actually, stacked with memories doesn't really cover it: the house, I realised, was a *manifestation* of my life with Cliff. I hadn't realised, up until that point, just how much *soul* was contained in all this material accumulation.

We sipped champagne, and nibbled the less-than-sophisticated Pringles that James had bought to go with it, and I struggled to appear convincing when I agreed that this was *nice*.

Luke phoned to ask if he could stay over at Cliff's, and because I realised that I was far from ready to see this new situation reflected in my son's eyes – my entire life as before, but with his father replaced by James – I agreed.

James and I reheated a ready meal, and then snuggled up on the sofa to watch a film: *Groundhog Day*. When we realised that neither of us was enjoying it – James had seen it, and I didn't much like it – we abandoned the film and went to bed to make love instead.

As I fell asleep in his arms that night, I dreamt unnervingly that he was Cliff, and then that he and Cliff were somehow the same person, and finally that the events of fifteen years ago had transpired in such a way that I had been living here with James all along. The really freaky thing about this last phase of the dream was that my life with James had been identical in every way to my life with Cliff. We had lived these fifteen years in this same house, had the same arguments, taken the same holidays, and ended up in the same stasis of predictable domesticity.

I awoke in the morning with a terrifying sense of inevitability, a knowledge I couldn't shake, that everything that had ever happened to me had been entirely my own doing, and that I was stuck in a Groundhog Day of my own creation that I would never be able to escape for the simple reason that no matter where I went, or who I was with, I would never be able to escape myself.

Watching James eat breakfast out of Cliff's bowl the next morning only magnified the feeling, and I wondered just what I would have to do to *really* change my life, and realised that whatever the solution was, it was going to involve living somewhere other than here. If James and I were to build our own story it would have to be somewhere different, somewhere preferably far, far away. And with an adolescent son, engineering that escape was going to pose a whole fresh set of problems.

41

That first morning, James looked up at me from his bowl of muesli and said, "Make me another coffee, would you Han'?" and without thinking, I paused eating my own cereal to do just that. It wasn't until I was standing over the kettle that the request struck me as cheeky.

When James finished his breakfast, he stood and started to leave, his bowl and mug still on the table.

"The dishwasher's empty," I told him with a big forced smile, and James just laughed.

"Right," he said, leaving the room.

And the problem now was that I had noticed, and once you start noticing it's impossible to stop. I had already begun to do what I suppose was inevitable: I had begun to compare the two brothers.

I had been married to Cliff for so long that I had ceased to really see him, but I began now to realise at least what a benign presence he had been to live with. Where James would "order" a fresh cup of coffee, Cliff would have made one just for me. Where James would refuse my hints at using the dishwasher, Cliff would fill and empty it without my even noticing. If we were watching a film, James was perfectly capable of heading through to the kitchen and returning with a beer without it even crossing his mind to ask me if I wanted something.

None of this is to say that I was in any way regretting the loss of Cliff from my life: our marriage had been beyond stale, and for all his faults I still found James to be novel and exciting, to be challenging and sexy. But I was starting to see that I had taken Cliff for granted too. I was beginning to realise that I had been asleep for much of the last fifteen years, and that, in a strange way, it had required someone precisely like James to wake me from my slumber. Whether

I was feeling aroused or irritated, in love or furious, I felt awake; I felt alive.

Luke, who had momentarily loved James during our French holiday, now seemed to see him with nothing but hatred. I knew this was to be expected; I knew that the child who doesn't resent a parent's new partner is a rarity. I could do nothing but batten down the hatches and hope that it was a passing phase.

James' rugged independence, his lapses into Aussie outback vulgarity, his, dare I say it, flashes of *selfishness*, did nothing to make life easier though. Within days, Luke was protesting everything from tidying his room to stacking the dishwasher with a new standard refrain: "Why? *He* doesn't."

"James is a guest," I would tell him repeatedly, but I knew that this explanation wasn't going to wash for long. I knew that, for Luke's sake, for all our sakes, I was going to have to house-train James.

For days I dropped hints: I tried witty remarks and I tried bitchy asides. I tried setting an example, and commenting on it loudly as I did so: "I'll just clear my plate away then," or "Hum, this dishwasher looks full. I'd better switch it on." But none of these had the slightest effect on James. He seemed entirely impervious to my training techniques.

I came to realise that I was going to have to deal with the issue head on; I was going to have to sit him down and talk about it. And yet every time I opened my mouth to do so, I closed it again, because I could never find the right combination of words that would express the problem without being confrontational. I had never been very good with forthright discussion.

In the end, it was Luke who forced my hand. It was a

Saturday, and he was eating his lunch. James, who had wolfed down his own sandwich, was reading a newspaper. He leaned back in his chair and rested his feet – encased in worn suede boots – on the corner of the table. His legs were positioned so that his boots weren't *actually* in contact with the surface of the table, but all the same – going against all of the rules he had had to follow himself – this clearly shocked Luke.

With his spoon in mid-air, he froze and looked from James' boots to me, and then back again. I shook my head gently and blinked slowly at him. The gesture was supposed to communicate "*Not now*," but Luke had had his fill of James' special rules. He placed his spoon in his bowl, shuffled his chair back from the table, and put his own socked feet on the table.

"Luke," I said, sadly shaking my head.

"Yes?" he asked, folding his arms defiantly.

"Take them off."

"My socks?"

"You know what I mean. Take your feet off the table."

"Why?"

"Because I asked you to."

"And what about him?" Luke said, nodding at James.

"Luke!" I said.

He lowered his feet, spluttered, "I *hate* living here!" and stomped from the room.

I took a deep breath and turned to James, ensconced in *The Guardian*, and seemingly unaware of the drama.

"James," I said. "We need to talk."

"Um?" he asked from behind the paper.

I reached for the edge of his newspaper and pulled it downwards so that I could see his face. "James. We need to talk," I said again. "We have a problem here."

He lowered the paper, glanced at me, then frowned and folded it up. "Sorry," he said. "Just reading about the bush fires in Tazzie. Bloody awful."

"Right," I said.

"So, what's up?"

"Did you catch any of what just happened there?"

James pouted and shook his head.

"I had an argument with Luke?"

"OK."

"He had his feet on the table."

"OK . . ."

"He's not *allowed* to have his feet on the table."

"Fair dinkum. Your house, your rules."

I glared at him now. "James," I said. "For God's sake. Stop being obtuse with me."

James laughed. "Obtuse? *Me*?"

"I can't tell Luke not to put his feet on the table if you're sitting there with your boots in his breakfast bowl, now can I?"

James was wearing a strange expression, a mixture of a frown and a grin. "So you want me to take my feet off the table," he said, glancing at his boots. "Is that what you're trying to say?"

"Yes."

He shrugged and removed them, then folded his legs beneath his chair. "Better?"

"Yes!" I exclaimed, exasperated.

"All you had to do was ask."

"Ask?"

He nodded and smiled at me. "I'm not a bloody mind reader, Han'."

"Right, but . . ."

45

"And I don't get why you never say what you want."

"What do you mean?"

"What I said. Why don't you ever say what you want? Why do we have to have all these bloody games?"

"I do *not* play games."

"Oh, you do. You're the biggest game player I've ever met, girl. And we're all supposed to sit around second-guessing you. Well it's not my thing."

"I really don't know what you mean," I said.

"Yes you do."

"Example?"

"OK. You say, 'Oh there's no room on the table,' and you mean, 'Please clear your stuff.' Or, 'Oh, I'll walk all the way up there to meet you then, shall I?' when you mean, 'Can you come and pick me up?' 'I can't tell Luke not to put his feet on the table,' means, 'Don't put *your* feet on the table.'"

"So you understand *perfectly* what I mean," I said. "You just choose to ignore—"

"Because it's bloody annoying," James interrupted, an incongruous smile on his face. "OK? I ignore it because it's a stupid way to talk to another adult. And I'm sick of trying to guess what you really want."

I stared at him for a moment, considering my position. His words seemed harsh, but his expression and his voice were calm. I felt tempted to justify myself, but in the end, there was something about his vaguely amused expression that just knocked the core out of my anger. "I didn't know," I said. "I didn't realise I did that."

"Well now you do."

"It's just how . . . how we worked. How we functioned. With Cliff, I mean."

"Fair enough, but it won't work with me."

"OK," I said.

"So what did you want to say to me?"

"Um. Well . . . Please don't put your feet on the table, I suppose."

"No problem," James said. "I won't. And if I forget, please remind me."

"And please clean up after yourself when you've eaten, and please put your dishes in the dishwasher and switch it on when it's full, and please put your dirty clothes in the washing basket in the bathroom rather than on the floor wherever you happen to be. Because all of these things set a bad example for Luke."

James nodded and smiled broadly at me. "Right," he said. "No worries. Anything else?"

I shook my head. "You're impossible," I replied, finally allowing my features to soften.

James shrugged. "Maybe," he said. "But at least I bloody say what I mean."

James was harsh, and sometimes vulgar, but the more I thought about it, the more I came to think that he was in the right.

Over fifteen years, Cliff and I had grown together from youth into adulthood, and during that time we had evolved our own special way of functioning, a method that provided workarounds for all of our personal quirks. But faced with James' shocking directness, his brutal honesty, I had no choice but to acknowledge that much of this was unhealthy and that, specifically, our methods of communication had become woolly if not actually dishonest.

But beyond my problems with honest communication,

there were issues of actual intent: I started to notice just how often I said "no" to things.

Cliff was a great convincer. He knew the way I functioned and would take my refusals to go to the cinema or my lack of desire to attend a dinner invitation with a pinch of salt. He would accept on my behalf and then chivvy me along.

James, on the other hand, seemed abnormally determined to take every word at face value. And though, for the moment, I was happy to spend my time at home as long as James was there, I couldn't help but notice how my life was contracting without Cliff to contradict me.

One sunny Sunday in October, I had a whole day to think about this, because when James asked me if I wanted to go for a long walk in the country, I said "no". I had too much to do around the house, I told him. Plus, it looked a bit like rain.

James, unlike Cliff, simply nodded, pulled on his coat, and left on his own.

Once he had gone, I sat down and stared out of the front window and wondered what had just happened. I asked myself, for the first time ever, why I had done this. Because in truth there was nothing that needed doing so urgently that I couldn't go for a walk. And in truth, what I really wanted was the exact opposite of what I had chosen.

Cliff would have offered to help with the tasks (thus revealing their non-existent nature) and then chivvied me out of the door, but whether James actually didn't mind that much if I went with him or not, or whether he was consciously training *me*, I couldn't tell. This thought led me to understand the first of the reasons for my strange behaviour: I wanted James to prove that he cared. I wanted him to show me that he wanted me there. I was also trying to make him aware of all that I did around the house.

As I thought about it further, I realised that deep down, I held a strange belief that accepting to do something frivolous too easily felt "wrong", naughty perhaps. So my refusal had been influenced by that as well. And finally, it was also, I realised, just a habit – something I had done for as long as I could remember, something I had learned, quite possibly, from my mother.

James got home three hours later to find me still sitting on the sofa, still staring at the switched-off TV.

"Tell me about your walk," I said, and he did just that, describing the barren fields and the leafless trees, a pheasant he had seen, a dog walker, and a group of inquisitive cows.

"And you?" he finally asked. "Did you get all your stuff done?"

I laughed sourly. "I didn't have much to do, to be honest," I told him. "I've been sitting here trying to work out why I didn't come with you."

James frowned. "Oh? And?"

"I have no idea," I told him. "Well, I can think of a few reasons, but none of them makes any sense."

"It's a girl thing, I think," James said. "Judy used to do the same thing. She liked to be persuaded."

"Maybe. My mother did it too," I said, shivering a little at the unusual mention of James' dead wife. "But it's very strange to suddenly realise that you can't explain your own behaviour."

"But you *did* want to come?"

"Yes. I think so. How stupid is that?"

James exhaled heavily. "Look, I know this is delicate," he said, his tone suddenly sombre.

"Yes?"

"But while we're doing the honesty thing . . ."

"Yes?"

"Have you gone off me?"

"Gone off you?"

"Yes."

"No, of course not . . . why would you even think that?"

"Well, we've only done it a few times since we got back from France, Han'."

I stared at him and thought about this and realised that it was true. "I haven't gone off you at all," I told him.

James sighed. "So why don't you ever want to . . . ?"

"I don't know," I said. "I'm sorry."

"Well, if you don't know, then I'm sure I don't."

"It's partly this house, I think. The fact that the bed was ours."

James nodded, then shrugged. "Sure. Well, I just thought I'd bring it up. I'm, um, gonna go make a drink."

"Make me a coffee, would you?"

"Sure."

While James made the drinks, I sat and thought about this new challenge. Because James was right – since we had got back, I had reverted to an old habit of saying "no" to sex. And now that I tried to think about why that might be, the only explanation I could come up with was that on top of my insecurities about my body – which hadn't, let's face it, held me back in France – saying "yes" made me feel embarrassed. It made the sexual act seem premeditated and for some stupid reason, that seemed wrong. I had always believed that sex should somehow just "happen".

50

Cliff had learned to ignore my protests and cuddle and coax me until I caved in, and again, that confirmation of desire reassured me. But there was no reason that James could know this, and no reason I could think of why he should have to put up with such strange behaviour on my part.

When he returned, he handed me my mug of coffee and asked, "Are you OK? You look a bit strange."

I laughed. "I'm just realising at thirty-eight that I don't know myself that well," I said.

"But you do still fancy me then?"

I looked at him now, masculine and farmer-like in a denim shirt and jeans over his worn suede boots. "Yes," I said. "How could I not? But do you fancy me?"

"Like crazy."

"Really?"

"You're beautiful, Hannah," James said.

"I worry about ... things ... My body. I'm not twenty anymore."

"Neither am I, Han'. But I still fancy the hell out of you."

I blushed and looked down at myself, but broke into a smile all the same.

"So," James said with a wink. "D'you fancy a bit of how's-your-father before Luke gets home?"

I laughed.

"We have the whole place to shag in," James said.

And though it was one of the hardest things I had ever done, I nodded. "Yes," I said. "Yes, let's have a bit of how's-your-father."

FOUR

Cliff

I found myself working late almost every day. Though it was true that my workload was heavy, the real reason I stayed so late was to avoid the yawning emptiness of the flat. When I did find myself alone in the apartment – and from time to time, it was unavoidable – I left the television on. Sometimes, when I woke up from a snooze, I momentarily believed that the noises surrounding me were the dulcet tones of family life. On these occasions, the reality revealed when I opened my eyes felt like an ice pack closing around my heart.

As soon as Luke reappeared, every other weekend and most Wednesdays, everything was fine. We would feed the lizard – a boring beast that barely moved – and go to the cinema; we would shop for must-have Adidas trainers and hang out in technology stores to play with the latest slick devices from Apple and Samsung. Surprisingly, my separation from my wife had created a space within which my relationship with my son – previously so stale – could blossom.

I realised that I was becoming increasingly dependant on Luke, and that this might not be entirely healthy for a man in his forties. But for now Luke was all I had, and so I let myself cling to him, spoiling the boy rotten to ensure his enduring love. There was only one threat to this relationship that I could identify, and that was the slowly forming storm cloud of blame over our separation. Hannah had already phoned me twice, spitting nails over her perception that I had been painting her as the bad guy in all of this. "If you don't share the blame fairly then I will tell him about you," she threatened. "I'll tell him what really happened in France. And then we'll see how much time he wants to spend in your bachelor pad." But the truth was that I hadn't said a word against her. Despite getting pretty much everything she wanted, she was so uptight that she was driving Luke away herself.

So far I had been able to manage the relationship with my estranged wife by, essentially, giving in to her every demand. So far, true to our word, we had not become *those* divorcees, but I feared that it was only a matter of time. With James in the middle of our lives stirring things up, I somehow couldn't imagine any way out that would avoid all-out war, because that was, and always had been, his way. And not for the first time, I wished that he had never existed.

On the Thursday of my second week in the flat, the landline rang. As this was the first time it had done so, and because the ring was both loud and unfamiliar, it made me jolt in shock.

The caller was Glen, the husband of Hannah's close friend Jennifer, but by default, being a man, Glen was officially *my* mate, not Hannah's.

"Hey," Glen said. "So how's life in the heart of the city? I hear you have one groovy little pad down there."

"It's fine," I replied, wondering who could have told Glen this. Hannah, after all, had never even seen the place. "You managed to find the number OK then?"

"Jennifer got it from Hannah for me," Glen said. "I was

thinking that I might be able to finally convince you to go on that fishing trip. Dad says I can borrow his camper van. What do you reckon?"

I was shocked. The famous fishing trip. How long had we been talking about this? Nine years? Ten? Why had it never happened? And why bring it up now? What had Hannah told Jennifer? What had Jennifer told Glen?

"Cliff?" Glen prompted.

"Yes, um . . ." I stumbled. "Yes, I'm still here."

"I thought the line had gone dead."

"No, I . . . I was just thinking about dates. I have Luke this weekend, that's all."

"Maybe the weekend after," Glen said. "Bringing the kids isn't really the point, is it?"

The trip tentatively organised, and the phone call over, I sat and stared at the muted TV screen and wondered what the point really was.

The fishing trip had first been mooted ten years before.

Jennifer had decided that Glen and I needed to spend more time together. We both suspected that what she really meant was that she and Hannah wanted more time alone, but whatever the reason, we complied by agreeing to take Luke, just two, and Charlotte, three, to the park.

It was a warm summer's day – August, perhaps – and the park was busy with people walking, picnicking and attempting to fly kites in the insufficient breeze.

"Well this is weird," Glen commented.

"It is a bit," I agreed. It felt strangely modern – a bit new man – to be the only two men with pushchairs. "So what do you think the ladies are getting up to in our absence?"

Glenn shrugged. "Drinking coffee and yacking about you and me, I expect."

"They'll run out of matter pretty quickly if they're talking about us."

"I don't know," Glen said. "I listen to Jennifer on the phone sometimes, and she can talk for hours – literally hours – without saying anything at all.

"Hannah too," I agreed. And it was true.

Once we had lapped the park – with the exception of a brief conversation about motorbikes, in silence – I glanced at my watch. "Too early to head back yet."

Glenn nodded at the green where a group of women were picnicking. "Let's go sit over there. At least the view is better."

Thirty yards from the women we pulled out a blanket and sat cross-legged. Luke was still sleeping so I left him in the pushchair. Charlotte, as ever, was awake but gurgling happily. Glenn lifted her onto the blanket so that she could crawl around. A worryingly late bloomer, she was walking, just, but only if forced.

A ginger, bearded guy in jeans and a red and white checked shirt started to cross the green towards the women and I watched him stride purposely across the grass, crouch down to talk, and then stand, stretch and leave.

As he walked away, Glen said, "Five women in various states of undress and you're watching Clint Eastwood. What gives, dude?"

It was only once he had said this that I realised that I had been quite attentively tracking him. In an initial attempt at an honest reply, I tried to examine my motives. Why *had* I been watching him?

It was something about his gait, something about the way he

walked, his bandy legs, his stride which had been purposeful and manly. Was I simply feeling jealous? Perhaps.

He had been wearing cowboy boots, and I had been thinking that in Farnham, on a Saturday afternoon in August, that somehow seemed brave. I had wondered if the pointy, heeled boots were as uncomfortable as they looked. I had pondered whether the boots were the thing that made him walk in such a determined, self-assured way. I even wondered what Hannah would say if I turned up at home in a pair. Would I look sexy, or absurd? Would I suddenly have groups of attractive scantily clad women to wander over to, or would it be one of those pointless purchases that Hannah so excelled in, one of those worse-than-pointless purchases where the second you put them on, you simply realise that you aren't that person, and that no amount of clothes shopping will ever make you into that person.

All of these thoughts drifted through my mind on that drowsy summer's day, but because not being sure if I wanted to dress more like the cowboy, or be the cowboy, or perhaps, just, be friends with the cowboy, all seemed a bit gay, I lied. "He's the spitting image of a friend I was at college with," I said, "that's all."

"I didn't know you had any friends," Glen said, "except for me."

I laughed. "I don't have a lot. Always been more about quality than quantity, me. Never been one for the big crowd."

Glen winked at me. "We should go fishing," he said. "Make a weekend of it. Just you, me and a camp stove."

I frowned as I tried to work out how that thought had linked to this one. Was there some subtext that I was missing here? "Yeah, maybe," I said, and an image of Glen and me dressed as cowboys around a camp fire came to mind, and I wondered if Glen had the same mental image, and if such manly camaraderie wasn't what I was truly craving.

The woman the guy had spoken to – an attractively curvy redhead – was now standing and pulling on her cardigan. As she crossed the green, following in the footsteps of the booted-guy, I tracked her departure. It was a conscious act to cover my tracks, to demonstrate that, "I'm just people watching, here, that's all." Once she had vanished from view, I glanced back at Glen and raised one eyebrow in a man-to-man kind of way.

"I wouldn't mind being her boyfriend tonight," he said, and I thought, *No, neither would I.* I wondered if it was for the same reasons.

"Watching these girls drinking beer is making me thirsty," Glen said. "Shall we go grab a pint before we have to take these monsters back?"

"Sure," I said, and as I stood I imagined wearing boots and wondered again, if I could get away with it.

* * *

Two weeks after the phone call, with Luke at Hannah's for the weekend, the camping trip finally happened. I threw my bag in the side door, and then climbed into the cabin of the camper van. It was far bigger than I thought. I had been expecting a funky VW van, but this was more like a small house on wheels.

As I buckled my seatbelt, I tried to ignore the fact that Glen was staring at me, pulling a face. After a few seconds of silence I turned to look at him and asked, "What?"

"Well those are a bit *Brokeback Mountain*, aren't they?" Glen said.

I looked down at my boots, still hideously shiny, conspicuously new. It hadn't been easy to find cowboy boots in Farnham. "These?" I asked, and from the heat I suddenly felt, I suspected that I was blushing.

"Yes."

"I never saw *Brokeback*," I told him, and it was true. "So I wouldn't know. I thought it might be muddy up there, that's all."

"It will be, which is why I brought wellies." Glen nodded over his shoulder to indicate the location of said wellies. "Big, green, rubber wellies."

"Shall I go and change them?" I asked, wondering why we were still sitting here discussing my boots instead of driving to Cumbria. The rules of what one could and couldn't do as a man were no clearer to me than they had been when I was an adolescent. And my embarrassment when I got it wrong was no less painful either.

"Hey, I don't give a shit what you wear, dude," Glen said, finally starting the engine. But clearly, he did.

As Glen glanced at my footwear again, raised one eyebrow, and then engaged first gear, I took a deep breath and steeled myself to regain my composure. "Anyway," I pointed out, "you can hardly talk about *Brokeback Mountain*. Not in that shirt."

"I thought you hadn't seen it," Glen said.

"I haven't. But I know it's about cowboys. And I know enough to imagine that they all wear checkered shirts."

"About cowboys, is it?" Glen said, with a snort.

Not wanting to get into a discussion about *Brokeback*

Mountain, I ignored this comment and so we drove in silence until we hit the motorway.

"It's gonna be freezing in Cumbria," I finally said, spying a patch of frost at the roadside.

"It is, but that's Britain. What are you gonna do? The fish don't care, why should we?"

"I bet I won't catch anything anyway."

Glen laughed. "Of course you will."

I had never been fishing before, and I wasn't sure I was going to enjoy the experience. I wasn't sure that I *wanted* to catch anything and was unable to imagine that I'd be able to kill a fish even if I did catch one. I have always preferred to buy my fish filleted and vacuum packed, always preferred to avoid those eyes, staring up at me from the fishmonger's counter.

During the drive north, we talked little, just brief summary conversations from time to time about our kids, or our jobs, or some passing sports car or truck. The rest of the time, I sat and wondered what this trip, so long in the making, was about. Could Glen really just want to go fishing. In Cumbria? In November?

It was three p.m. by the time we reached the fishery. At the farmhouse, I gave Betty, a ruddy-faced farming type, my credit card details and returned with a photocopied map of the grounds around the lake.

"She says to go there," I told Glen, pointing at a cross Betty had marked on the paper. "And she said we're brave. It's gonna be minus five tonight."

"The heater in this babe is great," Glen informed me, studying the map and then restarting the engine.

"We have to keep everything we catch apparently – no throwing back."

59

"That's standard."

"And it's a fiver a kilo. Seven if you want her to fillet it for you."

"What's that per pound?" Glen asked.

"No idea. A pound is two point two kilos, isn't it? Or is it one point eight? Actually, I think it's the other way around."

The van bumped and lurched and scraped across the frozen mudscape of the car park, and then developed a calmer, wave-like roll once we joined the gently undulating track around the lake. When we reached our pitch – a square clearing cut into a small copse of trees about thirty feet from the water's edge – Glen switched off the engine and we climbed from the van.

"Fuck me," Glen said, lifting his arms above his head and stretching. "That was a drive."

"I told you I was happy to do some of it."

"You're not on the insurance," Glen explained. "Anyway, we're here now."

"It's beautiful," I said, turning to face the sun, now setting beyond the lake in a fiery band of raw red brightness.

"*It's beautiful*," Glen parodied, in a soppy voice.

I shrugged. "Well it is."

"Red sky at night, fisherman's delight."

"It's freezing already." My breath was rising before me in little clouds as I spoke.

Glen nodded. "We had better get this fire lit."

"Oh, she said no fires on the ground," I said. "Only contained fires and barbecues."

"Did she now?" Glen laughed, already scanning the ground for firewood.

* * *

60

The steaks were burnt, but despite that, eating around the illicit campfire felt great. Surrounding us, the forest seemed dark and menacing, literally teeming with life. But here, within the circle of light from the flickering flames, it felt warm and safe. A primeval sense of well-being enveloped me.

"Another beer?" Glen prompted, and when I nodded, he reached into the cool bag, retrieved a can and threw it through the flames to me. Glen was working his way through the beers at quite a rate, and I was realising that I should have brought more. "It's good to be out here," I said, cracking the ring pull. "It's good to get away."

Glen nodded and then tossed the last piece of burnt steak from his plate into the fire where it crackled and hissed. "Yeah," he said. "Especially after all the shit you've been going through, I would imagine."

I sipped my beer.

"I admire you, dude," Glen said. "You know, the way you're holding it all together. If Jennifer went off with some guy, I don't know what I'd do. And your brother. I mean, wow. Like, fuck!"

"Yeah," I said, vaguely. This was the first time that my separation from Hannah had been mentioned, and I wasn't at all sure I wanted to go there right now.

"You must hate Hannah now, right?" Glen asked.

"A bit. Maybe. But it wasn't only her fault. I mean, it was mainly James' doing really. That guy is such a worm. But other stuff happened. Nobody's perfect. Not even me." I wasn't enjoying this conversation; it was making me feel angry. And nervous. And that was not what I had come fishing for.

"So are you gonna tell me what went down in France?" Glen asked.

I frowned at him. "Has Hannah said something?"

"No."

"Then why ask me that?" My voice was a little more aggressive than I had intended.

Glen raised his free hand. "Hey, calmos. She didn't say anything. I just know that something went down in France. Because you all drove off laughing, and by the time you came back it was like the apocalypse had happened."

I started to breathe again. "Well, James turned up, didn't he. Anyway . . ."

"If you don't want to talk about it . . ." Glen said.

"I don't."

"Then that's fine."

We sat staring into the flames for a moment then, attempting to change the subject, I asked, "So what's the best time for fishing?"

"Early. They wake up hungry and dozy. Perfect time to catch them on a hook."

"They sleep?"

"Joke, dude," Glen laughed. "But I always get the best results early on in the day for whatever reason."

I glanced at my watch. "Do we need to be up early then?"

"Six, seven, whenever dawn is these days."

"More like eight at this time of year then."

"Right," Glen said. "Then eight it is."

By ten p.m., it was too cold to sit outside, but finding that the light inside the van wasn't working and unable to find the torch, the only choices were to sit in the driver's cabin, or go to sleep. We agreed on the latter option.

"So how does this bedding work?" I asked, peering into the dark interior of the van. The sleeping arrangements had been on my mind since the sun had gone down.

62

"Well, there's a double up here," Glen said, his voice coming from a pitch-black ledge over the driver's cabin where he was wriggling into his sleeping bag.

"I take it there's a second bed down here somewhere?"

"There's a complicated thing that slots together where the dining table is, but frankly, pissed, in the dark, it's gonna be a challenge, even for a brainbox like you."

"OK . . ." I agreed, a little confused. "I could sleep in the cabin I guess."

"Don't be daft," Glen said. "There's loads of room up here. I don't bite."

"OK . . ."

"And if I do, I promise I'll be gentle with you."

*　　*　　*

I could not sleep. The roof of the cabin was oppressively close, and the heat rising from the gas heater was dispropor-tionate to the volume of the van. As the heater only had two positions – on and off – and because when we tried "off" we instantly froze, I was now lying on top of my sleeping bag in just boxer shorts and a T-shirt. Even in these I was sweating like a pig.

Beside me, Glen, one leg sticking out from his unzipped sleeping bag, was snoring with gusto – the gusto of a man who had drunk eight cans of Stella.

I hadn't been in such close proximity to a semi-naked man since my twenties. And now, as then, I felt nervous and uncomfortable and – these days, I can admit it – vaguely aroused.

Eventually the temperature outside plummeted to a point

where the heat loss from the van balanced out the perky little heater, and finally I started to doze.

When I woke an hour later, I discovered that Glen had moved across the foam mattress towards me, effectively sandwiching me against the freezing outer wall of the van. Glen, in his sleep, had somehow managed to drape one arm over my waist.

I lay there, paralysed, as I wondered what to do. I tried to guess what a blue-blooded heterosexual man would do in these circumstances. Wake Glen and push him away, presumably. And did the fact that I hadn't yet done this – that I was lying here actually enjoying the proximity, loving feeling nestled against the warmth of Glen's massive frame – did this mean, yet again, that I was not the blue-blooded heterosexual man I had pretended for so long to be? Then again, it was *Glen* who had moved to *my* side of the mattress here, Glen whose arm was draped over my waist. Perhaps blue-blooded heterosexual men simply didn't behave the way I had always imagined. Perhaps I was entirely normal after all, and the great unspoken secret was that all men – and perhaps even all women – enjoy physicality with both sexes alike. Perhaps it really was just morals and rules that keep everyone apart, that made actors of us all. Or maybe, more likely, Glen, as I had long suspected, was simply no more like most men than I was.

Glen's arm actually tightened around me at this point, winching me in, small spoon against big spoon, and it felt amazing, it felt like a homecoming, it felt suddenly like everything I had ever wanted, but I realised that my reputation depended on how I reacted here. Glen was Jennifer's husband, after all. This was too dangerous.

"Glen!" I shouted, sitting up sharply and whacking my head on the roof vent.

"What?"

"Shit!"

"What?"

"I hit my head!" I told him. "And you're taking the whole bloody bed."

In the pale moonlight I could just make out Glen's features looking up at me. "Um . . ." he murmured, drunk or sleepy, or perhaps both. "Sorry, I thought you were into that shit."

I blinked in surprise and watched as he rolled away, then opened my mouth to speak, to ask perhaps, "What do you mean, that shit?" or "And you, Glen, are you into that shit?" but instead, I closed it without saying a word and climbed down from the bunk pulling my sleeping bag with me.

I moved out to the driver's cabin and wrapped my sleeping bag around me and sat and stared at the shimmering lake until it vanished behind the misted windscreen. I wondered what Glen's words could mean. Was Glen, supposedly straight, open to whatever might happen here? And if he was willing, again, what did this mean about Glen, about men, about me? Had I been worrying needlessly for my entire adult life about these feelings? Realising that I was shivering with cold, I resigned myself to returning to the main part of the van. The alternative was death by hypothermia.

I sat at the tiny dining table for a while, hesitating over whether I should perhaps return to the bunk and simply let whatever was going to happen happen.

But I couldn't bring myself to do it. I was too scared of the consequences: ridicule, rejection, scandal, and so,

65

instead, using my telephone as a torch, I fiddled around with the table, hoping to convert the dining area somehow into a bed but managing merely to unclip it from the floor and the wall.

Finally, admitting defeat, I pushed the table to one side, dragged down some seat cushions, and curling up on the floor, stared up at the moon, and wished I was still sandwiched against the big guy snoring above.

* * *

"What the hell are you doing down there?"

I opened my eyes to see Glen, now clothed, standing over me. Grey dawn light was dribbling through the windows.

"I couldn't sleep up there," I said, rubbing my eyes and propping myself up. "It was too hot."

"And you can sleep *there*?" Glen asked.

"You took the whole mattress. I ended up squashed in the corner."

"You have to defend your territory, dude," Glen said, now opening the door to the van and stepping out. "Fuck it's cold out here," he shouted back, as he closed it behind him.

By the time we had eaten breakfast – instant porridge and coffee – dressed for the cold and set up, it was starting to sleet.

Glen was wearing waders, a waterproof mac and a yellow fisherman's hat. He was standing ten metres out, flicking his line with well-practised panache.

Without waders, I was stuck on the riverbank, but I can't say I minded. It was bad enough having frozen water landing on my head without having it sloshing around my feet as well.

After an hour, my fingers were numb and my nose was running. The sleet had turned to snow now, but not the crisp, white kind – the wet, sticky, all-penetrating variety. The only parts of me that were warm were my feet, encased, thank god, in my new boots. I glanced out at Glen, an absurd cliché of manliness, apparently impervious to the cold, happy as Larry, flicking the line around as he pursued his third fish.

"I'm frozen," I shouted.

Glen looked back at me. "It's actually warmer out here," he said. "It's minus something where you are. But the lake's about five degrees."

"I'm gonna go sit in the van for a bit." I was already reeling in my line.

As they thawed, my fingers started to tingle painfully, bringing back childhood memories of too much play in the snow.

It was another two hours before Glen appeared in the doorway of the camper van, brandishing three trout, and by this time my mind was made up – I hated fishing.

"So how's our hunter-gatherer?" Glen asked as he dumped the fish in the tiny sink, and pulled the door to the van closed.

"Better in here than out there. This is crazy weather to go fishing."

"Crazier than going on a fishing trip and sitting in the van the whole time?" Glen asked.

"I tried it, Glen," I told him, evenly. "But it's not my thing."

Glen nodded at the fish in the sink. "Do you think you can gut one of those for lunch?"

"Nope," I laughed, "I wouldn't even know where to start."

Glen rolled his eyes, and pulled a can of soup from a

cupboard and handed it to me. "OK, I'll do it later. But in the meantime, see if you can heat that up, would you, honey?"

Without a word of complaint, that's exactly what I did.

The weather alternated between rain and sleet all afternoon. I ignored Glen's taunts and remained in the van. I read the remaining chapters of my novel and then listened to Radio Four on the van's radio.

At five, the sleet turned to snow, proper: small, elegant flakes drifting downwards. This was apparently too much for even Glen to tolerate: he appeared in the doorway swearing.

"Shouldn't you leave them outside?" I asked, nodding at the carrier bag full of trout that Glen was brandishing.

Glen glanced at the bag. "Why?"

"It's a bit hot in here for storing fish, that's all."

Glen wrinkled his nose. "It'll freeze out there," he said, then backing out of the van he added, "But you're right. I'll stick them up front."

Outside, Glen climbed out of his green waders and removed his mac, then returned to the van carrying a single large trout. "Right," he said. "Time to taste the fruits of our labour. Well, my labour."

He tasked me with peeling potatoes and set about gutting the fish. We worked, side by side, to the sound of Radio Four. It felt strangely domesticated.

"So?" Glen asked, once the meal was served.

I forked a lump of the pan-fried trout to my mouth. "Wow. Amazing," I said. And it was true. It was the freshest, richest, most succulent piece of fish that I had ever eaten. "I guess she can't weigh this once we've eaten it either."

68

Glen winked at me and tasted the fish himself. "Fuck that's good," he said.

"I hope that snow doesn't settle. I hope we can still drive home tomorrow."

"It'll be fine," Glen said, pulling a fish bone from between his teeth.

We spent the evening playing cards, drinking beer, and then, when this ran out, whisky from a bottle Glen produced. "Time for some serious stuff," he said, and for tonight, I decided to go along with whatever Glen wanted. I decided to let Glen set the agenda just to see what would happen if I relinquished, for once, control. As long as I didn't take the lead, I figured, there was no way I could be blamed – there was no way this could come back to bite me.

Between us we drank the entire bottle of whisky, and then, with not inconsiderable difficulty, we laughingly climbed the ladder to the double mattress.

As the previous night, it was stiflingly hot, but I managed to persuade Glen to open the roof vent before I fell asleep and rolled away. As Glen began to snore, I couldn't decide if I was sad or relieved that this was all that was happening tonight.

I was awakened, again, by the weight of Glen's arm falling across my waist. This time, I did nothing; I didn't move a muscle, neither aiding and abetting, nor resisting. I waited to see if, as before ... Yes, Glen's arm tightened around me and winched me in.

I was fairly sure that Glen wasn't really asleep, but in truth I couldn't be sure. But whether Glen was dreaming of his wife beside him, or aware that he was snuggling against my back, one thing was sure: he was enjoying it. His dick, erect and hard, was pressing uncomfortably against me.

I remained rigid, terrified to move. Because surely for this fiction-in-progress to remain guilt-free, we both had to continue to pretend to be asleep.

Glen, behind me, didn't move. He even relaxed his arm a little for a while, but just as I concluded that he really was asleep, his hand moved down, then slipped under my T-shirt.

As it gently stroked its way up my chest, my body tingled all over. Every cell felt invigorated and alive with sensitivity to his touch, so incredibly, unreasonably sensual, so irredeemably ecstatically perfect, that there was no debate possible as to whether this really was what I wanted. Sex with Hannah, even at its best, even at its most frenetic, had never come close to this sensation of simply being held, simply being caressed by these heavy rough hands.

"Do you want me to fuck you?"

I ceased, momentarily, to breathe. "I'm sorry?" I said, stupidly, pointlessly. Because we both knew that I had heard exactly what Glen had just said.

"Do you want me to fuck you?" Glen asked again.

"Would you want to do that?" I asked, genuinely astonished.

I felt Glen shrug behind me. "Sure," he said, shuffling down until his dick was against my arse. "Why not?"

"I . . . I never did that," I admitted.

"Hum," Glen said, now reaching down and pulling down my boxer shorts. As he did this he lightly touched my dick, and it twitched and lurched towards the hand of its own accord.

"Have you done it before?"

"What?"

"Fucked."

"Sure."

"A guy, I mean," I said.

I sensed Glen shrugging again. "A hole's a hole," he said, and even if I remained as aroused as before, something bright, something hopeful that I hadn't even been aware of, faded, and I became aware of it now only by its absence.

"So?" Glen asked.

"No," I said. "No thanks. Sorry." I felt absurd for thanking Glen for the offer, for apologising, but I simply didn't know how I was supposed to respond.

Glen took my hand and pulled it behind me, and just for a moment, for no apparent reason except perhaps some childhood terror, some memory of James, I imagined that Glen was going to twist my arm – literally. In fact, what Glen did was pull my hand down and place it next to his own dick. I stroked it a little, then grasped it.

"D'you want to suck it?" Glen asked, and though the idea hadn't yet crossed my mind, though I hadn't yet projected any further than these adolescent fumblings, the second it became an option, it was exactly what I wanted to do.

After less than a minute, Glen pushed me away – had I been doing it wrong? – and started to bring himself off, vigorously. He groaningly, gaspingly came over his own chest, and then, astonishingly, rolled away.

I lay there on one elbow, peering, in the gloom, at Glen's back. "Glen?" I said eventually.

"Go to sleep, dude."

"But I haven't . . ."

"Go to fucking sleep."

I rolled onto my back and lay quite still until Glen began to snore, and then finished off myself in the hope that this, once done, would enable me to sleep.

But despite the whisky, and despite the late hour, sleep remained an impossibility, and so I lay there and frowned and fretted and wondered what had just happened, and tried to comprehend how I had been so efficiently reduced to the role of insecure adolescent.

In the morning, though the weather had improved, Glen wanted to go. As I had been ready to leave pretty much since we got there, I didn't argue, but Glen's sudden brusque nature concerned me, and I struggled to understand why he would want to miss out on fishing on the first sunny day that we had had.

At the farmhouse, Betty revealed that she was nobody's fool, and asked Glen to estimate the weight of the two fish we had eaten. "We only ate one," Glen told her, and Betty grinned at his admission, at her victory, and added a tenner onto the bill.

The first half of the drive took place in complete silence, but just past Watford Gap, I asked, "Are you annoyed about something, Glen?"

"Uh?" Glen said, without glancing over.

"Did I do something wrong last night? Because, you know, this is all pretty new to me."

Glen wrinkled his brow. "I don't know what you're talking about," he said.

I sighed and watched a few miles go past before I said, "You don't seem very happy this morning. Is it to do with what happened last night?"

I watched as Glen took a deep breath, held it for such a

long time that I feared that he might collapse at the wheel, and then, still staring straight ahead, said, "Nothing happened last night, Cliff. Nothing. So just shut the fuck up."

Unable to think of any reasonable way to proceed, I turned my body and watched the trees spinning past the side window. Eventually the blur tired my eyes, and so I closed them, and then at some point I fell asleep. When I woke up, Glen had opened the passenger door and was holding my bag. "This is your stop, cowboy," he said loudly, and I blinked and struggled to focus.

* * *

The first time I was called queer was at secondary school. It must have been about my third day and a guy called Stephen Hawking (not *the* Stephen Hawking, I hasten to add) told me to stamp on a worm. I said "no" and when he started to walk towards me, I picked it up and threw it into the bushes.

"Fucking queer," Stephen declared, and then, one hour later, when I got to the classroom, he told Nigel Ramsey, the class bully, "That's the one."

"Right," Ramsey replied, with meaning.

I had no idea what the word queer meant, but I could tell that it wasn't a good thing; I knew they weren't complimenting me on my empathy for worms.

From that point on, the die was cast. The class naturally separated out into different layers of sediment: the bullies at the top, the smellies and the queers at the bottom, and everyone else floating precariously in between. It seemed that there was no way to change category, or at least, no way to rise in the pecking order. The only direction, if you momentarily dropped your guard, was down. In fact, it later transpired, there was a way to beat the system, but I didn't know that yet.

I was constantly harassed, incessantly picked on. Some days someone would steal my homework and run across the playing field pulling out pages. This was called "paperchase". Other days, Hawking and Ramsley would grab my feet, pull me to the floor, and then, taking one leg each, run across the field, dragging me along my back, ripping my uniform, before finally running one each side of a tree. This was called "tree treatment".

My parents' reaction to all of this was to bully me further when I got home. My mother, generally drunk, or at the very least on her way to being drunk, would slap my face for ripping my clothes. My father, under instruction from my mother, would take his belt off to punish me for the homework failure, something for which I would invariably be punished at school too. And James, dear James, twisted the knife by coming up with the nickname Clifty Queer, and by telling a few choice people at my school that this was what he called me at home. It spread like wildfire, of course.

The first year of secondary school was purgatory, no less. I spent most of my time in a state of terror: fear of my parents, my brother, my teachers and my schoolmates. The rest of the time I was either distraught or working to replace lost homework, or plotting how to end my own life. I really did want to die, and faced with such a life, who wouldn't see that as the preferable option?

At some point, I came to understand what the word queer really meant, and felt confused as to why it was being applied to me. My dream, in those days, was to marry a quiet undemanding girl and live in the country as far away from other human beings as possible. We would have kids, and I would love them, and hug them. I would help them with their homework and I would never ever hit them.

At the end of my third year, our parents took us out for a meal – an almost unprecedented event – so rare, in fact, that I can still remember exactly what I ate: gammon steak with a slice of pineapple on top, served with chips and peas.

The meal was their attempt at smoothing the way for the big announcement: we were moving from Huddersfield to Reading. Reading was very posh, my father told us. It was our big chance to better ourselves. Mum, sipping at her third glass of wine, wobbled her head and agreed.

James was furious. He had a girlfriend two streets away, and a mate who grew marijuana three doors down. He had false ID and a local pub that obliged him by not looking too closely at it. James, almost fourteen, did not want to move.

As for me? Well, I was ecstatic. It seemed to me that no matter what life would be like in "posh" Reading, it couldn't be worse than the life that I was living. I might, I decided, not have to kill myself after all.

The new house was smaller but nicer, and for the first year at least, Mum and Dad seemed happier. Dad wielded his belt less, and Mum stopped drinking. For a while.

James was thoroughly miserable – the move had knocked all of the stuffing out of him, and he suddenly found himself King of Nothing-At-All. But even that worked for me. James' misery had somehow neutralised him, for the time being at least.

But the best thing of all was the change of schools. Highdown was perhaps one of Reading's rougher schools, and it certainly contained its fair share of bullies. But compared to Huddersfield, it felt like a paradigm shift. The boys here, for the most part, seemed to be acting, playing some kind of hardman theatre. Try as they might, they just weren't that scary.

About a month into the new school year, one of Highdown's overlords, the thick-set Gary Piper, came up to me in the playground and demanded that I hand over the chocolate biscuit in my lunch box. I had enjoyed four weeks of smooth, trouble-free, paradisiacal existence and the idea that this might be ending, that this might all be happening again, was too much to bear.

I looked at Piper's curled lip, then down at my lunch box. The disputed item was a Jacob's Club (with raisins) – my favourite.

"Give it to me now or get a beating," Piper said. Even his vocabulary seemed false. A beating? Nobody in Huddersfield said "a beating".

I glanced around, and noticed three or four boys watching the action, and realised that my fate was being sealed here, my reputation decided. As I reached into the box and grasped the Club, my skin prickled with swelling anger.

Gary Piper took the biscuit and leered at me. "Fucking queer," he said, and as he turned to walk away, he slapped me, gently, across the side of the head.

The final slap was his big mistake. My eyesight misted red, and my hand shot out, whacking him across the ear so hard that the lunch box, which I was still holding, split on impact. Piper fell, clutching his bleeding ear, to the ground.

I jumped on top of him and driven by years of bottled up rage, gripped his head and started to pound it against the tarmac. He offered little resistance. Perhaps he was just too surprised to react.

A teacher dragged me off him, and it's just as well . . . I fear I might have killed him if we hadn't been separated. I was in some kind of a trance.

Piper was sent to hospital, and my parents were summoned to the school. As Mum was "ill in bed" – an alias for "too drunk to stand" – Dad came instead. He nodded gravely as the headmaster explained the seriousness of the situation and assured him that I would be punished, and that it would never happen again.

Once we were in his yellow work van, though, he said, "Well there's a turn up for the books. Glad to see you finally found your balls. Now buckle up and let's get you home. I've got another job at four. And try to get that uniform cleaned up before your mother gets up. You know what she's like."

It was the first and last time that my father ever showed any sense of pride in my behaviour, and I realised in that moment what a stupid man he really was.

Gary Piper, not the sharpest knife in the drawer either, was off school for two full weeks. When he did return, proudly bearing stitches across the back of his skull, he walked straight up and proposed that we be mates. For security reasons, I thought it best to accept.

From that point on, with Piper's backup, I felt relatively safe at school. Though I didn't join in the bullying or extortion, I did stand idly by, I did watch. And I somehow gained a reputation for being the strong silent one, the quiet, dangerous brain behind the terrorist.

Back home, my position was more tenuous. My mother

lapsed from one alcohol-fuelled crisis to another and my father tried to manage her while hiding the natural disdain he felt for his bookish son.

James, though calmer than before, still knew that he held a trump card, and didn't hesitate to use it, threatening to tell my new schoolmates of my nickname. Now that I had repeatedly smashed the school bully's skull against the tarmac, I didn't know how much sway James might have in what was, for him too, a new school, but I wasn't prepared to risk it. I continued to give in to any and all of James' demands.

Around the same time, I became conscious that I looked at my classmates differently to other boys. I noticed the muscles the school athletes flexed as they ran and jumped. I glanced, more than once, at the bulge in Mister Simpson's shiny suit trousers. Where my peers laughed and joked around in the showers, I remained frozen in my efforts *not* to look. But even then, even from the beginning, what I desired was so confused with what I wanted to be that I couldn't even begin to think about where the one ended and the other began.

Silently lurking behind my "dangerous" facade, I watched the world around me and tried to decode who I was. I listened to the lyrics of Bronski Beat's "Smalltown Boy" and nothing had ever seemed so attractive to me as leaving in the morning to escape these people who would never understand. But then I would look at Boy George or Liberace and see that they were so totally, terrifyingly *other*, that if queer was what they were, how could that category possibly include me?

Occasionally, very occasionally, I would see a woman whose beauty I would find astounding. I would look at Joanne Whalley, or Debbie Harry, or Farrah Fawcett Majors and think, "Yes, I could marry her." But then AIDS outed Rock

Hudson and Freddie Mercury – to me, stunning images of masculinity – and suddenly I wasn't so sure.

But with the exception of a couple of eighties pop stars there were still no positive role models to be found. Every news mention of homosexuality was about someone being arrested, or someone catching a disease; an MP losing his job or someone abusing boys.

Perhaps if things had been different – if the world had been different – then I would have found the neutral space to consider the question objectively and then I might have made different choices. But by the time my intellect had developed enough to even consider the question, all the terms that could describe the concept – queer, gay, poof – had all been used as insults and only as insults, and were preloaded with so much fear and shame that no sane person could choose such an identity. And whatever I was, I wasn't insane.

And so, when I found myself on a crowded bus, squashed against a very Rock Hudson-style man in a suit, or opposite a moustached Mercury lookalike, I would force myself to think about the simultaneous equations I needed to hand in tomorrow, or the words to the school hymn, or anything that would enable me to avoid one of my frequent adolescent erections.

The first girl ever to ask me out was called Susan, and she didn't look a bit like Farrah. I felt no desire for her whatsoever, it has to be said, but she was a girl, and she wanted to date me, so we dated.

Susan and I spent many happy hours wandering around Reading together, and many more sitting on the sofa holding hands, and for a while at least, this stopped James from calling me a poof.

And then one day, Susan got to our house before me and found James alone in the house. He managed to wheedle out of her that we weren't doing much kissing, and then offered to fill in for me in my absence. By the time I got home, his bedroom door was locked, and by the time they stepped out of his room – even though he was still underage – they had become an item.

FIVE

Hannah

Once we had had our "honest communication" talk, things between James and me started to get better again, even if changing old habits wasn't easy and I frequently found myself slipping into my old ways.

I would say, "I'm not feeling that well" and James would raise an eyebrow at me. "OK, I just don't fancy it," I would admit, and he would give me a wink for having decoded my own riddle.

Sometimes, he would say, "Hey, d'you fancy a quickie before we go?" and out of habit I would say, "Now? Are you *mad*?" but then catch myself, and turn back to kiss him instead.

We still fought over the light switch – me switching it off, and James playfully flicking it back on – but he started to understand my complexes and did whatever he could to reassure me. He told me over and over that I was beautiful, that he loved my eyes, my lips, my hair, the little hollow on the inside of my arms that didn't seem to have a name ... And if I didn't suddenly fall in love with my own body, didn't magically begin to consider myself beautiful, I did at least begin to suspend disbelief. I did at least start to believe that James truly was attracted to me.

So the initial teething problems of our relationship – which

I had feared signalled a precocious beginning of the end – seemed to be behind us now. We were getting on well, communicating honestly, and having more and better sex than I had ever had in my life. Honesty, it seemed, really was the best policy.

Yet there remained the challenge of future destinations, a subject that I suspected still had the power to blow everything apart.

James was phoning Australia almost every night now, frequently talking until first light as he struggled to manage his farm from a distance.

In November, his friend Ryan, who had been running operations for him in his absence, announced that he would be leaving at the end of the year, and I could tell from James' ever more frantic phone calls that it was only a matter of time before he would be required to fly home.

Of course a trip to Australia was far from being the worst thing that I could think of, but I had been hoping that James and Luke would have the time to get over their relationship problems before attempting a family trip to the other side of the world.

None of these were James' fault, it has to be said: he made constant efforts to befriend Luke, offering to fix his bike, or drive him places, or teach him how to do stuff or help him with his homework. But he always seemed to go about it in the wrong way.

Luke was twelve now, and would have respected total disdain more than James' attempts at friendship. I tried to explain this to James; I tried to tell him that he needed to make less effort, to *care less* whether Luke liked him or not, but he could never stop trying for long. I think he desperately wanted Luke to become his friend, perhaps even his adoptive son. And that desperation was the last thing Luke was going to respond to.

In late November, James came to bed at three a.m.

"Everything OK?" I asked out of habit, still half asleep.

"Not really," James said, which was unusual enough to drag me from my slumber.

"Can it wait till the morning?" I asked.

"Sure," James said, but within ten minutes, it was clear that his tossing and turning would not allow any sleep that night.

I reached out and switched on the bedside light. "OK then," I said. "Tell me what's wrong."

"It's nothing," James said, characteristically, but then proceeded, for the first time, to elaborate a list of woe.

Ryan had confirmed he was leaving the farm on Christmas Eve, and was refusing to take responsibility for finding his own replacement; the roof in the cowshed was in danger of collapse, but there was no one to organise refurbishment; a number of the herd had some respiratory disease and James feared – because it had been going on so long – that Ryan hadn't been treating it properly. The list went on and on.

"OK. So you need to go home," I said once he had finished.

"I need to go home," he repeated.

"And how long do you need to go home *for*?" I asked.

"How long's a piece of string?"

"Sure, but you must have some idea?"

James shook his head. "However long it takes to find someone to replace Ryan, to fix the roof, and whatever else I guess."

I sat up in bed. "Do you need to go soon?"

James nodded. "I think so."

"That's OK," I said. "I understand."

"You do?"

I nodded.

"Thanks," James said, smiling weakly. "I'll have a look at flights in the morning."

"Christmas is coming, so we could always come out and see you for the school holidays."

"Sure," James said. "That's what I was hoping you'd say."

* * *

Luke wrinkled his nose in disgust. "No way!" he exclaimed. I hadn't even finished my sentence.

"Why not?" I protested. "It'll be summer out there. We can go sightseeing. You can go diving and . . ."

"No way," he said again.

I ran a hand across my brow. "*Luke* . . ."

"No!"

"You're not being reasonable."

"'Cos I don't want to go."

"Sure. But what if *I* want you to go?"

"You can't *make* me."

I sighed. "Well, actually I kind of *can*," I said. "You're twelve, dear. In four years you'll be sixteen and then you'll be able to decide where *you* want go on holiday and you'll be able to get a job and pay for it too."

Luke let out a gasp of disgust and shook his head. "There's no way," he said. "Really! Just go with James. Knock yourselves out."

"And now you're being rude. And I won't have it."

"Why do you even *want* me to go?" Luke asked.

"Because I love you, and I want to go on holiday with you."

"I don't like him," Luke said.

And I thought, *So, finally, it's out in the open.* "OK, let's talk about that. Why don't you like him?"

"He's creepy."

"He is *not* creepy."

"OK, he *isn't* creepy."

"Look, I really want this, Luke. I'd rather not have to *tell* you that you're coming. I'd rather you just agreed. So please just do this, for me."

"But why?" Luke asked. "I don't get it. If I don't want to go, and I can't stand James, then what's the point? It'll all be horrible anyway."

I stared at the top of his head – it was impossible to catch his eye these days – and in line with my new policy of honest communication, I considered telling him the truth: that I wanted to go to Australia to see if I might want to live there, and I wanted him to come with me for exactly the same reason. But I realised that honesty has its limits, and that there are truths that no one wants to hear.

Luke finished his breakfast, dumped his bowl unceremoniously in the dishwasher, then ran upstairs. When he returned he had his trainers on.

"Where do you think you're going?" I asked.

"Dad's."

"No. Not today you're not. You're with *us* this weekend," I told him. "Dad's is next weekend."

"OK, I'm *not* going to Dad's," Luke said pedantically. "I'm going out on my bike."

"Luke! Wait!" I said as he turned to leave. "I thought we could do something together today. Something nice. All three of us."

Luke paused in the hallway to listen, but didn't turn back.

"I . . . thought we could go to Thorpe Park," I said, plucking the idea of going to the theme park from the ether.

Luke turned back to face me now. His expression was one of utter disdain. "You can't *bribe* me with Thorpe Park," he said.

"You know what?" I said, finally losing my cool. "Just bugger off then. Go and see your father. I'm sick to death of you!"

Luke didn't hang around to argue.

A couple of days later, when Cliff dropped Luke off at the end of the drive, I ran out to meet them. I had been waiting.

"Am I late?" Luke asked, worried by my urgency.

"No, not at all," I told him. "I just need to talk to your dad."

Luke paused, glanced back at Cliff, then glared at me.

"It's fine," I said, holding my hand up in a stop sign directed at Cliff.

Luke glanced at me suspiciously and then loped indoors as I walked to the car. The window on the passenger side slid down and Cliff leaned over and looked up at me. "Something wrong?" he asked.

"Can we talk for a minute?"

"Sure," he said, reaching for the door handle.

I peered into the car, but the interior seemed to be somehow too constrained, too intimate. "Can we walk instead?" I asked.

Cliff looked puzzled, but complied, standing, pulling on his suit jacket and locking the car. "So what's up?" he asked, as we started around the close.

"Well, it's about Luke," I said.

"Australia?"

"Ah. So he told you."

"Of course. Quite frankly, I think you're fighting a losing battle."

"But not if we both agree, surely? Not if we *both* tell him he has to go."

Cliff sighed. "You know he's not a little kid anymore. I can't see how you can force him to go. Unless you cuff and gag him."

"Can't you just back me up on this?" I asked. "Would that be too much to ask?"

Cliff shrugged. "It's not like *I* want him to go. I enjoy having him round. He's good company."

"But . . ."

"And he'd ruin your holidays. Just think about what he would be like on a twenty-three-hour flight or whatever it is. I honestly think you're asking for trouble."

"I just really need him to do this," I said.

Cliff screwed up his features. "But why?" And then I saw him work something out. "You're not coming back, are you?"

"Of *course* we're coming back," I said.

"But that's what this is about, isn't it. It's about checking out Australia for you and Luke."

"No," I lied. "It's about a holiday in the sunshine at Christmas."

Cliff turned his head slightly sideways whilst still looking at me from the corner of his eye. He clearly didn't believe me. "How long are you going for anyway?"

"Three weeks. It's just three weeks."

He sighed. "Sorry, Hannah," he said. "But unless you can convince Luke, I don't think that there's much that I can do to help."

"You could tell him it would be a good idea. You could tell him he'll enjoy it."

"But he won't," Cliff said. "You know he won't."

"What's he said? Has he given you a reason?"

Cliff shrugged. "He hates James. Plus, it's Billy's birthday on Boxing Day. Same as every year."

"Of course. I forgot about Billy's party."

"You should just go. Really. Enjoy yourself. Don't spoil it all dragging a recalcitrant teenager around with you."

"I suppose," I conceded, starting to think that maybe Cliff was right, that maybe this was the best option. If I liked Australia, I could always lure Luke out at a later date.

As if he were reading my thoughts, Cliff added, "And you realise that you can't move to Australia with Luke. Not as long as we have joint custody."

"I've no intention of moving to Australia," I said. "None."

Cliff twisted his mouth, still clearly unconvinced. We had reached the end of the close, so we turned around and headed back.

"So how was the trip with Glen?" I asked, trying to change the subject.

Cliff paused, shot me a glare, and then started walking again, but with a furrowed brow. "What did he tell you?"

"Nothing," I said. "I haven't even seen him."

"And Jennifer? Did you speak to her?"

"No," I said, thinking, *But I will now.*

"It was pretty average. It was freezing. It actually snowed. I don't think fishing's my thing."

"But did you have fun?" I asked. "With Glen?"

Again, something flickered across Cliff's face. I saw it

happen, and I saw him disguise it. "I don't mean . . . I didn't mean anything," I said.

"Anything? Anything like what?"

"Anything like anything. I just meant did you two have a good time together?" I internally grimaced at the fact that this sounded slightly worse.

Cliff started to walk faster now, but I trotted beside him and reached for his sleeve.

"Cliff. I didn't mean anything. *Really*," I said. "Why are you reacting like this?"

"I'm not reacting like anything," Cliff said. "I just don't like what you're implying."

"And what would that be?"

"I don't know," Cliff said, now pausing and turning to face me. He was slightly red-faced. "That something happened with Glen maybe?"

"*Did* something happen with Glen?" I asked, shocked now.

"NO!" Cliff said. It was almost a shout.

"OK!" I shouted back. "Then calm down for god's sake!"

"I'm perfectly calm," Cliff said, his voice revealing that he really *wasn't*.

We stood looking at each other for a moment, and then I said, "*Are* you gay, Cliff?" The words came out of my mouth before I even realised I was going to say them.

Cliff looked shocked, or perhaps outraged. But I couldn't tell if he was shocked at the question, or at the fact that I had asked it outright. "What business would that be of yours?" he said.

"It's just . . . we've never really talked about any of this."

"Because it's no longer any of your business."

"So you are, then?"

"Oh, sod off, Hannah," he said.

"I'm not trying to upset you Cliff. I'm just trying to underst—" My voice faded because a dreadful thought had just popped into my mind. I was astounded that I hadn't thought of it before. "Cliff, did you do stuff? When we were together? With other people? With men?"

"*What?*" Cliff's voice whistled.

"Do I need to be worried? That's all I'm asking. Do I need to be worried about you? About myself?"

Cliff opened his mouth to speak, but then closed it again. When he finally found his voice, he said, very quietly, "You're losing it, Hannah, losing it!" and then started to stride towards the car.

"Cliff, I'm not . . . *judging* you," I said, now running after him again. "I just want to know if . . ." I had reached the car just as Cliff wrenched the door open. He glared at me over the top of the car, and ran his tongue across his front teeth before speaking.

"Do I have AIDS?" Cliff asked. "Is that what you want to know?"

"No. Not at all. But, if you took risks . . ."

"You're turning into a real bitch, you know that?"

"That's unfair," I said. "I . . ." But words failed me.

Cliff started to duck into the car, but then paused and straightened again. "For your information, Dear," he said. "You don't have anything to worry about. Because I never did anything with anyone, *ever*. Not in the whole fifteen years."

And then he slid into the car, slammed the door and drove away.

I watched the car until it vanished from view, and then murmured, "That went well. Nice one, Hannah."

Not only had I failed to get Cliff on side for the trip to Australia, but I had made him as angry as I had ever seen him. And I had learned absolutely nothing. Because of course, I didn't believe a word he had said anyway. Which meant that I would have to see the doctor and get myself checked out.

SIX

Cliff

I never did cheat on Hannah, not once – not with a woman, and not with a man.

I'd love to claim that such saintly behaviour was born out of steely self-control and high principles, but it wouldn't be entirely true. As far as the fairer sex was concerned, Hannah was the only woman I had ever wanted to sleep with. And men, well, that was so complicated for me, and my experiences were so limited, that it seemed a virtual impossibility to even *think* about it.

In fact my first-ever sexual experience of any kind had been with a boy. It had happened during a holiday to Skegness. I had been forced, through lack of space, to share a bunk with my distant cousin Will. We were both fourteen years old. One night, in the windswept mobile home we had rented, Will reached over and grasped my dick, and out of a sense of fair play, I had returned the favour. Around us the adults slept on.

It never happened again, and it was never once mentioned or alluded to in any way. And even though I had liked the experience, even though I hoped every night for the remainder of the holiday that it would happen again (it didn't) once we got back to Huddersfield, I pushed it from my thoughts. My mind's capacity to suppress anything challenging has never ceased to amaze me.

A few years later, Will's marriage to Eileen was the first wedding I attended as an adult. As if proof were needed that these events of our adolescence meant precisely nothing.

My only other experience with a man had been during the three miserable months during which I was separated from Hannah.

It was a terrible time for both of us.

We had lost our first child and Hannah, on leaving the hospital, had gone to her sister Jill's place rather than returning to me. I was feeling lonely and angry, yet horribly guilty and perhaps, yes, even responsible for the loss of the baby. I was heartbroken but wounded by her accusation of "near rape".

It had happened the night after James seduced her, and everything had been a little out of control. I had momentarily ignored Hannah's refusal to have sex and tried to force myself upon her before realising that she was deadly serious. The second I had realised I rolled away. The way I saw it, I hadn't done anything to Hannah that night that I hadn't done a hundred times before; after all, if I had never learned to ignore Hannah's protests about sex, I swear we would never have had sex at all. So it seemed unfair that she should leave me because this one time had been different, because this one time, "no" had meant "no", and I had failed to recognise that. Considering that I had caught her snogging my brother just days before our wedding was supposed to take place, it seemed utterly unfair that the blame for our separation should rest upon my shoulders alone, but that was how Hannah saw things back then.

So I was lonely, and angry, and guilty, and filled with hatred for James, and remorse for what had happened, and grieving for the loss of our first child. The mix of emotions was so

93

choppy, so confused, that I don't think I even knew *what* I was thinking. I remember sitting staring at the computer monitor at work and realising that the entire morning had gone by without my striking a single key, my mind entirely occupied by the ebb and flow of all these novel emotions.

One Friday after work, I found myself forced, with colleagues, to celebrate our secretary Sheena's birthday. The drinks were on the company, and I drank more than usual, enough, in fact, that I barely noticed as my work colleagues started to drift away to their families, to their partners, to their individual Friday nights.

By the time I did realise that I was alone in the bar, it was eight p.m. and I was too drunk to drive and yet still not drunk enough to face returning to an empty house. Because the sheer volume of beer inside me was becoming untenable, I switched, I recall, to whisky.

At closing time I staggered from the bar and started to stumble across the park in the vague direction of home. I needed to piss, so I headed for a clump of bushes, and though there were thousands of square feet to choose from, I was surprised to find myself sharing my bush with another man.

I would love to be able to say that he was cute, or that there was some kind of conversation, some cheeky, amusing seduction process, but I honestly have no memory of the guy, nor of quite how it transpired that we ended up touching each other. He climaxed quickly, I didn't (I was too drunk to climax at all I think), and then before I even realised it, he was gone and I was staggering home across the green with a sticky hand and a fresh burden of self-loathing resting squarely upon my shoulders.

By the time I got back, I was feeling thirsty and hungover

and yet still perfectly drunk. I washed my hands and drank a few glasses of water, and struggled to push what had happened from my mind.

As a distraction, I switched the television on, and on screen was a blurred Catholic bishop talking about the repeal of a law – it was Clause Twenty-Eight, I think. Though modern society accepted many things, he was explaining, homosexuality was still a sin; it was still an *abomination*. Clause Twenty-Eight was, in his opinion, still very much needed. Children, he said, still needed to be protected from the sodomites. I remember, he used that word: *Sodomites*.

That's when I vomited.

Beyond all of the pressures from mediaeval religions and rabid, shameful closeted politicians, beyond the constant bombardment of heterosexual imagery in the press, in film, in TV, in advertising, there was another reason that I had decided I *had* to be straight, and that was probably the strongest reason of all: I wanted children.

I know that in these twenty-first-century days of gay adoption and surrogate mothers, of turkey basters and test-tube implants, an act of fatherhood for a gay man might not seem, to the modern eye, to be an impossibility. But that was not the case where I grew up, and that was not the case *when* I grew up. And it still wasn't the case in southern England in the mid-nineties either.

I had always, from as early as I can remember, wanted to be a father. I'd even say that it was more than a want, I just never once imagined *not* being a father. And so with the information I had, and based on the logic of the time, I knew that I must be straight.

The second happiest day of my life was the day Hannah told me that she was pregnant, even if that did all turn to sadness so quickly afterwards. Secretly, alone at work, I had cried tears of joy, the first tears of joy I had ever experienced.

And the only day to beat that, even now, would be the day that Luke was born. I held him in my arms and looked down at him and felt my heart swell until it was bigger than me, until it englobed everything around me, as if I had been reduced to, or perhaps *expanded to*, nothing other than my love for my son.

That emotion remains today – it creeps up on me when I'm unaware. I will be watching Luke from the corner of my eye, perhaps feeling vaguely irritated by something he's doing, and wham, that same feeling will wash over me. Love, joy, pride, all mixed up. It's ecstatic.

I worried throughout Luke's childhood that he would be soft, like me; I was terrified that he would be bullied at school, as I had been.

When at seven he came home with a split lip, I went overboard and forced him, against both his and Hannah's wishes, to take up judo. Poor Luke got more split lips at judo than he ever did in the playground, and I needn't have worried: Luke had inherited not my docile pacifism, nor my desire to avoid conflict, but Hannah's steely determination, her fiery sense of justice. So outside of judo, no one ever managed to push Luke around. Not even we, his parents, managed that.

But everything was changing, I could sense things shifting in my head. After the camping trip, I found myself unable to push what had happened with Glen from my mind. I felt as if I was maybe going mad. Everywhere I went, I found myself looking at guys, sometimes with clearly identifiable feelings of desire, but mostly with that familiar sensation of intrigue. I was still, at forty, looking at other men and wondering what they were like, how secure they felt in their sexuality, if I could look more like them if I dressed differently, if I *should* be more like them. Only this time, I was watching myself watching them. I had gained a smidgin of self-awareness and, for the first time in my life, I was toying with the concept that I might be gay, and that, what's more, maybe, just maybe, in the twenty-first century that wouldn't be the utter horror I had always imagined.

Things had changed a lot in the last twenty years, that was for sure. There were gay guys reading the weather, gay guys hosting chat shows, lesbians winning sports events, men with boyfriends – men who would have been called *practicing homosexuals* when I was young — being elected as MPs by the public at large.

Even within my own circle of friends and colleagues I could identify Bill, the IT guy and his boyfriend Paul; Tristan, Jill's best friend with whom we had been on holiday when everything went pear-shaped; the couple of bearded guys at the end of our close with matching motorbikes ... And thoughts about these people and projections about how they lived their lives started to obsess me.

About a week after the argument with Hannah, I was standing in the coffee room at work thinking about all of this (Paul had sent Bill some flowers) when Ralph, one of the partners, came in.

"Cliff," he said. "You missed the meeting."

I glanced at the clock and realised that I had been standing staring at the flowers, propped in the sink, specifically staring at the label – "I Love You" – for over half an hour.

"Sorry," I said. "I got distracted, I guess. I have a lot on my mind at the moment."

Ralph nodded and rested one hand lightly on my arm. I wondered if he would still do that if he had thought that I was gay. I reckoned not. "We had a talk. In your absence," he said. "We all agree that you should take some time off."

I frowned at him. "Really?"

"You've been pretty useless lately if truth be told. And we know that's not normal for you."

"As I say, I have a lot on my mind," I said. "But I need to work on the . . ."

"John's happy to take over your workload for a bit. We all think that you should take a week off. Get yourself sorted out."

I nodded. "Oh," I said vaguely. I was trying to imagine how I could get through a whole week alone in the flat. It seemed like an impossible task, a terrifying desert of emptiness to be crossed.

Ralph slapped me on the back, said, "Anyway, just hand the files to John before you go," and turned and left the room.

Once the door had closed behind him, I said quietly, addressing the empty room, "My wife has left me for my brother. She wants to take my son to live in Australia. And I think I might be gay. It's not really something I *can* sort out in a week."

Just before twelve the next day, Hannah called me.

"Hi, Hannah," I said coldly.

"Hi, it's Hannah," she replied briskly, as if she hadn't heard me. "I wondered if we could have a word. About Luke."

"Luke . . . yes. Sure."

"I'm not disturbing you am I?"

"No," I replied, which was something of an understatement. Even though it was Hannah calling, and even though I was still angry with her, the telephone ringing had been the highlight of my day. Since getting up at nine, I had done nothing but watch breakfast TV. "So, Luke!"

"Now, I know we already discussed this, but would you have a word with him about this Australia trip?"

I must have sighed at this point, because Hannah said, "Don't *sigh* at me Cliff."

"I'll sigh if I want to," I said, thinking . . . *It's my party and I'll sigh if I want to.* My mind had been coming up with lyrical witticisms as long as I could remember, but I had learned at school never to say them out loud.

"Look, Hannah," I continued. "You're right. We already *did* discuss this, and you know that I don't much want him to go, and Luke *definitely* doesn't want to go. So quite why—"

"*Please* Cliff? It's really important to me," Hannah pleaded. She sounded like she might be close to tears.

I started to sigh again, but caught myself doing so, because something in her tone had registered, had reminded me that once, not so long ago, I had loved her. "I'll have a word with him," I said quietly. "But I really don't think it will help. You know what he's like."

"I do. But please try."

"I will. I promise," I said.

"Do *you* need anything?" Hannah asked.

"I'm sorry?"

"I presume you're off with the flu, are you? Everyone's getting it. It's sweeping the school like wildfire."

"No, I'm not sick at all."

"Oh. That's what they said when I phoned the office."

"Really? Well, that's incorrect."

"Then why *aren't* you at the office?"

"Sorry, I have to go now, Hannah," I lied. "There's someone at the door."

I ended the call and laid down the phone, then stared out of the window at the grey November sky, and tried to imagine Christmas here without Luke. That would be even worse than this horrible week off.

An hour later Jill, Hannah's sister, phoned. As she had never phoned me in my life, this was an unsettling development.

"I just phoned for a chat," Jill declared.

I pinched the bridge of my nose, and took a deep breath. "Did Hannah put you up to this?"

"Of course not."

"But she gave you my number, presumably."

"Actually I texted Luke for it," Jill said, sounding vaguely angry.

"Look Jill, I'm just gonna come out and say this. You have never phoned me. Not once. So this is weird. To say the least."

"Yes, I know."

"Then why now?"

"I'm worried about you, I suppose. Is that allowed?"

I softened my tone. "I suppose so."

"You're off work. Hannah told me that much. And she doesn't know why."

"So she *did* get you to phone me?"

"Not at all. I promise."

"OK."

"Anyway, I hardly talk to Hannah these days about anything. She's always going on . . ." Jill's voice faded.

"About James," I said, completing the phrase.

"Yes. Sorry. I get sick of hearing about him to be honest."

"But not as sick as me."

"No. I can imagine. So *are* you sick?"

"I . . . I'm . . . You know what, Jill. I don't want to offend you, but I can't really talk to you about anything that's going on in my life right now. You're Hannah's sister. I'm sorry."

"Can't I be a friend as well? Isn't that possible?"

"I'm not sure. But no, I don't think so."

"Even if I promise not to say a word."

"I'm . . . not sure I'd believe you," I said. Jill had never been much good at discretion. Hannah hadn't nicknamed her Blabber Mouth for nothing.

"Oh. OK," Jill said, sounding resigned. "Actually, I'm not sure I would either."

"But the . . . um . . . intention is appreciated."

"Sure. But you do have someone to talk to, right?"

"Of course," I said, realising only as I said it that I truly didn't.

"Right. Of course. Do you want Tristan's number?"

"Why the hell would I want Tristan's number?"

"I don't know. I just thought maybe . . ."

"So Hannah said something. She must have."

"She really hasn't."

"Then why Tristan?"

"Well, actually Tris' may have mentioned something. In passing. Something about Grindr?"

"He *told* you?! Then that's a really great reason why I don't want his number."

"He's just worried about you. We both realise that this hasn't been easy for you either."

"Thanks."

"OK, sorry. I suppose I shouldn't have called. But if you ever do need to talk . . ."

"I now have your number."

"I mean it, Cliff. I know I'm Hannah's sister and everything, but we've known each other forever."

"We have," I admitted.

"OK, bye then."

"Bye," I said, but then something caught in my throat. "Jill?" I asked urgently.

"Yes?"

"Just one thing."

"Yes?"

"If you were me . . ."

"Yes?"

"Who would *you* talk to about . . . you know . . . about all of that stuff."

"Oh. Me maybe? I'm surprisingly good at . . ."

"Too close."

"Fair enough. Then why not Tristan?"

"Too partisan. And indiscreet as well."

"What about a therapist?"

"A therapist?"

"Yeah. If you need someone detached, someone objective . . . if you need confidentiality. Well, that's what therapists are paid for, isn't it?"

"Right."

"You're not OK at all, are you?"

"Not really, no. But please don't say anything to Hannah."

"No. I promise. I promise on . . . On Pascal's life, OK?"

"Pascal the pool guy? Are you still seeing him?"

102

"On and off, yeah. He's coming over next week as a matter of fact."

"Blimey. I mean, he seemed nice enough. I just didn't think . . . I thought it was a holiday romance thing."

"I did too. Life's full of surprises, isn't it? Look, I'll send you a number. As soon as I hang up. A woman my friend Lisa sees. A counsellor. Lisa says she's great. And she's not too far from you."

"OK."

"Give her a call. We all have to talk stuff through sometimes."

"Sure."

"And at least you know she'll be honest and it'll be private."

"Right."

"Look after yourself, Cliff."

"Thanks, Jill," I said. "I'll try."

The text message arrived about a minute later. It said: "Jenny Church. Counsellor. Call her," and was followed by the number. I was still fingering my phone and thinking about phoning it when Luke got home at six.

"Hey, Dad," he said, dropping his rucksack on the floor. "What's up?"

"Nothing much," I replied. "Your mother called."

"Mum? Not Jill? 'Cos she texted me for your mobile."

"Yes. Jill called too."

"What did Mum want?"

"She just asked me to talk to you. About Australia. About Christmas in Australia."

"There's no way," Luke said. "I already told her a hundred times."

"Well, we both think you should maybe reconsider it a bit.

103

It would be a great experience for you. You've only ever been to France, and—"

"Don't you *want* me here at Christmas?" Luke asked, looking genuinely hurt at the idea. "Is that it?"

"Not at all. I love having you here. And you know it."

"Then I'm not going," he said. "End of."

I exhaled deeply and shrugged: I had neither the energy nor the desire to fight this battle. "OK. Whatever," I said.

Luke smirked.

"What?"

"Nothing," he said.

"No, come on. What?"

"You said, 'Whatever,'" Luke laughed. "You're always having a go at me for that."

"Well, I'm tired," I said. "And what exactly are you doing with that?" Luke had picked up the TV remote and was pointing it at the television.

"It's seven. *The Simpsons!*" he said.

I nodded. "Sure. Whatever."

SEVEN

Hannah

Cliff's mystery absence from work had me worried. I tried to interrogate Luke, but he was useless, insisting, simply, that Cliff was "fine". When I asked him what he was doing all day, he said, "Dunno. Watching *The Simpsons* and stuff."

In desperation, I got Jill to call him, but she drew a blank as well. He wasn't going to talk to my sister either, which was unsurprising really.

It was illogical and more than a little hysterical of me, I know, but I started to convince myself that Cliff had AIDS. I had always had hypochondriac tendencies (which I fought) but I now started to Google the symptoms and became persuaded that our various bouts of fever over the last few years had been not flu but HIV conversion symptoms, that the weight I had lost since France had been not caused by stress, or the endless long walks that James and I were taking, but some related wasting disease. I steeled myself and made an appointment at the doctor's.

The consultation was one of the most humiliating experiences I have ever undergone. I told him that I was in the process of separating from my husband, and before I could explain my fears, he assumed that I was suffering from depression. "So you need a little something to help you over the bump, do you?" he asked, his pen already poised to write a prescription for Prozac. Men!

I explained that, no, I wasn't feeling depressed at all, and then flushed with shame at the admission.

"Oh! Good!" he exclaimed, straightening in his seat and looking surprised.

Once I had managed to splutter the purpose of my visit, he explained that he could take a blood sample and give me the results in a week, or that I could walk into the private clinic on Weybourne Road and get it done instantly. Because a week of uncertainty seemed hellish to me, that's exactly what I did.

It was still only ten-thirty when I got there and, thankfully, the waiting room was empty. I had been wondering what I would say if I bumped into someone I knew.

Despite the morning lull in trade, I still had to wait fifteen minutes before I was seen, and during that time I convinced myself that the result would be positive. It seemed, in that moment, that it had to be positive – that the laws of karma required retribution for my having left my husband, for sleeping with his brother, for not being as depressed as I was supposed to be about the end of my marriage.

The nurse asked me a few embarrassing questions, finishing with *how would it change my life if I had a positive result, or a negative result?* I replied twice that I had no idea, and she seemed satisfied with this, which left me wondering why she had asked me in the first place.

And then she pricked my finger and transferred the blood to a stick that looked like a pregnancy test. She smiled at me stupidly during the entire thirty-second wait, whilst I sat and thought how, if it were positive, it would be the end of my relationship with James, of my new life, of everything.

"Well there you go," she finally said, sliding the stick across the table to me. It showed a single pink line.

"Which means?" I asked, momentarily confused. She had explained the test to me less than thirty seconds earlier, but so convinced was I that it would be positive, that single line made no sense to me.

"It's all clear," she said. "You're fine."

I burst into tears.

I didn't mention the test to James that evening, even when he asked me if I was OK, even when he commented that I was quiet. I pretended it was just because he was leaving for Australia the next morning, and in part that was true as well. I was nervous about missing him, and scared of finding myself alone in the house.

Once I had tearfully waved goodbye at the train station the next morning, I returned home. Luke was at school and in James' absence, the place felt like a museum of my marriage with Cliff all over again.

Within an hour, I had thrown myself into a cleaning frenzy that I continued every day that I wasn't at the school. I scoured and scrubbed and "simplified" – my code word for removing from the space anything that spoke too deeply of my time with Cliff. I thought of an episode from *Absolutely Fabulous* and muttered, "I want to see surfaces, sweetie, surfaces." But as every item of furniture was something that we had bought together, every bit of wallpaper a sheet that we had laughingly hung, it was an impossible task from the start. All I managed to do was to make the house feel even emptier.

On three separate occasions I tackled Luke about the Australia trip, but if it had been clear from the start that he would not come willingly, it became a little more obvious at each discussion that the only sane course of action was to travel alone and leave him with Cliff, and that is what I eventually resigned myself to doing.

When I finally phoned James to admit defeat, he revealed that he had booked my plane ticket weeks before. He had always known, he said, that Luke could not be convinced.

*　　*　　*

Finally, on the twentieth of December, Luke's last day at school, I closed the door on the ridiculously spotless house and started to drag my suitcase towards the car.

Amazingly, I had only ever flown four times in my life, and these flights had been short-haul trips, so I was as excited about my epic journey as I had ever been.

As the flight dragged on and on, punctuated only by bland meals and family-friendly films, that excitement turned to stress, boredom, discomfort and finally a kind of exhausted despair that I had never known before. My back ached from the confinement of the seat, my throat hurt from the putrid air being pumped through the cabin. Somewhere over Israel my head started to pound, and just as the pilot announced our descent to Hong Kong airport, my nose, somewhat explosively, began to bleed. By the time I arrived in Sydney, I felt like, and was pretty sure I looked like, a troop returning from Iraq.

I queued for my baggage, and then again for customs. I queued for immigration. I promised that I wasn't smuggling soil or fruit or insects, assured them that I wasn't looking for work or healthcare either, and then with a wave of the hand, I was free to step out into the arrivals hall.

James was right there – he had travelled down from Brisbane

to meet me. "You made it!" he exclaimed, bright as a button. He strode towards me and wrapped me in his arms.

"Only just," I said, resisting the urge to cry. "That was one of the most dreadful experiences ever."

"It's a bloody long way, huh?" James laughed.

"Yes, a *bloody* long way," I repeated.

"Come on, old girl," he said. "You'll feel better once you've had a shower."

"I'll feel better once I've had a shower, eaten, slept for a week and had a head transplant," I told him.

"It's all doable," James said. "Well, except the head thing. The hotel's lovely. We've got a sea view. You're gonna love it."

"Sounds great," I said. "Is it far?"

"Nah. Half an hour," James said, extending the handle of my suitcase and starting to drag it off across the concourse.

"Oh, and James?" I said.

"Yes?"

"Don't *ever* call me old girl again, OK?"

He squeezed my waist. "You've got it," he said. "*Old girl.*"

I shot him a glare and he pulled a silly face, and somewhere deep within me, I detected that, despite everything, my sense of humour was still alive. Just about.

The light in Sydney was amazing enough that it managed to pierce my daze. I had come from an English winter to an Australian summer, but even taking that into account, the light was exceptional.

As the train pulled out from the airport, I nestled against James and looked out at the cloudless blue sky, and the rich zinging colour of it all. "It reminds me of the south of France," I murmured.

109

"Really?"

"Not the view. The light. The way all the colours are so bright. Look at that bulldozer over there," I said, pointing. It was shimmering yellow against the green of the grass.

I sensed James nodding beside me. "It's kind of extra bright, isn't it," he said. "Like those old Daz adverts?"

"Yes. That's exactly it."

I watched the countryside slide by, and then the endless suburbs of Sydney, and slowly the city skyline rose before us.

We got off at Circular Quay, a port crowded with crazy criss-crossing boats, and bustles of people fighting their way to and from them. It was a hot day, in the high twenties, and I was overdressed for summer. But the air smelt fresh and salty, and my brain slowly started to come to. "It's a busy old port," I commented. "Where do all the boats go?"

"The beaches," James said. "And suburbs along the coast. They're just water buses really."

How wonderful, I thought, *to take a ferry to work instead of the tube*. "Can we take one tomorrow?" I asked. "Just for fun?"

"We sure will," James confirmed, squeezing my hand.

Our hotel, a Holiday Inn, was an impressive red building, dramatically modernised beyond its "historic" facade. My initial disappointment that we weren't staying in some romantic bijou hotel faded as soon as I saw the room. I dropped my jacket on the bed and ran to the window, from which I could see the whole of the port, the boats zipping in and out, the Sydney Harbour Bridge, and beyond that Australia's most famous landmark, the Opera House.

110

"My god," I said. "Now that's a room with a view."

"You like it?" James asked, lifting my suitcase onto a rack, then crossing to join me. "Did I do good?"

"It's gorgeous, James," I said, turning to kiss him. "Thank you!"

I took a shower and changed into light summer clothes – a pre-crumpled linen suit I had bought from French Connection for the trip.

"So what next?" James asked when I reappeared. He was lying on the bed, his arms crossed behind his head. "Sleep? Tucker? Drink? Or d'you fancy a bit of naughty?"

"Ooh a drink," I said. He looked so disgruntled I had to laugh. "Oh, I'm sorry, babe," I told him. "But the idea of a gin and tonic is just too much to resist. Is there a bar here where we can get one?"

James stood and took my hand. "Come on."

He led me to the lift, and when the doors closed he pulled me to him and kissed me. "I've missed you so much," he said, taking my hand again as the door opened.

The roof garden had a sparkling blue pool with half a dozen sunbeds along one side. We were the only people there. I strode to the edge and looked out at the bay. A gentle breeze was blowing from the sea, ruffling my hair, and the view was astounding in every direction.

"Nice?" James asked with typical understatement.

"Nice!" I confirmed, glancing up at the sun, and then at my watch. "Is this right?" I asked. "Is it three p.m.?"

James nodded. "Jet lag's confusing, isn't it. Plus the fact the sun goes the other way."

"It goes the other way?"

"Yeah," James said. "In England it does that . . ." he drew

111

an arc from left to right. "But in Oz it goes like that," he continued, doing the same gesture in reverse.

I frowned. "Can you explain that to me tomorrow when I've had some sleep?"

James laughed. "Sure."

I peered again over the balcony at the swarms of people below, then turned to follow him to one of the sun loungers. "It's so busy down there!"

"It's a big city. And it's high season."

A waiter appeared, so we ordered a gin and tonic and a beer, then I sank onto my recliner and closed my eyes. "This is heavenly," I said, reaching out with my left hand until it found James' arm.

"I'm glad you like it," he said, fumbling for my fingers.

"I am *so* tired though. I feel as if I have been drugged or something."

"It's tough," James said. "But worth it. I'm so glad you came, Han'. Oh, drinks are here already."

I opened my eyes to find the waiter rounding the pool with a tray containing a bowl of rice snacks and our drinks. My gin and tonic tasted like some magical elixir invented by the gods for the sole purpose of reviving weary travellers. The ice cubes chinked as I sipped it, the sun sparkled in the bubbles. "God, that's good," I said, taking a second sip, then putting down the glass.

I turned my face to the sun and let myself soak in the heat from that fabulous ball of fire, a ball of fire that, back in England, I had all but forgotten existed.

Sydney was gorgeous. We were only there for two nights, but I couldn't fault the place. We meandered through sunlit shopping streets, took a blowy, salty ferry out to Manly beach (which was aptly full of very manly bodybuilders); we sat in funky coffee shops and drank luscious Italian-style cappuccinos, ate gorgeous seafood platters in gleaming restaurants . . . With everything being in English, the place felt comfortable and familiar yet new and shiny and different, like a remanufactured version of home, only sunny.

A few times we walked past groups of drunken Aboriginals in doorways or on park benches – a stark reminder that all of this glitz had come at great cost to *someone*. But when I asked James what Australians thought about the Aboriginals, he said, rather brutally, "We don't much," and talked about something else instead.

That reply shocked me, and for half an hour or so I worried about that hard selfish streak I had detected in him previously. Despite my critical silence, James continued to be lovely to me, and he was so forthright and sexy and warm that I couldn't resist him for long. I finally reasoned that I understood nothing about Australia, and decided that I would just have to put the Aboriginal question in a box for later analysis. When a beggar asked us for money, I handed him one of my plastic banknotes, as much to see what James would say as anything else.

"He'll just buy booze with it," was his comment.

"If I were living on the street in my own country, surrounded by rich white people, I'd want to be drunk too," I replied.

"Fair dinkum," James laughed, grinning at me.

"What?" I asked.

"What do you mean, *what?*"

"What's with the big grin?"

"Oh, I just can't believe how lucky I am to have you here with me," James said.

That afternoon we went to Bondi Beach, smothered ourselves in factor fifty (the sun's rays were so strong they pricked the skin), and went swimming in the crazy waves.

Though the beach was vast, most of it was prohibited for bathers due to lethal rip tides. But being crowded into a tiny strip of sea along with hundreds of other people was fun. James and I ended up playing with some kids in a boat – people all seemed very friendly and open, it felt almost like a visit to a different era, to the fifties perhaps.

Then we spread our towels on the sand, and with my head resting on his rising and falling chest and his hand caressing my hair, I fell into a deep jet-lagged slumber.

When we got back to the hotel I took a shower to wash the sand and the sun cream off, and though I had been quite reasonably white when I went into the bathroom, I was a deep shade of pink by the time I came out. It was as if the cream had been not protecting me from sunburn, but hiding it.

"I look like a lobster!" I said plaintively as I stepped back into the bedroom.

James rolled over and looked at me with such desire that it made my heart race. "Sexiest bloody lobster I've ever seen," he said.

Once we had delicately made love – my shoulders and neck were raw – we headed back out and wandered through the narrow streets of The Rocks to Darling Harbour, a glitzy modern space of open promenades and waterside bars.

Along with tens of other people, we took off our shoes and paddled in a vast spiral water feature and then, after some debate, chose an Indian restaurant for a leisurely aperitif and a disappointingly bland Thali. By the time we had eaten, the sun had gone down and the lights from the bars were sparkling on the surface of the water and I felt, with the exception of the sunburn, as if I had stumbled into an advertising shoot.

"How's the jet lag?" James asked me once our plates had been taken away.

"It comes and goes," I said. "Sometimes I feel as if I'm going to collapse and have to be carried back to the hotel. And then ten minutes later I feel fine again."

"You'll be back to normal by tomorrow, I reckon," he said, stroking my hand. "If you can just make it through to bedtime."

"I think we're already there," I commented, glancing at my watch. It was ten to eleven.

"Unless we go dancing?" James said.

Dancing! I hadn't danced for over ten years. I wasn't even sure quite what the word meant these days. "Dancing," I repeated.

James shrugged. "It's our last night in Sydders," he said. "We might as well."

We ended up in a nightclub called Cherry, surrounded by people in their twenties. The music was strange, electronic, monotonous and yet, and yet . . . with a few drinks inside me, it was incredibly easy to dance to, and surprisingly euphoric. For an hour and a half we danced and shouted snippets of conversation, and laughed at the fact that even shouting we *still* couldn't hear each other. For an hour and a half I was not only in love, but twenty again, and, as James would say, it felt bloody great.

115

And then, while we were queueing at the bar, I caught sight of a twenty-year-old Kylie lookalike staring at me. The queue for drinks was slow, and initially I ignored her, but eventually her open-mouthed gaze was too much for me. "Can I help you?" I asked her.

"Oh, sorry," she said, slipping into a crazy grin. "I was just wondering how old you are."

I glanced at James, who frowned. "What business is that of yours?" he asked the girl.

"Oh, don't get me wrong," she said, still grinning. "It's just that I think it's really great . . . the way you're still dancing. At your age and everything. How old are you?"

"I'm thirty-eight," I told her. "So not actually ancient, you know?"

She nodded. "That's amazing," she said. "You're older than my mum. I hope I'm like you when I'm old. I hope I'm still enjoying clubs and stuff."

Her boyfriend, a spotty nineteen-year-old, tugged at her sleeve at that point. "Forget the drinks," he shouted. "You'll be there all night."

"This woman is thirty-eight!" Kylie told him loudly, pointing at me. "Isn't it great that she's still enjoying life?" And then, giving me a little fingertip wave, she turned and vanished into the crowd.

"Wow!" I exclaimed, scanning the youthful faces around me, many of whom were now looking at me. "Still enjoying life!"

"Silly bitch," James laughed, "She was off her head on drugs."

"Yes," I agreed. "Yes, I'm sure." I did my best to smile too, but from that point on, all I really wanted to do was leave. Which, less than five minutes later, is exactly what we did.

"Has that girl upset you?" James asked, as we headed back to the hotel.

"No," I lied, then, "Maybe. A bit."

"Don't let it get to you," James said. "You're more beautiful, and far more clever than she'll ever be, no matter how old she gets."

And though I felt instantly just a tiny bit better, the event troubled me, stupidly, the whole way back to the hotel and even on into the next morning.

* * *

Because it was midsummer in Sydney, it had entirely escaped my attention that it would be the wet season up in tropical Brisbane.

We were greeted with grey skies, thirty-degree temperatures and eighty per cent humidity. It was nigh on unbearable and every part of my linen suit started to cling to me before we had even stepped out of the plane.

Once we had negotiated the airport, we took a fast, modern train link into the city before checking into a smaller more mundane hotel in the centre.

"Sorry it's not as good as the place in Sydney," James apologised, "but I'm trying to get you prepared for the farm."

We showered and then made love, then, sweaty despite the air con, showered again before heading out. Once again, the humidity outside the hotel hit me like a brick and as the doors to the hotel slid closed behind me I could already feel beads of sweat sprouting on my forehead.

We wandered around the streets for a while, dipping in and out of air-conditioned shops and malls when the heat got to be too much for me (James seemed impervious) and eventually ended up in an area called Southbank, a stunning development of restaurants and museums, cinemas and bars set in a strip of tropical parkland right next to the beaches.

As in Sydney, the place was teeming with swanky restaurants offering just about every cuisine that the mind can imagine, and after some hesitation we chose a glitzy-looking place called The Jetty, which seemingly offered something from just about everywhere on a single menu: James ordered a beef burger and I plumped for risotto primavera.

As we sipped our drinks, the temperature fell a little and the empty tables around us filled with revellers. The ambient noise level began to rise and in response everyone simply spoke ever louder to compensate. James and I were soon shouting at each other just to be heard. Everyone seemed happy though, and the temperature was dropping, the wine was smooth and velvety – I was recovering from my jet lag and feeling good as if, perhaps, the tipsy, relaxed atmosphere of the place was infectious.

"So what do you think of Brissie?" James asked.

I looked around at the eating, drinking hordes, at the lovely waterscape beside us, and smiled at him. "It's lovely," I said. "It's a bit like the place we ate in Sydney. Only more relaxed, somehow. More languid maybe."

James nodded.

"And hotter, of course . . ."

"Yes, that takes some getting used to, huh?"

I looked around again and noted a vague feeling of unease within me, and analysed it to try to find the source. It was something to do with the newness, the shininess of everything, to do with the lack of history, or innate culture perhaps . . . It felt a little as if Ikea had been commissioned to "do" the whole town, and just as I always have a vague feeling of something lost when I enter an old building entirely gutted to make it "modern", I sensed here that something was missing. These chic hotspots of Australia seemed to be taking our whole culture of consumerism, our "out with the old and in with the new" obsession to a whole new level, and again, I thought about the Aboriginal Australians – one of the most ancient cultures on the planet, yet so entirely absent here.

James leaned down to look into my eyes. "Something wrong?" he asked.

I shook my head and smiled. Other than strange European cravings for old grubby decors, for tradition, for buildings older than myself, everything was lovely; it was as enjoyable an experience as I could have hoped for. "No, it's great," I said. "Really."

"Make the most of it then," James said. "Tomorrow it's back to real life."

I squinted at him and smiled slyly. "You've warned me about the farm twice now. Is it really that bad?"

James raised an eyebrow. "Things are in a bit of a mess, that's all. There hasn't been a woman around the place for a while, remember."

I nodded. For no apparent reason, a terrible thought popped into my mind: that perhaps this was what James needed most – *a woman around the place*. But I kept that to myself. "Well, I'm sure it'll be fine," was all I said.

Our charming and *very* camp waiter returned at that moment with our food, and the plates were so absurdly large, and the portions on them so inversely small, I couldn't help but laugh. But though tiny, my little mound of risotto was delicious, my second glass of wine as good as the first, and with James playing footsie with me under the table as he wolfed down his burger, it would have been hard to think of anything that could make the moment better. I felt as happy as I had been in years.

The next morning, we took a train to a suburb called Morningside, where James had left his battered four-wheel drive to be serviced during his absence.

The drive north took us through more suburbs, and then out into open country. Much of the highway was bordered with tree-lined embankments, but on the more open stretches I caught glimpses of vast sandy beaches and river inlets and lakes. As the high rises of the city shrank behind us the spooky forms of the Glasshouse Mountains rose ahead.

"It looks better on a clear day," James commented, and I nodded and imagined that without this oppressive blanket of grey over everything, the views would indeed be stunning.

"The beaches look amazing," I said. "You can see why they call it the Gold Coast."

"This is the Sunshine Coast actually. The Gold Coast is to the south."

"Is it like this?"

"Kind of. The beaches are bigger. It's more glitzy. These are more family oriented."

Once we left the highway and started to head inland, the countryside grew greener and opened out into gently rolling swathes of green. The road would rise to the top of a hill providing majestic views of grasslands and forests in the distance, then slip back down into a copse of trees. Every time we broke cover, the chimney-like forms of the mountains in the distance provoked a small intake of breath, and when at one point the cloud cover broke allowing shafts of sunlight to push through the humidity, illuminating a stretch of plain, I murmured a *wow* and struggled to pull my camera from my bag. As always with these things, by the time I found it, the sunlight had vanished.

My first glimpse of the farm also provoked a sharp intake of breath, but for a different reason. After a series of ever smaller roads and finally a bumpy muddy farm track, the car rolled and lurched through potholes and puddles, and then finally burst out of a strip of woodland revealing the farm in front of us.

Stupidly, the word "farm" had conjured up, for me, romantic images of stone cottages with roses around the door. I was expecting a dusty farmyard with chickens clucking around. The reality was a wide flat plateau of muddy grassland surrounded by industrial fencing to keep the grazing cows in place, a series of breeze-block cowsheds and beyond those, the house. This was an enormous single-storey building, the left half of which seemed to be the rotting original wooden construction, and the right half, a more recent, unfinished breeze block add-on. The grass around the house had been trampled to mud and various bits of rusting farm equipment were dotted around the place, seemingly left wherever they had expired. Virtually all of the paint had long since flaked from the wooden slats of the original building, whilst the newer section, lacking rendering and even a couple of windows, had clearly never been finished.

"Gosh," I said.

"I did warn you," James said with laughter in his voice.

But the truth was that he hadn't. Only a photo could have

prepared me for this, and it was probably for the best that I hadn't seen one before my arrival, as I'm not sure I would have wanted to come at all.

No sooner had we parked, than a man in his thirties, in grubby jeans and T-shirt, burst from the screen door and strode towards us. He bear-hugged James, and then glanced shyly at me.

"Hannah, Ryan. Ryan, Hannah," James said by way of introduction.

Ryan shook my hand, then smiled and looked down at his feet. It was a sweet, timid gesture, and I warmed to him immediately. "Sorry to have dragged your man away," Ryan said, addressing me.

"Had to happen sometime," James commented. "I couldn't spend my whole life on holiday, eh Han'?"

A number of flies were buzzing angrily around my head and when I swiped at them James said, "Here, come inside." He led me through the screen door into a large unfinished part of the newer extension. The walls here were still of bare brick, the roof above us uninsulated – rooms without ceilings or doors. Building materials were massed along one wall and yet the layer of dust over everything gave the impression that it had been in stasis for quite some time.

James must have been reading my mind as I glanced around because he raised one eyebrow and explained, "We were halfway through rebuilding the place when the accident happened. Everything just kind of stopped."

Of course it did, I thought, my heart lurching in sympathy for him. On a day-to-day basis James seemed so well balanced, so straightforward and reasonable that it was almost possible to forget that fact that his wife and child had both been killed in a road accident. Stupidly, it hadn't crossed my mind that I would be staying not only on James' farm, but on what used to be James' and Judy's farm, and even before that, Judy's parents' farm. We'd presumably be sleeping in James and Judy's bed too, and I wasn't sure, suddenly, how I felt about that.

"It's more comfy through here," Ryan said, leading the way into the original part of the building, and indeed, from the inside at least, this was much more the way I had expected an Australian farmhouse to look, albeit in a state of shocking disrepair.

We crossed a large lounge with tatty sofa and chairs and a rug that was so threadbare it was impossible to guess what the original pattern might have been. Beyond this was a large open kitchen with old-fashioned wooden cabinets on the walls and an enormous dining table in the middle.

"Big," I said. It was the only positive adjective I could come up with.

"It's a nice kitchen, ain't it?" Ryan said.

James laughed. "He's hoping you're gonna cook for us all. I wouldn't say a word if I were you."

Despite a rather pleasing image of myself ladling out stew from a huge pot, I took James at his word and simply smiled wryly.

"So where are the others?" James asked.

"Top end," Ryan replied. "Just heading up that way myself."

"They're planting," James told me.

"Corn," Ryan confirmed.

"I'll come up and see you all in a bit," James told Ryan. "I just need to get Han' here settled."

"Of course," Ryan said, briefly catching my eye, and then turning to leave.

"So, as you can see," James said, gesturing around him. "Lounge, kitchen . . . the bedrooms are through here."

He led me across the kitchen and through a door covered with flaking green paint and then along a dingy corridor. "Bathroom," he said, pushing open the first door to reveal an old-fashioned bathroom with a worn enamel bath and deep green wall tiles, of which a number were missing.

"Dunny," he said, knocking on the next door.

"Which is the toilet, right?"

"Yep. We'll make an Aussie of you yet."

James tapped with a knuckle on the following door and announced, "Ryan's room."

"He *lives* here?"

James paused and turned back to face me. "They all do, Han'. It's a way to keep the payroll down. Free board and lodging. Well, used to be. Just lodging these days really."

"Your wife used to cook for them all?"

James combined a nod and a shrug.

Judy's husband. Judy's farm. And now the men were hoping I'd be filling Judy's shoes in the kitchen. James' dead wife was becoming shockingly present.

"Charlie's room," James said as he continued on down the corridor. "Gio is in this one."

"Gio?"

"He's new. Giovanni. Italian guy. And then these two are ours."

He opened the left-hand door, revealing a double bedroom, which was clearly doubling as a store room. "Don't worry," he said, rapping one of the stacked boxes with his knuckles. "I'll get this all moved out."

I stepped around the boxes and crossed to the French

windows, pulled back the grubby net curtains and looked out. Beyond the window was a strip of trampled grassland on which sat the skeleton of a long-deceased motorbike and some kind of spiral drilling mechanism, both rusty and brown and tangled with weeds. Beyond the field was a ditch, a fence, and then a much deeper stretch of churned field curving down from the house and meeting, at the bottom of a shallow valley, an orchard of neatly planted trees. Beyond these, hazy, in the distance, rose the peaks of the Glasshouse Mountains.

"Great view," I commented.

"Yes," James agreed, moving to my side and enthusiastically yanking back the curtains. "Yes, it's a good one, isn't it?"

I could sense his relief at my having found something positive to say about the place. Encouraged, I asked, "Are those fruit trees?"

"Mangoes," James said.

"God, I love mangoes," I told him. "When's the season?"

"Right now," James said. "We can walk down and pick some if you want."

I was just about to say *yes* when James added, "Judy always reckoned that if you eat them straight off the tree, they're the best mangoes in the world."

"After lunch maybe?" I said, instead. "I'm pretty hungry. I think I need more than mangoes right now."

"I hope there's something to eat in the kitchen," James said. "Let's go look."

Despite my best efforts, I glanced around at the devastation of the bedroom. It looked like a squat really.

"I'm sorry the place looks so shitty," James said reaching out to touch my shoulder. "I just haven't had the time to sort it since I got back."

125

"It'll be fine," I told him. "I'll help you fix it up a bit while I'm here."

James pulled me against him and wrapped his arms around me. "That'd be great," he said. "Because I'm gonna be pretty full-on for a few days."

Though the refrigerator was empty, the freezer was full of ready meals and we were hungry enough that even microwave-in-the-box beef burgers managed to hit the spot. All the same, if this is what the men had been eating, I could understand why Ryan's eyes had twinkled at the idea of me in the kitchen.

After lunch, James headed to the top field to see Charlie and Giovanni and generally show that he was back in control, and hit by a sudden wave of jet-lag tiredness, I peered into the second of "our" rooms – it was a child's bedroom, untouched, I would guess, since her death.

I sat down – big Hannah sitting on little Hannah's bed – and stroked the pillow, and looked around at the toys and wondered how James had managed to survive so much trauma. And then, feeling rather sad, I retreated to the master bedroom to sleep.

The sheets were dirty and musty and I couldn't find any fresh ones anywhere. When I tried to sleep on top of the blankets I ended up having a sneezing fit – I doubted that James had changed them once since his return – so I quickly gave up and stripped the bed and went hunting for the washing machine.

In a trance, driven by the strange idea that the tidier the room was, the less of the past it contained, I began to blitz the place. By the time the daylight started to fade, I had not only washed and dried the bedding and curtains, but had also moved the stack of boxes (all of which contained plastic bags

126

of dried milk powder) out to the new, incomplete building extension.

There had been a lot of boxes, and they had been heavy, but I felt pleased with the result. Once I had tidied and hoovered the room and remade the bed, the room looked like a bedroom again and the process of making it that way had felt like homebuilding, something which gave me a warm feeling inside.

Once the bedroom was done, I set about cleaning the kitchen, and though what it really needed was stripping and redecorating if not gutting entirely, that too looked at least a bit more functional by the time I had finished.

Despite my reservations about replacing Judy, had there been a single natural ingredient in the house, I would have cooked a big meal for everyone too. But as it was, the best I could manage was to select five pizzas from the freezer and heat them in the oven along with some chips.

Dinner with the men that evening was a strange affair. Both Ryan and Charlie – a spindly balding man in his late fifties – seemed embarrassed by my presence. It was almost as if they had never seen a woman before. Even James struggled to find a topic of conversation that could include both the men and myself, and so alternated awkwardly between farm talk – I nodded knowingly – and discussions of things I might want to do and see around the area. Only the new guy, Giovanni, seemed at ease, and I think we all felt a sense of relief when he launched into an explanation of his roots. His parents' escape from the post-war depression in Italy made a great story and Giovanni, a five-foot mass of hair and muscle, told it with true Italian panache.

When he had finished eating, Ryan thanked me. "That was really great Hannah, thanks."

127

"I would have cooked something from scratch," I said, "but there wasn't a proper ingredient in the house."

Mocking me, James bowed then shook his head.

"I'd be happy to run you up to Costco tomorrow if you want," Ryan offered, grinning at James.

And though I knew exactly the trap I was stepping into, I said, "Yes, that would be great. But you'll have to tell me what kind of food you like."

"Anything proper," Ryan said.

"Pasta?" Giovanni said, predictably.

"Shepherd's pie," Charlie volunteered. "I'd kill for a decent shepherd's pie."

"Works for me too," Giovanni said. "If you can do it."

"I can," I admitted. "And you, James; any special requests?"

James shrugged and grinned at me broadly. "If you're really going for it, then a lemon meringue pie might hit the spot."

"Lucky for you lemon meringue pie is one of my specialities," I said.

"Hell, James loves lemon meringue pie, don't you, James?" Ryan said, and suddenly, the past was with us all over again.

In a way, James had been right. Once I had offered to cook that first meal, once I had delivered on my promise with such panache (that lemon meringue pie could have won top prize in *Masterchef*) the die was cast.

Almost every day, Ryan would ask me what would be for dinner that evening, and would ensure that any missing ingredients for the requested dish were efficiently supplied on time. He was a strapping young man who liked his food, who appreciated the finer points of any effort I made, but who seemed incapable of learning even how to boil himself an egg.

But the truth was that despite my unease at the idea the men were comparing my meals with Judy's, I enjoyed cooking for them all. The produce in Brisbane was as fresh and varied as I had ever seen anywhere, and the reception the men gave every meal I delivered, whether it be a prawn curry or a Sunday roast, left me on a high that lasted until the following meal. It was like cooking for a large family, only a special kind of family that actually appreciated the effort.

Sometimes, as I ladled out soup, I felt a little like Milly in *Seven Brides for Seven Brothers*, but that feeling was so different from anything I had known in what I was already starting to think of as my *previous* life that I couldn't get enough of it.

As the men got to know me they became less shy and more rowdy, cheeky and occasionally downright vulgar, but it was all light-hearted, it was all good fun if not particularly *clean* fun.

I frequently found myself singing while I was cooking, or laughing out loud at some vulgar joke or another, and once or twice, after a few too many glasses of the excellent Chardonnay that came out of a box, I laughed so much that my ribs hurt. And that hadn't happened since my teens.

On weekdays I cooked and cleaned and fixed the house up as best I could without burning the whole place down and starting again, and on weekends James took me on day trips to the stunning mountains, or nearby beaches, or to museums and restaurants in Brisbane.

But the ghost of Judy seemed to be at our sides ever more often. When I was cooking, I thought about the fact that she had perhaps cooked this meal, that she had used these same pots and pans . . . When I served up, I wondered if my lasagne was better or worse than hers. When I snuggled against James at night, I wondered whether he had preferred Judy's body to mine. She looked young and fit in the unique photo I had found in a drawer in Hannah's bedroom, and I was pretty sure her young farmer's body must have been firmer than my post-childbirth curves. When we visited restaurants, I wondered if James and Judy had ever eaten there together, and when the restaurant owner knew James by name, I felt convinced that he was comparing me with his mind's eye memories of James' dead wife. And thinking quite probably that I was no match. Because I was convinced that these obsessive ideas had nothing to do with him and everything to do with me, I didn't say a word to James. But try as I might to convince myself, this obsession continued to take form, and my fear that I was being shipped in as a replacement for Judy started to pollute almost everything we did together.

James picked up on it once or twice. He noticed me staring into the middle distance as I battled with myself, and asked me if I was OK, but I simply faked a smile and told him that everything was fine. He had enough on his plate, I reckoned, without dealing with my irrational fears.

For Christmas we drove down to the Gold Coast to spy on the nouveau riche types pretending to play chic (they looked the part until they opened their mouths) and on the way back visited a local casino where we quite literally threw away two hundred dollars. Surprisingly, throwing it away was the most fun I had ever had with money.

During the long drive home, James was quiet, and as always when things were quiet, my obsession with Judy began to fester.

As we drove back past Broadbeach, I asked, "So how long have you had this car, James?"

"The Toyota? Oh, about ten years," he said. "Why?"

"No reason," I answered. But it wasn't true. I was, of course, wondering whether James had driven Judy along this same route in this same car.

"And you've been to the Gold Coast a few times?" I asked. James seemed to know all the places we visited pretty well.

"Sure," James said. "Of course."

We drove on in silence for half an hour before James said, "Something's eating you, Hannah."

I didn't answer.

"Have I done something wrong?" he asked, after a pause.

I reached out and stroked his arm. "No," I said. "No, you really haven't."

"But something *is* wrong, right?"

I shrugged. "It's just some silly stuff in my head," I told him. "It's honestly not your doing."

"You've been quiet for days," James said. "I think maybe you should tell me what's up."

"I'm worried it will upset you," I said, feeling suddenly sick with stress at the realisation that there was no avoiding the subject now. "And it's *really* not your fault."

"Hannah," James said. "Please?"

"Look . . . It's Judy," I said.

"Judy?"

"You never talk about her much, so it's—"

"You want to me to talk more about Judy?" James asked, sounding vaguely annoyed.

"No. That's not it."

131

"Then what?" he asked, glancing at me briefly in puzzlement, then turning back to the road.

"Look, I know what I'm feeling doesn't make any sense, OK? So please don't blame me for it. It's . . . it's irrational. I know that."

"OK."

"But I worry that I'm some kind of replacement."

"A replacement?"

"A substitute. For Judy."

"Oh," James said.

"Do you understand what I'm saying?" I said. "I'm staying in her farm, I'm sleeping in her bed, I'm cooking the same meals for the same men that she used to cook for. So I feel – and, as I say, I *know* that this isn't rational – but I feel as if I'm some sort of replacement. Like I'm some kind of substitute."

"Right," James said. "Gotcha."

James' features closed up like a book and that was the last thing he said. And because he looked so angry, I didn't say another word until we stopped for coffee on the Pacific Highway an hour later.

We parked in front of a glass-fronted cafe and when we climbed out, I chose the end table. I sensed that an argument was in the air, and I wanted to be seated as privately as possible.

The waitress came and took our order, and only once she had gone did I dare say, "I'm sorry, James. I know I've upset you. It really wasn't my intention."

James shook his head sadly. "Nah, you haven't," he said. "I'm just not sure what to say. I'm not that good at this kind of stuff."

I nodded. "Try anyway," I said, softly. "Just tell me what you're feeling."

James rubbed his forehead. "Kind of tired," he said, unhelpfully, then, "Disappointed, too, I guess."

"Disappointed?"

"Yeah. That I haven't said enough."

"That's not what I was saying, though," I told him. "I don't need you to talk more about Judy. I—"

"That's not what I mean," James said. "I mean, I feel bad that I haven't said enough to convince you."

"To convince me? Of what?"

"Well, of how special you are."

At this instant, the waitress returned with James' beer and my coffee, and I raised one hand to my mouth, bit my bottom lip, and struggled to hold back a batch of tears that were suddenly pressing at my eyes.

Once she had gone, James continued, "The thing is, Hannah, that I loved Judy."

"Of course you did."

"She was an amazing woman. Strong, and clever and funny. Brash, some would say. But I loved her."

I sipped my coffee then swallowed with difficulty.

"But you've got it all the wrong way around," he continued.

I shrugged. "I don't see . . ." I said.

"It's a terrible thing to say about someone who's dead," James croaked, shaking his head. "And if she hears this, I hope she'll forgive me. But you've really got it all wrong. *Judy* was the substitute, Han'. She was the substitute for *you*. The only woman I ever really wanted was you."

He reached out to take my hand, and I could no longer hold back the tears. They flooded down my cheeks, and with them, all of the stress produced by my obsession – revealed, in an instant, as unreasonable jealousy of a dead woman – vanished.

133

It was the most wonderful declaration of love that I had ever heard, and the only thing I managed to say in reply was, "Oh, James."

His words were delivered so simply, and with such painful honesty, that I had no choice but to believe him.

By the time we got back all my worries about the ghost of Judy had blown away like so many storm clouds. Ryan had gone for good too, and with him another chunk of the past had been wiped. Only Giovanni and Charlie were left now, and, like me, had never met Judy.

James had to work long full days on the farm, but in love all over again, we ate well and laughed lots and drank too much and made love every night.

My life in England seemed a million miles away, and when I phoned Luke every morning, his tales of Christmas in England seemed absurdly familiar, ridiculously staid compared to the adventure I was living. I missed Luke, but perhaps not as much as I felt I should. And certainly not enough to want to be in England rather than here. Did that make me a terrible mother, I wondered?

EIGHT

Cliff

The therapist had sounded pretty nice on the phone. She had a warm voice and an easy manner that somehow made it seem as if anything, and perhaps even *everything*, was OK by her.

We had spoken three times before I met her, once to enquire and book an appointment, and twice to cancel. Each time I had phoned to do so she told me that this was perfectly possible in such a warm understanding manner that I no longer wanted to cancel at all.

Her house was just outside Guildford in a leafy lane of large houses, and I thought as I parked the car, *Wow! Therapy must pay well.* But when, through the December drizzle, I reached the front door and saw seven different doorbells, I understood that I had got that wrong.

Jenny Church's flat occupied the ground floor of the building, but her therapy room was a small wooden chalet at the bottom of the garden. This came as something of a relief, as I had been feeling nervous at the idea of potentially bumping into members of her family on the way in or out of her office.

Inside the chalet, Jenny offered me a coffee then sat opposite. She was a pretty woman in her thirties, wearing jeans and a wrap-around cardigan. Her hair was a little wild, which gave her a skitty, sympathetic air.

"So, lovely to meet you!" she said. "What would you like me to call you? Cliff, or . . . ?"

"Cliff is fine," I said, fidgeting to get comfortable. "I'm not sure how this works really," I told her. "I've never, you know . . ."

"Sure. Well, before we start, I want to reassure you that everything you say here will remain in the strictest confidence."

I nodded.

"The only exception to that rule would be if something you told me led me to believe that you or someone else might be in danger if I failed to act upon that information, or if you told me you were involved in money laundering or terrorism. In those cases, the law says that I would have to break patient confidentiality, but I would always tell you first. But other than those exceptions, you can be totally certain that anything you say in this room *remains* in this room. It's very important that you know that."

"Thanks."

"So sometimes it can be hard to get started in the first session; you don't know me and vice versa. If you find it easier to simply tell me what's going on for you then that's fine, but if it makes it easier I can ask you some questions. There's no right or wrong way of doing it, and I completely understand that you have to build up trust in me. What will work best for you?"

"Now that I'm here, well, I'm not sure that I know why I'm here," I told her confusedly. "So I'm not sure."

Jenny nodded. "So maybe a few questions to get us kicked off?"

I pulled a handkerchief from my pocket to wipe my brow and nodded.

"Is it too warm in here for you?" Jenny asked.

"No, it's fine. I'm just a bit nervous," I said.

"Of course you are," Jenny said with a smile. "Hopefully that will ease as we get more used to each other. So let's start with some basics."

Jenny asked me my age, occupation, marital status, and then moved on to my parents. I guessed that she was probably fishing for some Freudian obsession with my mother, but answered, "They're both dead. A long time ago. So I'm fine about that now really. Well, not fine, but I mean . . . I've had time to get used to the idea."

"Of course. And brothers and sisters?"

"Just one brother, James."

"Older? Younger?"

"Two years younger."

"Right. Am I hearing some anger in your voice when you talk about James? Or have I got that wrong?"

"Sure. There's anger," I told her. "But I'm really not here to discuss James."

"Right. That's fine too. So you said that you were separated from your wife?"

"Yes. We'll get divorced I expect."

"And how recent is the separation?"

"Three months."

"So very recent then. Is *that* something you'd like to talk more about?"

"Maybe."

"Maybe later, or maybe now?"

"Maybe later."

"Great. Well, we can come back to it any time you want."

"The trouble is, that it's all linked, isn't it?" I said, glancing out of the window at the rain. I turned back to face Jenny now, and she nodded at me encouragingly. "My wife. She's gone off with my brother. She's with James. Right now."

Jenny blinked. "I can only imagine how difficult that must be for you. It explains the anger I heard earlier. How do you feel about that?"

"Yep, angry pretty much sums it up."

"I'm sure."

"I hate his guts really. But then, I always hated his guts. He was a bastard even before."

"Before . . . ?"

"Before he stole my wife. But now . . . Well . . . There's no forgiving and forgetting that one, is there?"

"I can see that could be difficult . . ." Jenny said with feeling.

"Am I allowed to ask *you* questions?"

Jenny nodded. "You can ask questions if you like but I may not answer them if I feel that it will take the focus away from you. This session is all about you, after all. But go ahead."

"OK, so here's one for you. What makes someone gay?"

"What makes someone gay," Jenny repeated thoughtfully.

"Yes."

"I just want to be sure we're on the same wavelength here. The word gay has a few meanings, doesn't it."

"I mean, queer. Homosexual or whatever."

"Right. And when you ask what *makes* someone gay, do you mean how do they *become* gay, or what is it that makes society *define* them as gay?"

I shrugged. "Both, I guess."

"OK. So let's start with the first one first then. The truth is that no one really knows how people become gay. Some people believe it's genetic, like eye colour or hair colour. Some researchers are actually trying to track down the gay gene. But others think it comes more from upbringing."

"The old nature/nurture debate."

"Exactly."

"So what do you think?" I asked.

"Me? I don't know. If I were forced to guess, I'd say maybe a mixture of both. Really the question is the flip side of another question: what makes people straight."

I pulled a face. "What makes people *straight?* Surely being straight is just normal, isn't it?"

"Normal?"

"Yes. It's like a biological function. Otherwise the human race would have vanished. So it has to be normal."

"It's dominant. I'm not sure that normal is the most useful word."

"Normal, dominant. I don't see the difference really."

"OK, just for a moment, let's take a different example, eye colour, say. There are far more people with brown eyes in the world than with blue eyes. Brown eyes are genetically dominant. And normal. And people with blue eyes are a minority. But they're normal too. Normality contains a spectrum of dominant and minority traits. Do you see what I'm saying?"

"You're saying that being gay is a minority thing, but it still might be normal."

"Yes. Homosexuality has existed in all societies and all cultures as far as we know. So labelling it as abnormal perhaps doesn't make any more sense than saying blue eyes are abnormal."

"Sure. I suppose I was wondering if a child was told he was gay all the time. Would that make him become gay?"

"Why are you interested in that question?"

"It's just . . ."

"Yes?"

"It's just . . . well . . . If someone . . . Suppose someone . . . Look. James, my brother, he called me a poof. A queer. OK? When I was a kid. All the time. As an insult. He did it because it wound me up. He did it to upset me."

"I see."

"So I'm trying to work out if that could have made me . . . if that could have had an effect on me."

"If that could have made you what?"

"If . . ." I swallowed hard. My throat felt constricted. "If it made me . . . I don't know . . . less straight than normal guys, I suppose."

"Normal?" Jenny said.

"Sorry. Less straight than *most* guys then."

"I see. Do you feel that you are less straight than most guys?"

"I don't know. How would I know how straight most guys are?"

"Yes. I see the problem."

"So there's a question for you. From your experience, how straight are normal guys?"

"In most studies that have been done, the majority of people place themselves on a sliding scale somewhere between entirely heterosexual and entirely homosexual. There aren't that many people up in the one hundred per cents on either side," Jenny said. "But I'd say that anywhere on that spectrum would have to be classed as normal."

"James would definitely be a one-hundred-per-center."

"Did he tell you that?"

140

"I know him pretty well."

"And you? Where would you put yourself on that sliding scale?"

I opened my mouth to speak, but nothing came out. I tried again and managed to croak, "I don't know," I said.

Jenny smiled at me warmly and sighed as she offered me a box of tissues. "Would you like one of these?" she asked, and it was only then that I realised that I was crying.

"That's why I'm here, I think," I said. "To work out where I am on the scale."

The concept of a whole spectrum of normality was, though obvious to some, a revelation to me, and trying to reply to that question of quite where on it I belonged opened the floodgates to every fear, every hope, every doubt I had ever experienced. Mostly in tears, I told Jenny about my marriage, about my reasonably satisfactory sex life with Hannah, about my tentative fumblings with men, about Glen, and Tristan, and even about being caught looking at men on Grindr in France.

Jenny nodded and smiled sympathetically at me throughout, as though none of this shocked her, as though all of this belonged on her personal spectrum of normality.

The session went by too fast, and it ended too soon. I felt as if steam was gushing out of an escape valve and I wanted that to continue, but Jenny insisted that an hour of such intensity was enough and that having some time to decompress before the next session really was the best way to proceed.

She advised me to take the afternoon off if I could. She said I'd be feeling tired and emotional for a few hours at least and that I would need some time to digest everything that had happened.

I told her that I couldn't possibly do that, that I needed to get back to work, that I had things to finish before the Christmas break, but though this was true, when it came to it, I couldn't face work. Instead, when I got back to Farnham, I walked right past the office entrance and headed on to the park where I walked, impervious to the faint drizzle, and tried in an unfocussed manner to think about the subject of my sexuality. But it seemed, that day, as if the more I tried to think about it, the vaguer my thinking got. It felt as if the subject was too big to be held in my head at one time, like trying to remember a rapidly fleeting dream the morning after. I felt exhausted and depressed, but also, deep down, aware of a tiny sprouting seedling of hope that, with Jenny's help, everything might be all right.

When I got home that evening, Luke was already back from Billy's house. His first question, before I even took my coat off, was, "Dad, can we go get the PlayStation from the house? I *need* it."

I looked at him and smiled weakly. This intrusion of normal life into my brain, exhausted with self-analysis, felt like a gift.

"I'm not sure that's a good idea," I told him. "If you start carting it back and forth, it'll end up getting damaged."

"But—"

"What *I* was thinking, is that maybe we need to get another PlayStation for here," I told him. "I thought that might be your main Christmas present this year."

"Wow."

"Good idea?"

"Yeah. But can we get an Xbox instead?"

"But all your games are for the PlayStation."

"I know, but Billy's got loads. I could borrow them."

I pulled a face.

"Oh go on, Dad!"

"How much is an Xbox?"

"About the same as a PS3. Oh go on. That would be so cool."

"Maybe. Let's have a think about it. See if you're sure that's what you really want."

"I *have* thought about it," Luke declared. "I'm a very quick thinker. Please, Dad?"

"We'll see."

Luke glanced at the clock. "Can we go get one now? Argos is open till five-thirty."

"Luke! Calm down. I said 'maybe.' And I said for Christmas."

"But it could be my Christmas present. And I could use it this week while I'm off. Oh come on. *Please?*"

Because rushing out to buy an Xbox was such a very welcome distraction from the machinations of my own mind, that's exactly what we did – Luke's timing for the request couldn't have been better. It was clear from his wide-eyed expression that he couldn't believe his luck.

* * *

By the time the next appointment came up, it was a week before Christmas. Luke was off school, and with Hannah away in Australia, he was living full time with me in the flat. This meant that Billy, who only had a portable TV screen for his own Xbox, was almost permanently at ours as well.

On the Wednesday, I left the two boys under strict instruction to do nothing other than continue slaying the insurgents in their on-screen, Middle East hellhole, and made my way to Guildford.

Jenny got me to run through how I had been feeling since the previous meeting, and this led us straight back into our discussion about the great sexuality continuum and where I would place myself upon it, a question I was still unable to answer.

I had spent fifteen years in a heterosexual relationship, I pointed out. Even if, perhaps, I did find myself looking at men from time to time, how could I quantify these two separate and opposite aspects of my life into a single point on a graph?

It was at this point that Jenny introduced another concept to me: that my sexuality didn't have to be a fixed point in space and time; that she wasn't asking where Cliff, once dead, would be situated by some all-seeing power, but where Cliff the Living would place that dot right now, at this instant, even if he suspected that it might change again in the next ten minutes.

The idea brought me so much relief that I started to cry again as I forced myself to admit that, at least for the moment, I was finding myself more attracted to men, and that, in truth, it had been many years since I had found any woman other than Hannah sexually attractive. If ever.

I asked Jenny if that meant that I was gay after all, and she said again that at this point in my debate with myself, fixed labels that defined one-hundred-per-cent sexualities weren't helpful. She asked me whether I felt that exploring this other side of my sexuality was something that I might want to put into practice, and when I said "no", she asked me why, and the only answer I could come up with was shame.

As after the first session, I came out of the meeting feeling emotionally shattered. I returned home and fixed soup and cheese-on-toast for the boys, who were luckily still far too engrossed in mass slaughter to notice anything strange about me as I sat staring out of the window.

For the next few days, as we went Christmas shopping, as we bought and then decorated the tree, I tried to imagine a scenario whereby I might do something with another man. But as all of the situations my imagination came up with involved me going to a gay bar or club to actually meet someone – something so clearly beyond the bounds of possibility – the whole concept remained very much a virtual fantasy.

And then, on the morning of Christmas Eve, while Luke was still sleeping, I looked at my phone and remembered Grindr – after all the drama it had caused in my life, I could hardly believe that I had forgotten it. Even if I didn't actually go to meet anyone, I could look and see who was around; I could at least see what other gay men in Farnham *looked* like. And I thought, *Why not?* It wasn't even a bit of fun – it was research.

So I started looking at, and eventually chatting to, guys on Grindr and it was an eye-opener in so many ways.

Most of these men seemed to be looking for sex, nothing more. Many of them seemed to be in relationships already. So many were looking for "no-strings fun" that they had reduced it to an acronym: NSF.

It was as if sex, so complex to me, was to them no more or less important than a bar of chocolate – to be consumed, guilt-free, whenever they felt the urge. The conversations I had with these guys quickly went nowhere because, though I tried, I couldn't simplify my view of sex to their way of thinking.

Whether it was Christian morality or societal conditioning or a combination of both, I still saw sex as something special and sacred, and yes, complicated.

As I continued my visits to Jenny Church, we attempted to explore and decode my feelings about sex, and though at times I could glimpse a broader truth – that it was perfectly OK for others to see sex in an entirely different way – that didn't mean that I agreed, and more importantly, I came to realise that I didn't *want* to agree either.

Of course, not everyone I "met" on Grindr fitted this stereotype. My conversations with Paul (alias FarnhamBear) and Dan (SurreyLad) reassured me that I wasn't, at least, an alien. There were other guys out there who felt the same way that I did, people who thought sex was not unimportant, and a few who even seemed to want to take me on a proper date.

Of these, Dan was the most interesting, and it was Dan who explained to me that by its very nature Grindr attracted the section of the population that wanted instant hook-ups, and drove away those who wanted a real relationship. I had to realise, Dan explained, that it wasn't representative of gay men in general any more than a survey undertaken in a swingers club would be representative of the heterosexual population at large.

Dan also introduced me to his very own classification system for the various types of time-wasters he had come across on Grindr. Amongst the many categories were the 5AD (five-a-days), people who required on average five different partners a day (yes, an exaggeration, but in some cases only just); the FIBBERS (people who posted photos of themselves ten years earlier, or even photos of other people entirely); and the LURKERS (men who never came out from behind their computers, preferring to live in the textual fantasy land of Grindr).

My talks with Dan left me feeling guilty about my own behaviour. After all, I had posted a headless photo of myself, and lied about my name. For the purposes of the web, I had become "Fred".

I discussed all of this during my weekly sessions with Jenny and came to the conclusion that, as my primary purpose was not to deceive but to create a safe space in which I could explore my feelings, a little deception could be permitted. But inevitably, both Dan and Paul got bored trying to get me to provide an actual photo of myself, or a phone number, or an address, or a date for a proper meeting. Eventually they both gave up on ever meeting "Fred". I'm pretty sure Dan must have classed me under "LURKERS", and he would probably have been right to do so.

Only once – and this was the most dishonest of my Grindr sins – I arranged to meet a pleasant, good-looking tree surgeon called Rob, only to chicken out at the last minute and, sweating and trembling with nerves, stride right past the pub.

Rob sent me a message the next morning telling me that I was a "wanker" and I couldn't really blame him for that. He then blocked me in some way so that even when, a week later, I was wracked with guilt and regret, I was unable to apologise to him. I swore then never to arrange to meet anyone, at least not until I was ready to follow through.

For weeks, as Hannah returned from Australia and as Luke returned to school, I continued to chat to the various bits of anatomy that would pop up on my Grindr screen, but no one was ever as interesting as Dan, and no one ever looked as cute

147

as chunky, bearded, brown-eyed Rob. I felt that I had wasted the two best opportunities I had stumbled across.

And then one day, whilst sitting on the loo, I glanced at the screen and saw Tristan.

I stared at his photo for ten minutes then, suddenly conscious of where I was, moved to the lounge, and stared at it some more.

I felt strangely drawn to the photo, compelled to send him a tiny message of recognition if nothing else, but I wasn't sure quite why. Though Tristan had always been pleasant enough to me, it would be a stretch to claim that we had been friends. He had always been Jill's friend, and by extrapolation more of Hannah's side of the family than mine. And yet, as I stared at that photo, I couldn't help but wonder how much of that lack of closeness had been due to my own "issues" with Tristan's sexuality, my issues with my own sexuality for that matter. Perhaps Tristan and I could have been allies.

Grindr was informing me that Tristan was three-point-two miles away, which meant that he had to be at the house, so on top of everything else, I couldn't help but wonder what he was doing with my wife.

I crossed the room and looked out over the rooftops of the houses opposite. It was a cold, grey January Saturday and with Luke absent, the weekend yawned in front of me.

My phone chirruped with a message, so I crossed the room and peered at the screen. The message, amazingly, was from Tristan: *Hey there. How's it hanging?*

I sat down and frowned at the screen, then clicked through a number of screens to check my own profile. But no, there was no possible way that Tristan could know he was talking to me.

I pondered what to do for a moment longer then decided that I needed to come clean quickly before Tristan sent another message, potentially something compromising that would embarrass us both.

"Hi Tris'. It's me, Cliff. PLEASE. Not one word to anyone there."

Tristan replied almost immediately with, "Oops! Not one word!" and I wondered if I believed him.

"You at the house?" I asked.

"Dragged here for lunch. Bored out of my mind."

"I'll bet."

"And U?"

"Home. Bored too."

"Come join us. That would liven things up. Lol."

"No ta. Not keen on the company."

"Me neither! Pint?"

Pint! I stared at the phone and wondered why on Earth Tristan would want to have a pint with me. It felt like some kind of a trap, like something from my schooldays, and this reminded me of my most recent session with Jenny Church. She had pointed out how low my self-esteem was, how unattractive and uninteresting I believed myself to be, and suggested that this belief might be holding me back. Perhaps Tristan really *did* want to have a pint with me. Perhaps he really did think that would be more interesting than lunch with Jill and Hannah.

My phone beeped again. "Hello?"

Of course there was only one way to find out. I swallowed hard, and thinking, "Jenny will be so proud of me when I tell her," I typed, "Sure. Now?"

"Where?"

149

"The Jolly Sailor? West Street?"

"How apt! In half an hour?"

"Yes."

"I'll be wearing a carnation."

I glanced at the clock, then dropped the phone onto the couch and strode to the bedroom. I changed my shirt three times before settling on a beige corduroy number. I was aware that I was behaving like an adolescent girl on a date, but I couldn't help but think, *But what if it is a date?*

By the time I got to the pub, Tristan was already ordering at the bar.

"Cliff," he said when I reached him. "What you having?"

"A pint of Abbott, please," I replied, half to him and half to the barmaid.

"That'll put hairs on your chest," Tristan commented, taking and sipping his own pint of lager.

"Not much hope of that," I retorted. "I didn't see your Jeep outside."

"I swapped it for a Mini. Too big. Too brash. So how have you been? You look well. If a little beige."

I looked down at my clothes and realised that I was indeed wearing beige chinos, a beige shirt and a beige jacket. "Is beige some kind of fashion no-no?" I asked.

"Like you don't know," Tristan laughed, handing the barmaid a ten pound note. But he was wrong. I didn't know.

We settled in a corner table as far from the Saturday eaters as possible. Tristan looked around and pulled a face. "Not so jolly, is it?"

"The pub?"

"Yeah. I was expecting something a little more, well, gay, I suppose. With a name like the Jolly Sailor . . ."

"I don't think they do gay in Farnham," I said.

"No. There's some private bar in a guy's cellar, so I hear."

"In his cellar?"

"Yeah. All sounds a bit *Pulp Fiction* to me. But I'm assured it's legit."

"Pulp Fiction?" I asked, starting to feel a little uncool.

"Yeah. You know. Bring out the gimp. The gimp's sleeping . . ."

Even though I had no idea what he was talking about, I faked it: I smiled. "Right!"

"Never been there though. A mate mentioned it once. I think it's in Farnham anyway. You've not heard of it then?"

"I haven't heard of anywhere," I replied. "So how did you know it was me?"

Tristan frowned. "I'm sorry?"

"On Grindr. How did you know?"

"I didn't."

"Oh. So why did you contact me?"

"Precisely because I *didn't* realise it was you."

I must have frowned at this, because Tristan added, "Sorry. That came out wrong. I just meant that I wouldn't have propositioned you. I would have respected your privacy. That's all."

"Right. So that's what that was? A proposition? I'm kind of new to all this."

"It was just a contact, Cliff. No offence, but I sent the same message to ten guys. I was just bored, that's all. Hannah was banging on about her holiday. You know what she's like."

I nodded, and felt a little deflated.

151

"But I'm happy to be here having a pint with you. I've been feeling bad about France, so . . ."

"Bad? About what?"

"About telling Hannah you were on Grindr."

"So it *was* you that told her?"

Tristan grimaced. "Oops. I thought you knew."

"I suspected. But . . ." I shrugged.

"Anyway, sorry."

I sighed. "It hardly matters now I suppose."

"So how have you been coping?"

I shrugged again.

"Not so well, huh?"

"It's a big adjustment to make."

"Sure. Coming out's hard whenever you do it," Tristan said, nodding knowingly.

"I just meant living alone, actually."

"Of course. Sorry. I just assumed. What with you being on Grindr and all."

"That's just . . . well, it's research really."

"Research?"

"I'm still trying to work out how I feel about everything."

Tristan nodded. "And?"

"I'm not sure. It's becoming clearer. Slowly. But as I say, I haven't . . . taken steps, or anything."

Tristan grinned. "Taken steps," he repeated. "I've heard some euphemisms in my time, but never *taking steps*."

"Sorry. But I find it hard to talk about all this. Especially to you."

"Because?"

"Well, you know Jill for a start. I know you told *her* about the Grindr incident as well."

"Oh. It was only because she was worried about you."

"All the same."

"Well, I promise I won't tell her anything else. OK? About time I showed a little solidarity with the sisterhood."

"Not sure about being in the sisterhood. But thanks."

"So what *steps* have you taken? Other than posting a faceless pic on Grindr."

"None really. I'm seeing a shrink. That's helping a bit."

"That's good. And dates?"

I shook my head.

"You been out at all?"

"Out?"

"Pubs, clubs. Gay ones, I mean."

"No. Not yet."

"Wow."

I sipped at my beer. "I don't think I'd have the nerve to be honest."

Tristan sighed. "Would it help if I took you?"

"Took me where?"

"We could meet up in Soho or something. I could take you to a few gay places. Just for a drink."

"Really?"

"Sure. Why not."

"That's nice of you Tris' . . . But as I say, I'm not sure I'm ready, really. I'm not sure I ever will be."

Tristan laughed. "Ready for what? It's just like here." He looked around and wrinkled his nose. "OK, it's like here, but without the football on the telly, without Sacha Distel on the sound system, without the pensioners, and without the kids. Other than that, it's identical."

"Sounds OK when you put it like that," I said.

"So let's do it."

I half-smiled. "Maybe. Some day."

From that point on, Tristan and I became Grindr buddies. We exchanged messages regularly, and that felt good. Having a friend in cyberspace made the whole experience feel that much less threatening.

Tristan would ask me who I was talking to and make witty comments about the profile in question; he would ask me repeatedly if I had "taken steps" yet, endlessly amused by my invented euphemism. He also attempted, tirelessly, to convince me to go out with him in London, and it took under three weeks before I capitulated.

It was on the first Saturday in February that Tristan rang my doorbell as arranged. He had been attending a business meeting in Guildford, and was to drive us both into the city.

I opened the door and noticed, perhaps for the first time, how very good-looking he was. Perhaps I somehow hadn't allowed myself to see him that clearly before.

He was wearing a sleek, blue checked suit over a light blue shirt with a cutaway collar and a blue striped club tie. The overall result was entirely traditional, and yet, each of the ingredients, the shirt, the tie, the suit, the overcoat, the cufflinks being so visibly *expensive*, he looked outrageously dandy as well. "Wow!" I said. "Now I feel *totally* underdressed." In an attempt at avoiding beige, I had opted for blue: jeans, a denim shirt and trainers.

"Work gear," Tristan said with false modesty. "But it's always good to go out in a suit. You get to meet all the suit sluts."

"Suit sluts?"

"Everybody likes a man in a suit, Cliff." He stepped into my flat and looked around. "Nice pad," he said.

"So do I need to change then?" I asked, closing the door.

"No, you're fine," he said, giving me the once over. "Maybe lose those if you can." He nodded at my feet.

"No trainers?"

"Not *those* trainers anyway. What are they? Tesco trainers or something?"

"Not far off." I crossed the lounge and entered the bedroom, then slid open the wardrobe door. "Brogues?" I asked loudly.

"Yeah, brogues are quite in," Tristan commented, his voice shockingly close behind me – he had followed me into the bedroom. "Especially if they're a bit knackered."

"Are you sure I shouldn't wear a suit or something? Won't I look a bit ridiculous next to you?"

Tristan shook his head. "Better this way. We have all the bases covered."

I stooped to pick up the brogues, but Tristan pointed at the wardrobe and asked, "What about those? They're cool."

"The boots?"

"Yeah. They'll get you noticed. Full cowboy combo. You'll have 'em queuing"

"Aren't they a bit too much?" I asked. I wasn't sure how much I wanted to be noticed.

"A bit too much *what?*"

"A bit too much . . . *dodgy.*"

Tristan laughed. "When you're going to a place where everyone's already accepted the fact that they're a bit dodgy, you have to adjust your whole concept of dodginess."

"Are you serious though? Should I wear them?"

Tristan nodded. "Put 'em on. Let's have a look."

I swapped my trainers for the boots and then stood and looked at myself in the mirror. "I look like James," I commented.

"Yeah," Tristan agreed. "But that's no bad thing, believe me. They make your arse look good in those jeans too."

As Tristan drove us into London I became more and more anxious about our night out, but Tristan either failed to notice my silence or pretended not to. He chatted incessantly during the entire journey about Jill and Pascal, her French boyfriend, and how amazing it was that they were still together when neither of them could string more than three words together in the other's language, about the staffing problems he was having at his Brighton restaurant, about a guy called Steve he had met two weeks ago who just might be boyfriend material . . . He just didn't stop. Even so, by the time he pulled into the car park on Lexington Street, I had broken out in a nervous sweat.

We walked as far as Compton Street then Tristan asked, "So where to start? That's the question."

"Don't ask me," I said, looking at an all male group of smokers standing outside a bar opposite. They were clearly giving Tristan and me the once over.

"Comptons? The Duncan? G-A-Y?"

"Maybe not G-A-Y," I said. "At least, not just yet if that's possible."

"A pub or a wine bar?"

I shrugged. "Pub? Maybe?"

Tristan laughed. "You look like you're about to faint or something," he said, fiddling with his tie.

"I *feel* a bit that way."

"There's only one thing to do then," Tristan laughed. "Jump right in."

"You won't abandon me will you?" I asked, as he linked his arm through mine and started to march me across the street, past the group of staring smokers, and through the door into Compton's.

"Of course I won't," he said. "I remember exactly how scary this is."

The pub was packed with Saturday-night revellers, and in truth, with the exception that there were very few women present (I counted three) it truly did feel much like any other London pub.

Tristan and I ordered pints and then moved to an area beneath the stairs where there was both standing room and a table for our drinks.

"So what do you think?" Tristan asked, undoing his overcoat. "It's not too scary, is it?"

"It isn't," I admitted. "But that doesn't stop me being terrified."

"Of what though?"

I shook my head. "I have no idea really."

"It's busy. Happy hour," Tristan said, sipping his drink. "It empties pretty quickly once happy hour is over."

"I see," I said, reaching for my pint and noticing that my hand was trembling.

Tristan laughed. "Relax, won't you? You look like you're waiting for the dentist. Or euthanasia."

"I'm sorry. I can't help it."

"Then drink more or something. I can't, I'm driving, but there's nothing to stop you getting blotto. I'll make sure you get your train home. I promise."

I downed my pint quickly, and then made good progress with the second one, and did start to feel a little more human.

I studied the men around me and kept asking myself the question over and over: am I like them? There were guys in suits (though none as chic as Tristan), and guys in jeans. There were bald, bearded men packing a few extra pounds, and skinny camp boys who moved like John Inman. But none of them looked, to my eye at least, much like me.

Once he had fetched me a third pint, Tristan headed for the toilets, leaving me momentarily alone. This increased my stress levels exponentially, but as the only alternative was to follow him to the toilets or beg him to stay, I forced a fake smile and watched him go.

A guy with a crew cut in a black leather jacket immediately took his place at the table. He smiled at me. ". . . Like your boots," he said.

I felt myself breaking into a sweat. "Thanks," I muttered, glancing down.

"I'm into boots," he said, stretching his leg out so that I could see his own beautifully polished motorcycle boots.

"They're nice," I stammered.

"I wish I had worn my cowboy boots now though," he said with a wink.

"My, um, friend told me to wear them," I spluttered, already grimacing at just how gauche I was managing to sound.

"He was right," the man said. "They're hot."

"Thanks," I replied, deciding that it was best to keep my idiot splutterings to the bare minimum.

"So where's your friend?"

I nodded towards the far side of the room. "Gone to the loo."

The man nodded. "Is he your boyfriend then?"

"Oh, no. No! He's just a friend."

158

"Right. Good." He smiled broadly at me, then held out his hand. "Peter."

"Um, Fred," I replied, shaking it.

"You live in London, Fred?"

"Surrey."

Peter nodded. "I live just around the corner."

I cleared my throat nervously. "That's nice," I said, groaning internally at my inability to make conversation.

"It is actually," Peter said. "D'you want to come and see?"

"No, I . . . I can't. As I say, I'm with a friend."

At that moment, I saw Tristan heading back through the crowd. He spotted Peter talking to me and started to divert to the right, but I waved and beckoned him over.

"Tristan, this is Peter," I said when he arrived.

"Hi," Tristan said, shaking his hand.

"Nice suit!" the man said.

"Thanks."

"Can I get you two boys a drink?"

"No, we're just about to, um, go somewhere else, aren't we?" I said, sending Tristan my best begging stare.

"Yes," he said, seamlessly getting my drift. "Sorry. But nice to meet you. And thanks for the offer."

Once outside, we continued our way down Compton Street, which, at eight in the evening, was now crowded with people, mainly men.

"So what was that about?" Tristan asked. "Was he not your type?"

I shrugged.

"He wasn't bad. Looked pretty fit to me. Nice smile . . ."

"I know."

"So what *is* your type?" Tristan asked.

"I don't know. I'm not sure I have a type."

"But you didn't fancy Peter there?"

"I'm not sure I fancy anyone, to tell the truth."

"Are you actually gay?" Tristan asked. "Or are you still trying to work that one out?"

"I'm not sure," I said. "Sorry."

"Maybe you need to suck it and see," Tristan sniggered.

"Maybe," I agreed. I wasn't really listening to him. I was too busy analysing my feelings about Peter, about Tristan, about Compton's, about the street. Jenny said that sometimes, when you don't know what you're thinking, it can help to note the physical sensations in the body, and I was trying to do that now. But the only feeling I could identify was an enormous ball of fear in the pit of my stomach that was wallowing in beer, making me want to puke.

"So, another bar?" Tristan was asking, pausing briefly outside another venue.

"I'm pretty hungry actually," I said, glancing up at the sign above the door. "Could we just go get something to eat?"

"Sure, I'm hungry too actually. There's a tapas place down here if that works for you?"

"Tapas sounds great," I said, relieved that at least I wasn't going to have to stride through the doors of G-A-Y.

The tapas restaurant was friendly and efficient. We took the last free table and I did my damnedest not to stare at the couple to my right – two forty-something men clasping hands across the table, staring dreamily into each other's eyes.

Of course I knew that gay couples existed, and as they were on home turf here I accepted that their behaviour was absolutely fine. But again and again I felt the need to sneak a peek as I asked myself, *Am I like these people?* and *If I am, would I ever have the courage to do what they're doing?*

Tristan chatted easily about food and the restaurant trade and then Jill and Pascal. He asked after Luke, wanted to know what we had done for Christmas ... It was easy and friendly but all the same, by the time we left the restaurant, all I wanted was escape.

Though I felt incredibly grateful for his efforts escorting me on my first adventure in Soho, just as after a session with Jenny, I was left feeling suffocated, left gasping for the mental space required to analyse my own feelings, or perhaps the space to not have to analyse anything further at all.

Tristan offered to take me to another bar but accepted readily, happily even, when I insisted that I wanted to go home. He had had a hard week himself, he said. He wanted to get back to Brighton.

And so we awkwardly hugged, promised, dishonestly I think, to do this again, and went our separate ways – he into the car park, and me back down Compton Street towards the tube station.

As I walked past Compton's, the strangest thing happened though – I ducked back inside. I wasn't quite sure why I had done this, but it felt right, it felt as if now the taboo of entering the place had been broken it might be easier to find out what and where and how I wanted to be if I was alone, unaided, unseen. I had been craving, I suddenly realised, anonymity.

I bought another drink at the bar and returned to the exact same spot under the stairs. I could see Peter on the far side of the bar chatting to a man in one of those fleece-lined denim jackets. I watched them together, and sipped my drink and started to do what in Tristan's presence I had been unable to do: I started to imagine going home with him.

I watched his gestures, his easy manner, his confident smile; I studied the fluid way he held himself, the opposite of my own rigid gait; and I started to feel attracted, I began to feel aroused.

I went to the toilet, and admitting to myself finally that I wanted to speak to him again, that I wanted, very possibly, to go home with him, just to see what would happen, I returned to my drink.

But he had vanished. I scanned the room and saw the guy he had been talking to now installed at the bar alone.

I stepped outside to see if Peter had joined the smokers, and then, realising that this particular boat had been missed, I grinned in relief and not a little amusement at myself, and started off, once again, in the direction of the Underground.

I felt happier though, as if something had perhaps been resolved. I felt comfortable, here, alone, walking along Compton Street in my boots. I may even have swaggered a little.

NINE

Hannah

Without James, and more and more frequently finding myself without Luke either, the house felt like a black hole that might swallow me up at any moment. I started to hold my breath when I woke up in the mornings so that I could listen to the eerie silence; I started to hesitate before stepping over the threshold when I got home at nights.

The school asked me if I could work some extra days to cover for one of the other secretaries away on maternity leave, and I jumped at the chance. Unsure of what the future held, I felt I needed the extra money, but even more than that, I needed the distraction.

It wasn't only that without James, I was forced to face up to the family life I had given up when I broke up with Cliff, but also the fact that in contrast with my technicolour adventures with James, every other part of my life seemed like monochrome.

Whether it was my job at the school which, though unchallenging, I had always managed to enjoy, or listening to my friend Jennifer complain about the builders, or entertaining my sister and her new French boyfriend for dinner, I was unable to sum up any real enthusiasm. I felt increasingly like an actor in my own life, feigning interest in those around me, going through the motions of normal life – a normal life that suddenly didn't interest me at all.

I knew, through Jill, that Cliff was seeing a shrink, and I wondered from time to time if I didn't need to see someone myself.

The ninth of February was Luke's friend Peter's birthday, and as it fell on a Saturday when Peter's dad was working, I took both boys to Thorpe Park for the day.

I was so desperate by that point for any sense of connection with my life that I anticipated the trip for days in advance, turning it, in my mind, into a pre-visualised cliché of family bonding with my son. The reality, when it came to it, couldn't have been more disappointing. Luke's attention, at twelve, was with Peter and Peter alone; his attitude to me was one of barely disguised disdain.

The boys wanted to go on all of the most terrifying rides, and *only* on the most terrifying rides, which reduced me to a lonely figure standing on the tarmac, shivering against the chill. I felt as if I had been reduced to a taxi driver to and from the park, a credit card to pay for everything, someone to hold the camera while the boys swung upside down, and a parental figure to be ignored on the way home.

When we got back to Farnham, I dropped the boys off outside Peter's place – his mother was taking them out for pizza. "Cheers, Mum," Luke said as he slammed the door and ran across the road.

I gritted my teeth and drove away. I would wait until I had closed the front door behind me and only then would I let myself do what I had been wanting to do all day: bawl my eyes out.

The following Monday, during a quiet moment at work, I phoned a divorce lawyer to book an appointment. He couldn't see me until the Friday, which gave me plenty of time to realise that no matter what he said, there were no good solutions here. The best-case scenario was that I could take Luke wherever I wanted *whenever* I wanted, but that was so unreasonable, so cruel towards Cliff, that I couldn't see how I could possibly go through with it even if it were possible. The worst-case scenario – that I wouldn't be able to leave at all – didn't bear thinking about.

The lawyer, a certain Steven Bower-Reddington QC, was young, beautiful, exquisitely dressed, visibly wealthy and nauseatingly sure of himself. But he knew his subjects – divorce law and parental rights – just as the teacher who had given me his details had assured me.

Within the first ten minutes of that outrageously expensive half an hour, he informed me that not only would I be breaking the law if I took Luke on a mere day trip to Calais without Cliff's permission, but that a family court – which would make any decision in case of dispute between us – would be unlikely to authorise any emigration plans given Cliff's regular access history, the lack of any problem aspect to Luke's relationship with his father, and above all, Luke's own desire to stay put.

Feeling rather desperate, I offered him my only potential trump card: my husband's some-might-say-dubious sexuality.

Bower-Reddington sat up straighter in his chair and rubbed his hands together with something akin to glee. "Homosexuality isn't considered a crime or even an illness these days," he told me, "so that might not have much sway over a family court, but given the right judge, it could certainly help us obtain a handsome divorce settlement. What would you say your husband's estate is worth?"

I gave him an overview of our finances, and he settled quickly back into his chair. We were hardly poor, but I don't think our riches were of the kind required to maintain the glint in Bower-Reddington's eyes.

"What's the timeframe for your relocation to the antipodes?" he asked, fiddling with a diamanté cufflink.

"I'm not even sure it's definite," I told him. "I'm just trying to get an idea what my rights are in all of this. But my partner, James, is already there. So if I do decide to go, I expect it will be sooner rather than later."

"Your new partner is Australian?"

"No, he's English. He's my husband's brother, in fact."

"Ah," the lawyer said, and his shoulders slumped a little further.

" 'Ah'?"

"Though I obviously have no judgement about it myself, the fact that you've left your husband for your brother-in-law is unlikely to sway a family court or a judge in your direction. In the hands of your husband's lawyer, it's all likely to sound a little tawdry. And that's putting it mildly."

"Yes," I said, blushing deeply. "Yes, I can see how that could pan out."

"Still, we can always have a bash. As long as you have the funds to cover costs should we lose."

By the time I left his office, I felt as if I had been supping with the devil. His clammy handshake somehow lingered with me, and I ached to get home to wash my hands. In fact, by the time I got back, my disgust with both him and myself felt so acute that I headed straight for the shower. Whatever the solution to my divorce with Cliff was, it wasn't something I was going to let Bower-Reddington sully with his beautifully manicured hands. At least the consultation had made me aware which path I *didn't* want to take.

I phoned James that night and told him what the lawyer had said.

"I guessed as much," was his blokey reply.

I had been feeling fraught and emotional all evening, as I had waited until it was late enough to call, and I doubted I would get through the conversation without tears. Indeed my throat started to constrict mere seconds into the conversation.

"So unless I can convince both Luke and Cliff then . . ."

"I don't wanna upset you Han'," James said, "but that simply isn't going to happen."

"I know, but I can try."

"Sure. Try by all means. But we need to work out a plan B."

"I can't leave him James. You get that, right? I can't just up and leave my son."

"Of course! But I can't come back either. I mean, I can *come back* – of course I can, for *visits* – but not to live."

"I know that."

"So what do you want to do?" James asked.

I frowned. "What do I *want to do?*" I repeated.

"Yes."

"I can't even see any options."

"Well there are a couple."

"Are there?"

"Yeah. I mean, the obvious one is that we carry on going back and forth. When we have the time and the money."

"Or?" I asked, bracing myself. I had a bad feeling about option number two.

"Or I guess we can give it up as a bad job."

I held my breath and squeezed my eyes tightly against the welling tears.

"Han'?"

"Is that what you want?" I asked, struggling to control my voice, which, unable to decide if it wanted to lurch into outrage or sobs, was instead wobbling madly between the two. "Do *you* want to give it up as a bad job?"

"Well . . . No. No, that's not what I *want*. What I *want* is for you to be here with me."

"And you know that's what I want too."

"But I don't want to see you unhappy. And lately we seem to be heading that way."

I couldn't speak, and eventually James continued, "So, if that's what's best for you . . . if you want to call it a day, well, I'd understand."

I lowered the phone, swiped a tear from my cheek, then lifted it again to my ear.

"Hannah?"

"It's just . . ."

"Yes?"

". . . It's just that I don't think I *would* meet someone else," I said. "Ever."

"Of course you would."

"That came out wrong. It's not what I mean. I mean that I don't *want* someone else. You're not just *someone*. You're you. It was . . ." I gasped as a batch of free-flowing tears began to cascade down my cheeks. "It was always you," I croaked. "From that first time."

"I know. I know that," James replied softly.

"What we have is so *special* James. So I can't just give you up, any more than I can give Luke up."

"Then there's your answer."

"Where?"

"We carry on as is for the time being."

"For the time being?"

"That's all anything ever is Han'. As long as it's bearable . . . as long as it works, as long as we can."

"I suppose."

"You'll come out during holidays. I'll come back whenever *I* can. And we'll see what happens next."

"I can't come out till Easter either," I announced. "I only get a week for half-term and it looks like I've got Luke. Cliff can't take him because he'll be finishing all the accounts. But I could maybe come out at Easter. It's right at the end of March this year, so it's after the financial year end."

"I don't think I want to wait until then," James said.

"Do you think *I* do? You do believe me, don't you? I really can't . . ."

"What I meant was that I was thinking about the last week of February."

"For what?"

"For a visit. I reckon most of the big stuff will be sorted by then. I could probably manage two weeks, maybe even three."

"Really?" I asked, starting to cry again, but with different, happier tears.

"Sure."

"That would be wonderful, James. Oh please do."

"But it doesn't fix anything. You need to realise that. It's gonna be difficult."

"I know."

"Being apart all the time is hard. But financially it's gonna

169

be shitty too, Han'. These flights are a grand a pop. There's only so many I can afford in a year."

"I know that. But please do. I can pay half this time if you want."

"No, you're all right. I can manage this one, but eventually it's gonna be a problem."

"I know. God I miss you."

"I do too. Oh."

"Oh?"

"Gio has just appeared. I've gotta go do farmer stuff."

"Right. Go on then."

"You're OK?"

"Now that I know you're coming I am!"

I laid down the phone and crossed to the kitchen calendar so that I could count the weeks between now and the last week of February. *He's coming back,* I thought, then, *he really must love me.* It was only then that I realised I had been doubting it. I chewed the inside of my cheek and allowed myself to break into a smile.

I worried about the conversation with Cliff all week, running and re-running various scenarios, practising useful key phrases in my head over and over to the point where two of my work colleagues commented that I seemed distracted.

I finally plucked up the courage to phone him to request a meeting. James had just booked his next flight, and I was feeling bold and optimistic.

Cliff agreed immediately and offered to call in that very night on his way home from work, so I packed Luke off to Billy's for the evening and cooked one of Cliff's favourite meals: cauliflower cheese. By the time he arrived at seven though, I had decided against the meal. I was worried it would appear to be little more than a cloying attempt at softening him up so that I could get my way – which in fact it was – and as such, I feared it was likely to have the opposite effect to that desired.

On arrival, Cliff walked quickly through the house to the kitchen, glancing left and right as he did so, as if to check for hidden assailants. "You've had a clear out, I see," he commented once we were both in the kitchen.

"Yes. I had one of my spring cleaning frenzies," I admitted. "The stuff's just in the loft. I didn't bin anything important."

Cliff nodded thoughtfully then sniffed the air. "Something smells good. Cauliflower cheese?"

"Yes."

"I'm pretty hungry. I don't suppose you have enough for two, do you?"

I smiled. "I think I can probably manage that. I made enough for Luke and me, but he's gone over to Billy's now, so . . ."

Cliff took a seat at the kitchen table whilst I plated up. "So how have you been?" he asked.

"Good. Fine. And you?"

"I'm OK," he said unconvincingly. "How was Australia?"

"Lovely actually. It was summer, so . . ."

"A nice way to spend Christmas then?"

"Yes. We were on a beach. On the Gold Coast."

"You went all the way up to Brisbane?"

"Yes. That's where we spent most of the time. On the farm. It was lovely."

"Good."

I placed the plates of food on the table, and Cliff reached

behind him to pull knives and forks from the drawer. "Well this is strange," he said as he handed me my cutlery.

"Yes, it is a bit."

"Just like old times."

"Yes."

"So I'm assuming this is about the house?"

"The house?"

"This place."

"In a way, I suppose it is."

Cliff looked confused. He opened his mouth to say something, but then changed his mind and forked a lump of cauliflower cheese instead.

"Well," he said, once he had swallowed. "Your cauli-cheese is as good as ever."

"Thanks," I said, hesitating over my next move. Everything was going so well, I was loath to spoil the atmosphere.

"So . . ." Cliff prompted.

"This is hugely difficult," I murmured.

"Yes, I know."

"Could you . . . I know it's an ask, but do you think you could try to forget that you're my husband, my ex, whatever, just for a moment?"

Cliff raised one eyebrow at me quizzically.

"I'm in a bit of a bind, and I'm not really sure what to do."

Cliff nodded vaguely. "I can try," he said, "go for it."

"The thing is that I really liked Australia. I felt like a new me when I was there. And that felt good."

"Right. Well, that's great."

"I *really* liked it," I said.

Cliff chewed his lip. "So you want to move?"

"I think so, yes."

"So we have to sell this place."

"I guess we do."

Cliff shrugged. "It's fine, Hannah. I already said I don't want to fight you over any of this. We'll sell the place and split the proceeds fifty-fifty.'

"That's generous but . . ."

"No buts. That was always the deal. It was always ours and there's only twenty-grand or so left on the mortgage, so if we sell it, we split it."

"Thanks," I said, stumbling in the face of Cliff's generosity. "My problem, my concern, isn't so much about the place. It's about Luke."

"Yeah . . ." Cliff said slowly. "You're worried he'll hate you if you leave? Is that it?"

"No, I . . . Will he? Would he, do you think?"

Cliff wrinkled his nose. "Probably not. Not if we deal with it properly. Not if we keep everything civilised. He's pretty adult now. I'm sure he'd understand."

"Actually, what I wanted to say is that my concern, my worry . . . is that I don't think I can bear to leave him. I love him so much."

"I know you do. We both do."

"So the obvious answer would be for him to come with me." I swallowed hard and watched him for a reaction, but he remained poker faced.

"Yes, that *would* be the obvious solution," he eventually said, sounding business-like.

"Oh," I replied, momentarily flummoxed. "Oh, well, I'm glad you agree."

"It *would* be the obvious solution if Luke wanted to go with you. But he doesn't."

"But don't you think he needs me? Honestly, Cliff?"

Cliff nodded. "Yes. He probably needs both of us. But he'll manage only seeing one of us. He already does to a certain extent during holidays and such."

"I just can't leave him behind," I said.

Cliff smiled at me strangely. "OK, let's play the pretend game the other way around. Let's pretend you're not my wife, but a friend. What would you advise me to do?"

"Oh. I'm not sure."

"I am," Cliff said, flatly. "You'd ask me what I want, and you'd ask me what Luke wants, and then you'd advise me to fight you every step of the way. I don't want to fight you, Hannah, I really don't. But you need to know that if you try to force Luke to go with you to the other side of the planet, that's exactly what will happen. I will fight you, I will throw everything I have, every penny at fighting you, and I will win."

"I consulted a lawyer," I told him, hardening my tone of voice. "Just to get an idea. He said that family courts tend to favour the mother."

Cliff laughed falsely. "And I'm sure he told you that, at twelve, Luke's wishes would be considered paramount."

"They did say they'd be taken into account, but . . ."

"I consulted one too, Hannah. I think it's best if I'm absolutely clear here. So you need to know that hell will freeze over before I let you take Luke to Australia. And I'm not saying that because I want a war with you. I'm saying it because I love him."

"But so do I."

"I know that. It's a tough one. You've chosen a guy who lives as far away as anyone ever could. If he lived any further away, he'd be coming back. Now maybe you can get James to move

174

here, though I doubt it, he was never that—. Actually, I'm not going to go there. Suffice to say, maybe you can convince him to move here. But I doubt it. And if you can't then you'll have to choose. If you choose Australia, then we could think about Luke possibly coming over in the holidays. Summer, Christmas – that kind of stuff."

"Would you even let that happen?"

"If we're being civilised about it all, then yes. But be warned, Hannah. I've taken legal advice. There is no way you could keep him out there. It would be seen by a court as child abduction. You could end up in an Ozzy prison. And I'm not making that up."

I ran a finger across my brow and shook my head. "I'd never do that, Cliff. You know that."

"I don't think you would either. But I'm telling you, just in case. You can't. It's not an option."

"I don't see I have any options. That's the trouble."

"You have a few. You can stay here and continue to see your son. You could get James to move here perhaps. You and I can divorce in a civilised manner, and you can go live on a farm with wonder boy and take a hundred and fifty to two hundred grand with you. Or you can drag me through the courts, lose everything you have, and then go to Australia with nothing. The choice is yours really."

"Nice, Cliff. Really nice."

"Just honest."

"Well, it's *helpful* to know where you stand," I said smiling coldly at him.

"Your food's going cold there," he said, nodding towards my plate.

"I've lost my appetite, I think."

"Yes. Me too," Cliff said, pushing his plate away and standing. "I think I might leave now."

I waved towards the hallway. "You know the way out."

"Great seeing you, Hannah. Just great."

"You too," I said. "Thanks so much for coming!"

I barely slept that night. Random images kept popping up in my head: Luke in a car accident and me unable to reach his side; Luke crying for his mum after some kind of heartbreak but not daring to tell me he needed me; women at the school gates talking to Cliff, saying, "She left for Australia? What a terrible mother!"

I finally drifted into a tortured sleep around three a.m., and awoke feeling thoroughly wired just after six, with a single thought in my mind: that until I had spoken to Luke, my options were not exhausted. I needed to have an adult chat with my son. And that, I knew, wasn't going to be easy.

I prepared my speech studiously, even making notes in the back of my diary. I knew I would only have one chance at this conversation, and I was determined to get it right.

By the final day of the week-long half-term break, I was ready, but as Luke was in a particularly sullen mood I made myself wait for a more auspicious moment. In the end I had to wait until the following weekend for whatever adolescent cloud Luke was under to lift.

My chance came on a cold, sunny Saturday morning. Luke looked up and spotted me watching him.

"Everything OK?" he asked.

I nodded. "Yes. Everything's fine," I said.

"Will James be coming back again?"

"Yes. At the beginning of March."

Luke nodded.

"Is that OK?"

He shrugged. "Sure," but then he managed a small smile, and I knew that now was my moment.

"Luke," I said. "I need to talk to you about something."

He spooned Rice Krispies to his mouth. "OK . . ."

"It's a pretty big thing, and I want us to have a proper adult conversation about it. I really need to know what you think. OK? Whatever you say is fine. But I need to know what you really, honestly think."

Luke straightened in his seat. He looked proud that he was being consulted in this manner. "OK."

"You know that I'm with James now."

"Sure."

"And you've probably worked out that your dad and I will get a divorce."

"Yeah. I know that."

"So the question is, what happens next?"

Luke frowned.

"The thing is that I want to see James more often than I do."

"Is he moving here, like, permanently?"

I shook my head. "He has a farm to run. It keeps him pretty busy. And I had a really great time in Australia. I really loved it there."

"Why can't you move *there* then?"

I swallowed hard. I was struggling to remain composed. "I *could*, in theory. But I'm worried about you."

"I'll be fine," Luke said matter-of-factly. "I can live with Dad."

"But I don't want to lose you. I don't think I could bear that."

"You wouldn't *lose* me."

"If I couldn't see you, I don't think I could stand it."

"Oh."

"Now the thing is that I know you're not keen on the idea, but I really want you to come out to Austra—"

"I don't want to."

"Let me finish. I really want you to come out *for a visit*, just to see what it's like. I know you don't think you'd ever want to move there, but I think you might be wrong. The weather's lovely, the beaches are lovely. There would be loads of fun things for you to do on the farm, and along the coast . . ."

Luke looked disconcerted. "I'm *never* gonna want to move to Australia, Mum. You know that."

"But how can *you* know that? You haven't even been there."

"I just do. That's all."

"How?"

"The same as you know you do. It's never gonna happen, Mum."

"Then I have to stay, don't I?"

Luke sighed. "You said to tell you what I think. What I really think."

"I did."

"Well, I think you should go, Mum."

I covered my mouth with one hand. "How can you say that as if it's so easy?" I whispered through my fingers.

"It's not *easy*, Mum. But I'd be fine with Dad. You'd be happy with James. It's the best deal for everyone."

"Wouldn't you even miss me?"

"Course I would. But I could come and see you and stuff. And you could come here."

"You make it sound so easy. But I'd miss you so much. I'd miss you too much."

"We could talk on Skype. That's how Billy talks to his dad."

I shook my head and blinked back tears. "But I love you so much, Luke," I said.

"I know," he replied. "But you've got a life to live, Mum. And so have I."

I shook my head and then rested it on one hand. I stared at my son in sorrow that the idea of my moving to the other side of the world touched him so little, and in wonderment at how adult he had become. Had my separation from Cliff forced that upon him, I wondered.

"Are we done here?" Luke asked. "'Cos I told Billy I'd be over by ten."

I nodded slowly. "Yes," I said. "We're done here. Thanks, Luke."

"No probs."

TEN

Cliff

One Saturday afternoon, I drove out to Billy's council estate to pick up Luke. Though it was mid-March, the weather was unpredictable and unseasonably cold, and because it had begun to sleet, Luke phoned requesting an emergency pickup.

Unusually, when I arrived at the house, Luke wasn't ready. He couldn't, he claimed, find his trainers, so after a full five minutes of polite conversation in the hallway, Brenda invited me into the lounge.

One end of the sofa was occupied by a pretty woman with cropped orange hair – the result was more than a little Milla Jovovich – and the armchair was taken by an enormous, curled-up Alsatian.

"This is Sue, my partner," Brenda announced, nodding at the woman, not the dog. "Take a seat. She's quite tame."

Sue smiled up at me and patted the sofa, so I perched beside her. She reached for the remote control and muted the television.

"Please don't do that on my behalf," I said. "I'm sure Luke won't be long."

"It's fine," Sue said, wrinkling her nose. "It's just a documentary."

"We wanted to go walking," Brenda explained. "But the weather turned nasty."

"I know. The forecast said sunshine," I commented.

"So how have you been?" Brenda asked.

"Fine thanks."

"Luke told us. About your divorce," she said.

"Yes. Being single takes some getting used to, but I'm getting there."

"His mum's going to Australia or something?" Brenda said.

"Yes. He told you about that, huh?"

She nodded knowingly.

"What did he say?" I braced myself for an unveiling of Luke's long-suspected angst at our divorce.

"Just that he'll be moving in with you and going to Australia for his hols. He seems pretty happy about it all."

I sighed in relief.

"He wants Billy to go with him," Sue added. "On holiday but—"

"But we could never afford it," Brenda interjected. "The flights must cost hundreds."

I raised an eyebrow. "Well, if Luke plays his cards right, he might well be able to get Hannah and James to pay for that," I said. "She wants him to go so much. And she wants him to enjoy it too. And Luke's very good at playing his cards right."

"He's a clever boy, that's for sure," Brenda said. "He's been helping Billy lots with maths."

"Anyway, nothing's settled yet," I said. "Hannah hasn't even decided, I don't think."

At that moment, Billy entered the room, followed by Luke, who sat beside me and started to pull on his shoes.

"So did you get your homework done?" I asked, as that was the official reason for the visit.

"Mainly," Luke said.

"It didn't sound much like homework to me," Sue said. "It sounded a lot like *Grand Auto Theft*."

"We had to have a break," Billy said earnestly. "Didn't we, Luke?"

Luke nodded and stood to pull on his coat. "And it's *Grand Theft Auto*," he said.

We said our goodbyes and headed out to the car. As we folded down the seats for Luke's bike, an idea came to me. "Hang on, Luke," I said, returning to the house and ringing the bell.

Brenda opened the door. "Did Luke forget something again? He always does!"

"No. I was just wondering . . . as we've got the seats folded down and everything . . . do you want us to drop that off at the tip?"

"The washing machine?"

"Yes."

"Oh that would be amazing," Brenda said. "It's been doing my head in. But without a car, it's just stuck there. Would you mind? Will it fit? With Luke's bike, I mean?"

"I think so. The Mégane is pretty vast once all the seats are down. I can drop it off tomorrow on my way into work. I drive right past the tip."

Once the machine was loaded and we were on our way, Luke said, "So you met Sue then?"

"Yes, I did," I replied, frowning vaguely at something in his tone of voice – a false naivety perhaps.

"She's Brenda's partner," Luke said, and I nodded and started to listen extra attentively for whatever message Luke was trying to deliver in this mock-casual tone.

"Yes, I got that," I said. "What's she like?"

"She's great," Luke said. "She's funny."

"Well, that's good. Does Billy like her too?"

"Of course. Well, except for the school thing."

"The school thing?"

"Yeah. They came to the open day together, and now Billy gets loads of aggro about it."

"About what?"

"About Sue."

"I'm not sure I follow."

"About living with lezzas," Luke said.

"Right. He gets bullied because of that?"

"A bit. They call him Ellen. But I stand up for him."

"'Ellen'?"

"Yeah, she's some famous lesbian on YouTube or something."

"Do you need me to talk to someone about it? Someone at the school?"

"Nah," Luke said. "That would make it worse. We've got it covered, I think."

"They came to the open day, you say?"

"Yeah," Luke said. "Sue said it was a politics statement or something. But Billy said it was just stupid."

I thought about Luke's "intervention" – for that was how I saw it – over the next few days.

I wasn't sure which of the possible interpretations corresponded with his intended meaning, but whether he had been telling me that he *knew* about me, or that it was OK to be gay, or that there was, quite simply, a life after divorce, I was touched by his concern.

It forced me to realise, again, that the world had indeed

moved on since my own adolescence. If Brenda could casually introduce Sue as her partner, if they could go to the school open day as a couple, and if at least some of Luke's generation thought that was just fine, then things really had changed. On the other hand, the bullying of Billy revealed that they hadn't completely changed either. Perhaps Luke had, in fact, been firing a warning shot across the bows, pleading with me to be discreet.

Whatever he was trying to tell me, I continued to see Jenny, and I continued to gently push my boundaries, returning to Compton's repeatedly, daring myself to talk to people, hoping vaguely that sexy Peter would return and chat me up again so that I could make a better job of responding. But he never did reappear.

The fourth time I returned, I had planned to meet Tristan, but just as I rounded the corner into Compton Street my phone beeped with a message from him. The freezer in one of their biggest restaurants had broken down, he said. He would be firefighting all evening in an attempt at saving the thousands of pounds of produce stocked within. There was no way he could make it.

Disappointed, I continued to Compton's anyway, where I ordered my customary pint. My usual table was occupied by a couple of guys in City suits. They didn't, to my eye, look gay at all, which was something that always cheered me up. I took a stool in the window and stared out at the fading daylight of the street.

I knew via Luke that James was back at Hannah's, and as I watched the evening light turn red and the streetlights flicker on, I thought about this. I was a little surprised at how much effort he was putting into their relationship if truth be told. I had always assumed that he wanted Hannah simply because she was mine, simply to spite me, but I was having to modify my beliefs on that one. If James was repeatedly spending thousands of pounds to fly across the world to be with her, then it clearly had to be about more than a simple victory over his brother. This admission that James' soul might contain even a smidgin of humanity hurt my pride, and I was trying to analyse why this might be when a voice to my left said, "You *can* smile you know. It is allowed."

I turned to see a very short but good-looking man with a crop haircut and a full beard, wearing bright red one-piece motorcycle leathers. He waved his crash helmet towards the window. "So what ya watchin' out there?" he asked. His accent was very East End.

I glanced back at the street. "Oh, nothing really," I said. "I was miles away."

"Daydreamin'?"

"Yes. Kind of."

"Were you daydreamin' about all the fings we're gonna get up to together?" he asked.

I blinked at him in surprise. "I wasn't aware we were going to get up to anything," I laughed.

He grinned broadly. "Well you are now," he said, holding out his hand. "I'm Mo, by the way."

I shook his hand. "Cliff."

"Cliff," he said. "That's not a name you hear much."

Mo's repartee was so polished that within ten minutes we were walking through the streets towards his flat. Part of me felt excited that I had taken this bold leap, and the other part of me was watching the whole scene with disdain and a little shock. It felt as if I had split in two.

It was only as we walked past some parked motorbikes that I asked, "So where's your bike?"

"Bike?" he said.

"Yes. Your motorbike. I assume that's what the leathers and the crash helmet are for?"

"Oh! Of course," Mo said, looking shifty. "I, um . . . had to leave it at the garage."

"What kind of bike is it?" I asked. I knew nothing about motorbikes anyway – I just wanted to see his response. Because, for some reason, against all logic, what I was picking up here was that Mo didn't have a bike at all.

"It's, um, a Suzuki," he said, leading me down an alleyway behind an electronics shop, and in through a side door to a grubby staircase.

"What kind of Suzuki?"

"One of the big ones," he said unconvincingly, pausing before a door and pushing his key into the lock.

The second he opened the door an ageing white poodle rushed to greet us, and by the time I had stepped inside, I knew definitively that the whole thing was a mistake.

The flat was only slightly cleaner than the communal staircase, and with walls adorned with dreadful reproductions of teary-eyed children, and a sofa covered with a hand-crocheted bedspread, it felt more like a retirement home lounge than a motorbiker's pad.

The poodle was of the needy, whimpering kind, with tear-stained eyes that oozed the same sadness as his master, the same sadness as the flat itself. Indeed, when I went to the bathroom, I spotted an empty Prozac blister pack in the dustbin, and that lack of Prozac seemed indicative of the whole setup.

When Mo led me through to the kitchen – complete with a

186

stained electric hotplate and flowery melamine mugs – to offer me a cup of tea, I made a feeble attempt at escape, muttering something about not realising how late it was, but Mo grasped my elbow and looked pleadingly into my eyes. "Please stay," he said. "At least stay for a cuppa." And because I felt sorry for him, I capitulated.

Once the tea was brewing (he placed a tea cosy over the pot) Mo said, "Do you wanna see my collection?" and without asking, led me through to his bedroom. He slid the wardrobe door open, revealing five or six brightly coloured motorbike outfits hanging there.

"Wow," I said. "You have a lot of those."

"I know," Mo said, grinning unnervingly. "I'm really into bike leathers. That one's too big for me, but it might fit you."

I laughed nervously.

"Do you want to try it?" he asked.

"Um, no thanks. You're all right," I replied. I had no intention of taking up motorbiking that day.

"You should," he said, lifting the hanger from the cupboard and laying it on the bed. It was lime green and said "Kawasaki" on the arms. "Bike leathers feel amazing," he said, nodding at me encouragingly. "The leather's really thick, you see."

"No thanks," I said again, forcing a fake smile and turning to leave the room. "I reckon that tea must be ready by now, no?"

Mo caught up with me in the kitchen. He had the green Kawasaki suit draped over his arm. It looked like a huge, deflated body. "You'd look great in bike leathers, I reckon," he said. "Look, I'm hard just at the idea."

He slid his free hand down over a bump in his crotch and right there, right then, something snapped and, sorry for him or not, it all became too much for me. I glanced at my wrist, remembered that I hadn't worn a watch for years, and then pulled my phone from my pocket. "Oh, god," I told him. "I had no idea it was so late. I really do have to go."

I retrieved my jacket from the chair back and made a dash for the door.

Mo and the Kawasaki corpse followed me into the lounge. He had a confused expression on his face. "You're leaving?" he said.

"Yes."

"Well, that was a fucking waste of time, wasn't it?"

"Yes," I agreed, as I gently kicked the poodle to one side and opened the front door. "Yes, I'm sorry about that. But I really do need to leave now."

Once I had left Mo's, I headed straight for the train station. I was feeling hollow and worthless – tearful almost – at the cheapness of what had just transpired, at the visible hopelessness of Mo's life, and somehow, by abstraction, at my own prospects for happiness.

My thoughts were confused but underlying all of them was a worry that gay lives seemed to be hopeless, and that if this was the path I chose, the rest of my life would be an endless series of meetings with men like Mo, until I became, by association, a Mo myself.

With hindsight this was what Jenny would call "dramatic thinking", but it was what was going on in my head that day and I suffered as a result.

Once I was on the train to Farnham, Tristan phoned to see how my evening was panning out. I told him that I was already on the way home, and he asked me why. After standing to check that the seats around me were empty, I explained my horrific visit to Mo's flat.

"Bike leathers are hot," was Tristan's frivolous response. "You should have gone for it."

"I don't think he even has a bike."

"Who cares?" Tristan said. "You need to let yourself live a little."

"Only I don't call putting on a set of motorbike leathers in a grubby flat *living a little*."

"I do."

"Well that's where we differ. I'm not like you."

"You might be more like me than you realise, if you let yourself go," Tristan said, sounding vaguely piqued.

"You know what, Tristan?" I said, my angst unexpectedly morphing into anger. "No matter how much I let myself go, I'm never going to be the guy who puts on bike gear for sex, because I'm never going to be a slut."

"A slut?" Tristan repeated.

"Yes."

"Like me, presumably?"

"If the cap fits," I said, wincing at my own harshness.

"Have a nice trip home, Cliff," Tristan said. And then the line went dead.

I felt bad. Of course I did. But I was in the middle of a drama of my own, and being pushed by Tristan to "loosen up" simply wasn't the answer. I would, I decided, phone him the next day; I would apologise.

In fact it was Tristan who phoned me the next morning. "I just wanted to check you're OK," he said, which under the circumstances, I thought surprisingly selfless of him.

189

"I suppose I am," I replied. "I'm not sure why, but the whole thing yesterday has left me feeling miserable. I actually feel a bit depressed to be honest."

"When you say the thing yesterday, you mean the conversation with me? Or . . ."

"No, the conversation was my fault. I'm sorry about that. But the date, if you can call it that. The whole thing was sad. There's just no other word for it. Sad."

"I've had a few of those," Tristan said. "There are some sad people out there, and sometimes you're going to meet them."

"And the whole fetish thing. It's just all a bit pathetic really."

"One man's pathetic is another man's hot."

"I know. I get that. Honestly I do. And I really am sorry for what I said, you know."

"It's fine," Tristan said. "You're right in a way. I am a bit of a slut. But that's how I like it."

"You know I'm really *not*," I told him. "I've been thinking about it, and it's not because I'm uptight. I mean, I may be uptight, but that's not the reason. I'm really just not built that way."

"I know. But you don't have to be," Tristan said.

"I'm not sure I'm cut out for this at all."

"Cut out for what?"

"For the whole gay thing."

"You don't *have* to be slutty to be gay, you know."

I laughed. "Except that you kind of *do*. Everyone I meet, everyone I talk to online. They all think more like you than me. They're all into *something*."

"Well that's just the law of probabilities," Tristan said. "The slutty ones are all online hunting for fresh meat. They're all hanging out in the bars waiting to pounce. My single girlfriends have exactly the same problem. The slutty guys are the ones you're going to stumble upon. But there are plenty of nice guys at home watching TV, dreaming of their perfect partner, believe me."

"Are there?"

"Sure."

"So how does one go about meeting *those* guys?" I asked.

"Ah," Tristan said. "If I knew the answer to that one, I'd be a happy man, wouldn't I?"

Tristan went on to say that Grindr wasn't ever going to work for a "wallflower" like myself, and suggested a different website called OKCupid, and after a brief discussion about it with Jenny at my next session, I took the leap and signed up. It was free, after all.

The men on OKCupid did seem to be, by and large, a more relaxed, less frenetic bunch than the men on Grindr. They appeared to be open to wider-ranging, non-sexual discussions and, for the most part, to be looking for actual, old-fashioned dates.

The setup process required the answering of literally hundreds of random questions about tastes in pop music and favourite colours, but it also allowed me to identify as bisexual, which for the moment, at least, struck me as less daunting than having to assume a one hundred per cent gay pigeonhole.

I quickly got chatting to three nice-enough-sounding guys, but before I could even arrange to meet any of them (the closest, Tom, was on the south coast) a far more exciting romantic possibility dropped, almost literally, from the sky.

I was walking back to my car carrying two work suits, freshly retrieved from the dry cleaners, when it happened. As I crossed Castle Street, I walked past a ladder leaning against a tree, and as I glanced up, a man in a red nylon harness dropped quite speedily to the ground, landing less than two yards from me.

He lifted off his safety helmet and unclipped the rope, and then frowned at me, and because I felt that I knew him from somewhere but couldn't quite work out where, I stopped walking and frowned bemusedly back. And then it came to me. He was Rob, the tree surgeon I had stood up less than two months earlier.

Rob squinted at me, then smiled lopsidedly before asking, "Do I know you from somewhere? I know you from somewhere, right?"

I nodded. "We, um, talked online. A couple of months ago. Rob, right?"

Rob nodded but continued to look confused.

"I stood you up," I admitted.

Recognition slipped across his face. "Ah! That was you was it? Fred, isn't it?"

"It's Cliff actually. I lied about the name as well."

"Right," said Rob, his smile fading.

"I tried to apologise, but the system wouldn't let me send you a message."

"I probably blocked you."

"I guessed that. I don't blame you really."

"So where you heading with the suits?" he asked, inclining his head to indicate my dry cleaning.

"My car. It's parked up there."

"And after?"

"Just home."

Rob nodded. "You could buy me a pint then," he said. "That would be a proper apology."

I swallowed and steeled myself to be brave. "OK then," I said. "I'll just dump these in the car."

When I returned, Rob had finished loading his equipment into his van. "Over there?" he asked, nodding towards the Nelson's Arms in the distance.

"Sure. Why not?"

"So what happened?" Rob asked as we started to walk. "Why did you leave me sitting there like a lemon?"

"I chickened out, pure and simple. I'm a bit new to all of this."

"Me too," Rob said. "But I still don't stand people up."

Though not classically good-looking by any stretch of the imagination, there was something very attractive about Rob. From his bandy-legged walk to his calloused hands to the way he fiddled with his beard while we were waiting for our drinks, he oozed manliness, and that was something I realised I found very attractive. It was the same thing that had initially drawn me to go home with Mo, only with Rob, one sensed that it was not theatre, not make believe, but a genuine ruddiness that came from working outdoors all year round.

We took seats in a corner of the bar and sipped our pints. Rob followed each sip of his Guinness with a wipe of his beard on his sleeve.

"It's nice of you to give me another chance," I said to fill the silence as much as anything.

"I'm not," Rob said, grinning cheekily. "I'm just letting you buy me a pint."

"All the same."

He shrugged. "Life's too short to stay angry," he said. "And if you fell out with everyone who ever behaved like an arsehole you'd pretty soon fall out with yourself. We've all been there."

I nodded. "I like the attitude. Where's the accent from?"

"West Country. Yeovil."

"It's a good accent. We used to go down that way a lot for holidays."

"We?"

"With my family," I said vaguely.

"So what happened that day?" Rob asked. "Did you just fail to achieve lift off from your sofa?"

I shook my head sadly. "I honestly did chicken out. I came to the pub, but then panicked and walked right past."

Rob smiled. "I saw you then. I was watching out the front window, and I thought I saw you go past. I thought you were just heading to the hole-in-the-wall or something. I assumed you were coming back."

"I'm sorry."

"So you keep saying."

"Well I am. Honestly. You seem nice."

"You reckon?"

I nodded.

"Nice to talk to, or nice as in cute?"

I coughed. "Um, both," I said, feeling embarrassed.

"You're cute too," Rob said. "I like the whole banker thing you have going there."

I laughed. "I'm an accountant. I'm on my way home from work. So it's just standard uniform."

"Well this is my uniform too," Rob said, glancing down at himself. He was wearing green combat trousers and a darker green cable-knit jumper.

"It suits you," I said. "What's it like being a tree surgeon?"

Rob shrugged. "Pretty OK really. Except when it rains. Which is most of the time in this bloody country."

"Yeah. That must be tough."

"I'm joking. I like it. I'm outdoors and it's low stress. That suits me. What's it like being an accountant?"

"Boring," I admitted. "Well-paid but boring. But I like the order. I like the predictability of numbers, I suppose. At this time of year, of course, it's pretty stressful."

"Year-end accounts?"

I nodded.

"I have to do mine soon."

"You're self-employed then?"

Rob nodded. He had already reached the end of his pint, and I realised that his thigh was now touching mine – an experience it would be impossible to deny that I was enjoying.

"So, another one here?" Rob asked. "Or are you gonna offer me a theoretical coffee at yours?"

I blinked. "Oh," I said. "Um, yes. Yes, I guess we could do that. I think I have coffee and stuff."

Rob grinned. "You don't need actual coffee for a theoretical coffee," he said. "That's the point."

"Oh. Right," I sputtered.

"Let's do that then," he said, standing. "Come on."

Rob followed me home in his van, and then as soon as we entered the apartment, pushed the flat door closed behind us, grabbed my arm and boldly pulled me in for a kiss. I'd been waiting so long for something like this but was still feeling horribly nervous, so I was relieved that Rob was making the moves. All I had to do was let it happen.

He slid his arms around me and pulled me tight against his

chunky frame, and as his beard met my lips, I thought, *Oh my god! This is what I need.*

That first kiss lasted about a minute, and then we separated and Rob asked, "Do you have any coffee of the non-theoretical kind? Because I'd kind of like one, to tell the truth. It's been a long day."

I nodded and broke free. "I do," I said as I made my way to the kitchen.

Rob followed me and leaned in the doorway, watching me as I switched on the espresso machine. He had a strange expression on his face, half smile, half leer, as though he was feeling particularly pleased with himself right now, and that felt flattering.

Once the coffee was made, we returned to the lounge. "Nice pad," Rob said, sitting down on the sofa. "You live alone?"

"Most of the time. I have a son. He's twelve. He stays every other weekend, and occasionally during the week too. He's at his mother's today."

Rob nodded. "That's cool."

"And you?"

Rob smiled and shook his head enigmatically. "You couldn't actually sit any further from me, could you?" he asked, ignoring my question.

"Just nerves," I said.

"Come here." He patted the sofa beside him.

I moved to his side, and we drank our coffees before Rob turned and kissed me again and the taste of Guinness was now replaced by that of sugary coffee. He undid my tie and unfastened the buttons of my shirt.

"Very smooth," he commented before pulling off his own T-shirt and jumper in a single movement to reveal a mass of brown hair. "I hope you don't have anything against bears," he said, looking down at his own chest and running his fingers through the hair.

"I don't think so," I said, reaching out towards him. "Can I?"

Rob nodded. "Sure. That's what it's for."

My hand hesitated mere millimetres from his chest, because that reaching out to touch, here, now, in daylight, between consenting adults, felt monumental. Absurdly, at forty, I had no idea how I was going to feel about it. Rob took my hand and squashed it against him. "You've got great hands," he said.

"Have I?" I questioned. I had never really thought about them.

"Yes," he said, removing his hand. I looked at my own hand nestled there and started to move it gently through the forest, and I shivered, because it felt amazing, it felt right, and once I had started there seemed to be no way, no matter how much we undressed, or how much we pressed our bodies together, that I could find a position that yielded sufficient contact between Rob's hot body and mine.

The whole experience was so warm and sensuous and good-humoured, I really couldn't have hoped for a better first date. There were no requests to dress up in strange uniforms, and no requirements to do anything that I might have felt to be challenging physically. It didn't feel slutty; it felt romantic. We just cuddled and kissed, and stroked each other's bodies until, one after the other, we came.

Once it was done and we had shared a shower, Rob returned to the sofa and beckoned me over once again, whereupon he wrapped his animal-furred arms around me and pulled me down into a horizontal position beside him. "You don't mind, do you?" he asked.

"Not at all."

"If I separate too quickly, I end up feeling horrible. You have to give yourself time to come down, I reckon. You have to be gentle with your soul."

And as he started to doze and then, gently, to snore, it felt so good, so wholesome, that I swear I had to blink back tears.

At seven, Rob awoke with jarring rapidity and declared, "Shit, it's gone seven. I need to get going."

I sat up. "Sure," I said. "Will I see you again?"

"Yes," Rob said, dressing quickly. "Definitely."

I found a business card and handed it to him. "My number and my e-mail are on there."

"Cheers," he said, stuffing the card into a pocket in his combats.

"Can I have yours?"

Rob smiled. "I'll call you. Don't worry," he said, which I took to be a polite "no".

He glanced at the clock again, swiped his coat from a chair, and crossed the room to the door. Once he had opened it though, he paused and glanced back at me. "I'm glad we finally met, Cliff," he said.

"Me too."

Then the door closed and I didn't know whether to feel happy that he existed, or sad that he was gone.

I couldn't stop thinking about Rob after that. Why hadn't he wanted to give me his number? Did he already have a partner? Would he ever call me again?

I checked my phone and e-mail frenetically, I glanced at trees in case I might catch him hanging in them – I felt nervous and excited and expectant all at once. And I felt vaguely ridiculous because of it, because, surely, a father, in his forties, should be emotionally more mature than his son.

After a few days, the precise image of Rob I had in my mind's eye started to fade a little. Though I remembered that I had liked him, though I could still recall the memory of his body pressed against mine, like a blurred, shifting Identikit image, I could no longer picture him. After a week, I stopped thinking about him constantly, and after two, my sense of excitement had been replaced with a kind of grey disappointment that tainted everything around me. Everything felt pointless. I even stopped checking my messages on OKCupid.

And then, one Saturday, I was eating a late breakfast when my phone rang with a hidden number, and, unusually for a weekend, I answered.

"Hey Cliff, it's Rob," he said. "How's tricks?"

"Hang on one tick," I said, moving to the kitchen – the farthest room from Luke's bedroom – before I continued the conversation. "Right, that's better."

"So how's things?" Rob asked again.

"Fine. Good. I didn't think you were ever going to call to be honest."

"Really? Even though I said I would?"

"It *was* over three weeks ago."

"Yes. Sorry about that. I was away. On holiday."

"Oh. Right. Anywhere nice?"

"Lanzarote."

"Good?"

"Sunny. That's all I wanted, so, yeah."

I wanted to admonish him for not telling me he was going

away, for not warning me to expect such a long wait, but I restrained myself, because above all, at the sound of his voice, I simply wanted to see him again.

"So are you free this afternoon?" Rob asked.

"My son's here," I said, glancing out through the kitchen doorway in case Luke had unexpectedly surfaced – which at nine a.m. was unlikely to say the least.

"Oh. OK."

"His mate's coming round later, so I could probably get away for an hour or so. I could come to yours."

"Nah, that's not gonna work for me," Rob replied.

"I could meet you outside somewhere. A pub. A park . . ."

"Not really what I had in mind."

"I know," I said despondently.

Rob sighed. I heard his breath hit the mouthpiece. "But I guess a walk in the park never did anyone any harm."

Once the meeting had been arranged – Farnham park, two p.m. – I could barely contain myself, so I paced around the apartment until Luke surfaced, whereupon I convinced him he wanted a cooked breakfast, just to give me something to do.

I was nervous as to whether Rob would still appeal, but when I got there, he looked even better than I remembered. He was tanned and relaxed after his fortnight in the sun and, unsurprisingly, looked at home amongst the greenery of the park.

We were both wearing jeans and similar green hiking jackets. "We look like a team or something," I said when I arrived.

"We do," Rob agreed, starting to walk across the park. "So your kid's OK on his own, is he?"

"He's very mature. He really doesn't give me any trouble

at all," I said. "He has a friend round and they're playing *Grand Theft Auto*, so they won't even move from the sofa is my guess."

Rob nodded. "When we were that age we were out on our bikes," he said.

"I know. It's a shame. But you can't really fight it."

"Not if you want to stay friends with them you can't."

"So, do you have kids too?"

"It's a shame we can't go to yours though," Rob said, and I wondered if he had even heard me. "I was hoping for a cuddle."

"Me too."

"I've been thinking about it since the last time."

"Even when you were on a beach in Lanzarote?"

"Especially when I was on the beach in Lanzarote."

"So who were you with? I take it you didn't go alone?"

"Shall we go over there and get a coffee?" Rob asked, nodding towards the cafe.

"Sure. Why not."

It was a cold, bright spring day and as we crossed the park, Rob bumped his hip against mine and grinned at me. "You've gone quiet," he said after a few minutes.

"I don't know what to talk about now," I said. "You don't seem to want to talk about *you* that much."

"Don't I?"

"No. You never tell me anything about yourself."

"OK. So what do you want to know?"

I shrugged. "I don't know. How about who you went on holiday with? How about where you live?"

Rob laughed. "You're right," he said. "I'm not that keen." He pointed to an oak tree. "That branch needs lopping off before it falls on someone. I used to work for the council, but then they outsourced it all. As you can see, it's very much minimum service these days, what with all the cutbacks."

"So you're never going to tell me *anything* about yourself?"

"I just told you I used to work for the council," Rob said, grinning cheekily.

"You're right. You did," I laughed. Because despite my annoyance, all I really wanted to do was kiss him.

The frustration, as we sat, knee to knee in the park cafe, was almost unbearable, and apparently the feeling was mutual because twice Rob glanced furtively around and ran his fingers over my hand, and as soon as we stepped out of the cafe, he scanned the horizon and pointed at some bushes in the distance. "Over there," he said.

"Over there what?"

"In the Photinia."

"What?" I asked, matching his stride and peering at the bushes in search of a clue.

"In the bushes!"

"What's in the bushes?"

"My kiss!"

As we pushed our way into the greenery, I flashed back to the drunken sexual fumblings of many years earlier in this very park and felt momentarily disgusted with myself, and ashamed at what I was about to do. But Rob was perfect. He really *did* just want to kiss. Which was just as well, as I don't think I could have refused him anything. We kissed and hugged and kissed again. He ran his hands beneath my jumper and pulled me tight. And then finally, he declared, "Actually, this is worse than doing nothing. It's just too frustrating!" and pushed me laughingly away.

As we clambered out of the undergrowth an elderly woman walking her dog glowered at us, and I didn't need a diploma in psychology to guess what she thought we had been up to. If only I could have put her right; if only I could have explained to her how loving that hug felt, how right.

As we headed across the green towards the car park, I asked Rob again if I could have his phone number.

"I'd rather just call you," he said.

"Are you a spy or something? Is being a tree surgeon just a cover?"

"Something like that," Rob said with a chuckle.

"Seriously, Rob. This isn't funny. You have my number. You know where I work. You know I have a son. You know I'm divorcing."

"Divorcing, are you?" Rob asked. "No, I didn't know that."

"You see, there you go. Another question avoided."

We had reached Rob's van. He fished his keys from his pocket, then turned and smiled sadly at me. "Look, Cliff," he said earnestly.

"Yes?"

"I will tell you at some point. I'll tell you everything, OK? But not yet."

I swallowed and nodded. "It's OK. As long as you tell me if it's going to be another month before I hear from you again, it's OK."

Rob looked me in the eye. His forehead wrinkled as he considered something, then relaxed as he asked, "When are you free? I mean, free-free. When's your son go back to his mum's?"

"Monday. After school."

"So how about Monday night?"

I slipped into a broad grin.

"I'll take that as a yes then, shall I?" Rob said, touching my cheek, and then remembering he was in public, dropping his hand and glancing around.

I nodded.

"Sevenish?"

"Sure. I'll get some food in."

"I wouldn't bother on my account. I will have eaten by then." He reached down and unlocked the door to his van, folded himself inside, and then wound down the window.

"Rob. Just one thing," I said.

He looked up at me, and seeing him from this new angle, I was stunned, again, at how sexy I found him. "Yes?"

"You don't have, you know, a boyfriend, do you?"

Rob laughed. "No Cliff, I don't have a boyfriend."

"OK," I said.

"So, Monday?"

I nodded. "Monday."

He winked at me, then started the engine and drove away quickly, his tyres spitting gravel, but just as he turned the corner, when his van was almost out of sight, something caught my eye: the phone number on the back of his van. I couldn't believe I hadn't noticed it before.

Oh-seven-seven-four-five . . . I chanted until I had fished my phone from my pocket and typed it in. I wouldn't ever use it, I promised myself. Not until Rob gave me the number himself. But all the same, creating a new entry in my iPhone and typing "Rob" gave me the warmest feeling I had had for years.

That Monday, Rob arrived as promised at seven p.m. sharp. We drank a few beers and chatted and kissed and cuddled and again brought each other to a climax, and as before, it felt blokey and relaxed, wholesome and right, even if Rob's continuing secrecy hovered at the edge of the landscape like a storm cloud threatening rain.

But from then on his visits were regular – every third evening as long as Luke was elsewhere – and I began to settle into an uneasy relationship with a man I barely knew at all. A relationship with a man! This was a revolution for me, but it felt surprisingly easy, perhaps because Rob's reticence enabled me to pretend that it wasn't really a relationship at all.

Once, Rob phoned when Luke was holding my phone – he had exhausted his own data plan – and Luke asked me, once I had hung up, who I had been talking to.

"A friend," I said. "From work."

"Your voice went weird," Luke commented.

"Weird?"

"Yeah."

"How?"

"Dunno. Just weird. You didn't sound like you."

"Well he's a work colleague," I said, as if this somehow explained that.

Luke nodded and went back to checking his Facebook account, but I couldn't help but wonder what special voice I had used to talk to Rob and quite what that might have revealed to my son.

The next time Rob called, I listened to myself, and heard the soft, quiet voice I used with him. And I decided that I rather liked it.

His fifth visit to the flat turned out to be the watershed moment when everything shifted. Not only had he brought condoms so that we could "try something new" – but he asked, afterwards, if he could stay the night.

After months of sleeping alone, having his arms around me felt amazing. I barely slept a wink, and purposely so – I didn't want to miss a minute of the experience.

In the morning I awoke at first light to find that we had reversed our positions and Rob was now nestled against me, his head lying across my arm.

I yawned, and Rob said brightly, "You awake then?"

I cleared my throat. "Just about."

"Did you sleep OK?"

I snorted. "Not really," I said. "But I'm not complaining. It's the nicest night I've spent in a long, long time."

Rob turned his head and kissed my arm then said, "Well, don't get used to it or anything. I can't do this often."

"Because?" I asked.

The pause was so long that I assumed that Rob had simply decided, as was his way, not to answer the question. But he had apparently been weighing up his answer the entire time, because he finally said, "Well, I'm married, aren't I."

Despite the fact that I no longer wanted to hold him in my arms, I remained frozen as I waited for my thoughts to clarify. I was aware that he had finally told me something, and that this was something I had been asking for since we met, even if it was the last thing that I had wanted to hear him say.

"Cliff?" Rob prompted.

"Yes?"

"Did you hear me?"

"Yes."

Rob rolled away, then bounced until he was facing me on

the pillow. He stared at me questioningly, his big brown eyes oozing concern.

"You said you're married," I said.

Rob nodded and bit his bottom lip.

"Is that married as in married-but-divorcing, like me?"

He shook his head.

"You're still together then?"

A nod.

"Kids?"

"Two. A boy and a girl. Eleven and fourteen."

I thought about this for a moment. "I'm assuming she doesn't know about you."

Rob shook his head.

"And last night?"

"She's at her sister's place with the kids. She gets back tonight."

"I see."

"And now you're angry," Rob said. "You see, I shouldn't have told you."

I shrugged as my reply. Because I wasn't sure what I was feeling at all.

The fact that Rob was married provoked a whole raft of feelings I felt ill equipped to deal with. The imagery went from the intellectual – the lies I knew he would be telling his wife about where he had been – to the graphic: the taste of me in his mouth as he kissed his wife, the odour of my sweat on his skin as he helped his kids with their homework. So I felt guilty. Of course.

More surprisingly, seeing as I had never once acted upon them, I began to feel guilty because of my desires during my time with Hannah. Ironically, I also managed to feel ashamed that I *hadn't* acted upon them, that I hadn't been as brave as Rob, who, it seemed, accomplished his own duplicity without the slightest hint of discomfort. "The way I look at it," he would say, when asked, "as long as no one knows, then no one is getting hurt."

I knew and I hurt for them all, but still, I couldn't give Rob up. Not only did the sex we were having move from *revolutionary* through *gymnastic* before setting into *amazing* as the weeks went by, but I started to admit to myself, and to Jenny, that despite all of the limitations that Rob's circumstances imposed, I was falling in love with him. I could sit in front of a work spreadsheet and go glazy-eyed thinking about his dimples, about the downy fur on his upper arms, about the sensation of his hairy legs against mine when, at the beginning, we had fucked, and more lately, whenever we *made love*. It all seemed unexpected and immature and absurd, but that was what was happening to me.

When he was around the flat, he was thoughtful and tactile and funny and sexy. The rest of his life remained as opaque as the opening scene from a spy movie, but as Rob himself once said, I was perhaps the only person on the planet who could understand, empathise with, and yes, tolerate his situation. Because though I had never once gone looking for a Rob during my fifteen years with Hannah, I knew why. I knew that I had been scared shitless. I had known that if I met a Rob back then, I would do exactly what Rob was doing now. It had been a tightrope walk over a terrifying precipice, and I had managed, just about, to keep my balance. And knowing how difficult that had been, how could I possibly blame Rob for having wobbled and fallen off?

One day in April, while I was waiting for him to arrive, the front door opened and Luke's head peeped around the door.

"Luke?!" I exclaimed, standing to cross the room and already fumbling in my pocket for my phone so that I could text a warning message to Rob. He had, by then, accepted the use of anonymous, non-specific text messages.

"Mum's going to Australia," Luke blurted, looking red-faced, perhaps from the bicycle ride, perhaps with emotion.

When I reached him, I glanced at my phone screen, on which I had attempted to type, "Luke's here," but on which – after the iPhone's overactive auto-correction facility had had its way – was frustratingly displayed, "Liked jets."

I deleted the message and crouched down in front of Luke. "What's wrong?"

"I said!" Luke said in what was almost a shriek. "Mum's going to Australia. She's on her way here to convince you."

"But we knew she was going to—"

"But she's going to tell you something to convince you to make *me* go. I heard her on the phone."

"Luke, there isn't a single phrase in existence that Hannah could say to convince me to make you move to Australia," I said. "Not one. Now, just give me ten seconds and—"

But it was too late, because, there, on the landing, right behind Luke, was Rob. The second Rob caught sight of us both, he turned and scooted back down the stairs.

"Luke, everything's going to be fine. Just give me ten seconds . . ." I said, and I ran after Rob, pulling the front door closed behind me.

I caught up with him at the back of the building just as he reached his van. "Rob!" I called, and he paused, and turned, then broke into a reassuring smile. "Looks like a change of plan," he said.

"I'm sorry. There's some family crisis going on. Hannah's on her way over apparently. Luke's almost in tears."

Rob nodded. "It's fine," he said. "I understand."

"You do?"

"Of course I do. If I don't get that family comes first, who does, eh?"

"Sure. Well, I'm sorry, anyway."

Rob reached out to touch my arm, but then glanced at the building behind me and withdrew his hand sharply. "We're being watched," he said. No trace of the smile remained.

I turned to look up at my balcony just in time to see the bay window sliding closed. "Was it Luke?" I asked.

"A lad. So yes, I guess so."

"I'm so sorry, Rob. I really have to go," I offered with an embarrassed shrug.

"I know," Rob said. "Just go and sort it out. I'll see you on Wednesday as usual."

Back indoors, I found Luke in the kitchen drinking juice from the carton.

"Don't drink out—"

"I know, it's *unhygienic*," Luke said mockingly.

"It makes it go off. The backwash from your mouth makes it go off faster."

"But I don't backwash."

I rolled my eyes.

"Who was that?" Luke asked, his voice studiously casual.

"Who? Oh, Rob?" I said, managing my own "casual" less convincingly.

"Who's Rob?"

"He's a friend."

"How come I never saw him before?"

I shrugged. "I have lots of friends you don't know."

Luke frowned. "Do you?"

"Yes."

"Who?"

"You don't know them, Luke. That's what I'm saying. Anyway, what was all that about? Why are you here?"

"Is he a good friend?"

I rubbed the bridge of my nose. "He's just a normal friend. Someone I have a pint with sometimes."

"When I'm not here."

"When you're not here. Anyway, what—"

"What does a tree surgeon do?"

"I'm sorry?"

"It says 'tree surgeon' on his van."

"Yes. He's a tree surgeon. He cuts bits off trees."

"So he's a gardener?"

"Yes."

"Why doesn't it say 'gardener' then?"

"Because a specialist gardener who climbs up trees to cut off branches is called a tree surgeon."

"That's stupid."

"Yes, it is a bit. Now, what was so urgent you came rushing in here?"

"It's Mum," Luke said, looking concerned again. "She's a bit mad today. And she's coming here to convince you to send me to Au—" He was interrupted by the intercom buzzer.

I sighed heavily, then crossed the room to buzz her in.

"I thought that was your bike outside," Hannah said, addressing Luke the second I opened the door. "What are you doing here?" Then as an aside, she added, "Hi, Cliff."

I nodded and forced a smile.

"I needed this," Luke said, miraculously producing a geometry textbook that I knew he hadn't looked at since the previous autumn. "I needed it for my homework."

Hannah nodded. "OK. Well head back and I'll see you at home."

"Is *he* there?" Luke asked.

"Yes. You know he is. He's leaving tomorrow."

"I'd rather stay here then," Luke said.

"Can you STOP . . ." Hannah took a deep breath, then continued, "Can you please just go home Luke. I need to talk to your father."

"Dad said we could get pizza," Luke said, flashing me a glance of desperation.

"Maybe. I said we needed to phone Hannah first," I explained, thinking on my feet. To Hannah, I added, "I was getting one for me anyway, so . . ."

Hannah sighed, then fumbled in her purse and pulled out a twenty pound note. "OK. Go get pizzas then. But don't come back before . . ." she glanced at her watch. "Before seven-thirty."

"For all of us? Three pizzas?"

"No. Just for you and your father."

"So what's so urgent," I asked, once Luke had been successfully dispatched.

"Urgent?"

"Yes. We usually phone before dropping in these days."

"Do we?" Hannah asked, looking genuinely confused. Her eyes had a glassy madness about them that somehow reminded me of Tony Blair.

"We do," I insisted, studying her features and surprisingly asking myself if I felt any residual desire for her. Though I could see that she was still a good-looking woman, the answer was "no".

"These came today," Hannah said, pulling a clutch of paperwork from a folder. "I ordered them from the Citizen's Advice because they had run out. So they sent them on."

I took the paperwork from her grasp. "Divorce papers," I said.

Hannah nodded.

"And after almost nine months, this is suddenly urgent, because . . . ?"

"It's not *suddenly* urgent," Hannah said. "But it needs sorting out. I need everything sorted out. I want the divorce filed and the house on the market. I've been thinking about that too, and I don't want half. Half wouldn't be fair . . ."

"I told you I'm quite happy with–"

"But it wouldn't be fair. I only worked half time, and not at all for the first seven years. I thought a third would be fairer."

"Well, I'm hardly going to fight you on that one, am I?" I said. "But are you sure you're all right? You seem . . . I don't know . . . Agitated?"

"I'm not *agitated*, Cliff," Hannah said. "I just want all of this done so that we can move on with our lives. I can't stand it any more."

" 'It' being?"

"This . . . stasis."

I nodded and glanced at the paperwork again. Although

Hannah did seem particularly agitated that day, I understood that the desire to move on is not one that manifests in a linear, progressive fashion – it comes in fits and starts. "OK. I'll look at these and get them back to you in a couple of days," I said.

"And . . ." Hannah said, looking even more stressed, as though she perhaps might burst.

"Yes?"

"I want you to come clean with Luke," she said, sounding nervous.

"'Come clean'?"

"About . . . you know."

"No, I'm not sure I'm following you."

"I want you to tell him about . . . you know . . . About the reasons we split up."

"So you could be with James?"

"I want you to tell him the other reasons."

"I'm really not following you, Hannah," I said, even though I was, in fact, following her perfectly.

"If you want Luke to live with you full time, then he needs to know about the rest."

"The rest?"

"I know you've been going to gay bars with Tristan."

"Jesus!"

"I don't think it's anything to be embarrassed about, Cliff. But I think Luke needs to know."

"He's twelve, Hannah! It's none of his business. Actually, it's none of yours either. Tristan needs to keep his mouth shut."

"Only I think it *is* his business. If he's going to be living with you then he needs to know who he's living with. It's only fair. And if you're going to be bringing men back to the flat—"

I stared at Hannah, wide-eyed. "I have not been *bringing men back*," I spat.

"Well, I'm sure you will at one point, won't you? And Luke needs to decide if he can cope with that now, before I'm so far away that I can't help him."

"He copes with you bringing men back," I said.

"What?"

"James is a man. Well, I assume so."

"James isn't *men*, Cliff. He's one man. He's the man I love. And he's your brother, so he's hardly a stranger. It's hardly the same."

"The same as what?!" My veneer of steely self-control was slipping away here.

Hannah pulled a face – goggle-eyed I suppose one might call it. "Look, I don't know what you get up to, but . . ." she said.

"I'm not getting *up* to anything! Jesus!"

"Well you still need to tell him."

"What? Hannah, what do I need to tell him?!"

"That you're gay."

"I'm not."

"So the nights out with Tristan—"

"I'm bisexual. Not that it's any of your business."

"Oh . . ." Hannah looked momentarily confused. "Oh, well, then you need to tell him that."

"For god's sake, woman. He's twelve."

"Cliff. I'm not backing down on this one. If you want Luke to stay with you, you have to come clean about who and what you are. I'm not having him trying to deal with this when I'm on the far side of the planet."

"No way."

"And if you're too ashamed to tell him, then maybe you need to reconsider if you're an apt guardian after all."

"Hannah, I'm not telling a twelve-year-old boy that his dad's bisexual. And it's not because I'm ashamed, it's because it's inappropriate."

"If you don't tell him, then I will," Hannah said.

And there it was. The ultimatum.

ELEVEN

Hannah

I had awakened feeling edgy that day, it's true.

James and I were coming to the end of a three-week visit, a visit that had been blissful. I was horrified at the idea of his leaving the next day for Australia and worried about when he would next be able to return.

During our weekends, all without Luke, we had gone away on three separate mini-breaks. James had suddenly realised that there were parts of the UK and swathes of Europe that he had never seen, and seemed determined to make the most of his time over. This newfound urgency made me nervous that he wasn't sure if he would be coming back at all.

So we had spent two nights in Brighton, staying in a quirky, old-fashioned bed and breakfast with flock wallpaper and a nylon bedspread – we walked along the blowy pier eating dribbling ice creams with chocolate flakes. The second weekend we drove up to the Lake District, where we walked until we could walk no more, much of the time through drizzle, before warming ourselves up with cream teas and mugs of hot chocolate. And then finally, and best of all, we had jumped on the Eurostar and spent a weekend in Paris, wandering around the Marais, drinking rocket-fuel espressos in Notre Dame and generally falling in love all over again. Because that was the result of our three weeks of mini-trips. I felt as if I were in my twenties being wooed all over again, perhaps wooed properly for the first time in my life.

In Paris, sitting in a colourful brasserie on the Canal St Martin – watched by the seemingly obligatory glowering waiter – James said, "Hannah, I need to ask you something," and just for a moment, I thought that he might be about to ask me to marry him. I surprised myself by realising that if that *were* the question, I was going to say "yes". I really shocked myself in that moment, because that was when I realised that not only had I sworn – without ever acknowledging the fact – never to marry again, but that I was now so in love with James that my never-again-marriage-ban no longer applied.

Why was I so in love with James? It was difficult for me to put a finger on it. A part of it was that he was just so straight-forward. There really didn't seem to be any hidden agenda with James. Ever. He would tell me exactly what he wanted, and he expected me to do the same. That honesty had the result of removing complexity from things, of demystifying everything, whether it was planning a trip, choosing a restau-rant, or having sex. Everything seemed easier, everything, to do with James at least, seemed stress-free.

I'm sure a psychiatrist would say that my attraction to James' abrupt honesty was a reaction against the complex nature of my relationship with Cliff. Because, let's face it, there had been more than a little sleight of hand in *that* relationship. So James' up-front nature provided a welcome contrast to Cliff's years of deceit. But more than the way James behaved himself, I think I fell in love with the way he made me feel about *myself*, the way he made me *be* myself.

I had spent most of my life adapting my desires in an attempt at second guessing what everyone else wanted. Being able – no, being *forced* – to be who I wanted to be, forced to say what I really felt/wanted/desired was a liberation, a rebirth. And that's not overstating it.

Dating James had turned me into a new version of myself, a new Hannah that I was also just a little in love with – a new Hannah who looked back on old Hannah with almost complete incomprehension and not a little disdain.

The question James had *actually* wanted to ask me at that brasserie in Paris wasn't, in the end, about marriage at all. "Are you really going to come to Australia?" he said. "Or are you just going to string things out forever more?"

"I'm really coming," I replied, struggling to hide my disappointment. "Why would you even ask me that?"

"Even if Luke won't come?"

"Yes. Even if he won't come," I said, unconvinced myself that it was true. "But I haven't given up on that one yet. You know that."

"I think you have to."

"There's one last conversation I need to have with Luke," I said. "Then we'll see."

"And will you actually start things moving then?" James asked. "Because, not being funny, but the fact that neither of you have sorted the divorce papers yet . . . well, it means what it means."

I reached across the table and laid my hand over his. "I will," I said. "As soon as we get back. I promise."

James winked at me. "OK," he said, allowing himself a hint of a smile.

The waiter caught my eye and smirked and started to whistle as he wiped the tables. Yes, they're grumpy as hell in

Paris, but unlike the British, who are embarrassed by love, the French like nothing more. And you have to respect them for that.

When we got back, I went into overdrive, reading about divorce law on the internet, making appointments at the Citizen's Advice Bureau and cataloguing what, within the house, I would need to take, what would need to be sold and what, hardest of all, would need to be discarded.

It's strange what love does to us: I read somewhere that whole chunks of the brain cease to function, and that's certainly how it felt. Everything that didn't involve James, whether it was the friends I used to see or the pastimes I had used to fill up the hours, seemed pointless. And this didn't feel like a temporary malfunctioning of the cerebral cortex, it felt like a revealed reality. It was as if I had been duped all these years into thinking that all this clutter was what life was about, when, in fact, it was really about nothing more than cuddling on the sofa with James.

My only remaining tie to England seemed to be Luke, and though I suffered constant bouts of soul-racking guilt over it, I was even beginning to imagine leaving *him* behind. Perhaps I can blame that upon the love drug too? Perhaps it's not my fault if the part of my brain that linked me to my son had started to malfunction too?

Of course, I loved Luke. That much was never in doubt. And leaving him behind would be like amputating a limb – this much I knew. But unless I could convince him to come with me, unless I could make him admit the same love, the same *need* for me that I felt for him, then perhaps, just perhaps, amputation, no matter how painful, really was the answer.

A part of me doubted I would ever go through with such a thing, sneering at my forms, at my lists, at my plans for a new life, saying, "Huh, there's no *way* you can leave Luke behind, and you know it." But I told that voice to shut up and wait and see. "We're not there yet," I said.

The reasons I wanted Cliff to tell Luke about his sexuality were multiple. Some of these were born of honesty and reason, and some of selfishness and a desire to manipulate. Old habits die hard.

I really *did* think that Luke had a right to know. And I still think that this was a reasonable, honest point of view. We were about to force our son to make the decision of a lifetime: to stay with his father or travel to a new country with me. And if we deigned that he was old enough to take such a decision then we had to trust him with the information he needed in order to take it.

It was, I thought, stunningly unfair for Luke to be expected to choose to live with Cliff if Cliff would not reveal who he really was. That, after all, had been precisely the data that had been missing from my own life, and that lack of information had cost me the last fifteen years.

I'll admit too, that, yes, of course, I hoped that Cliff admitting he was gay might sway Luke in my direction. And that wasn't because I thought he would turn against him because of his sexuality per se. It seemed to me that all of the negatives of choosing to live with Mum had been exposed and no doubt exploited to the full by Cliff. Luke knew that choosing me would involve changing schools, changing countries, leaving his friends behind and living with James. Yet none of the negatives of living with Cliff had been allowed to slip into visibility. Cliff would not, as Luke imagined, remain celibate and one hundred per cent available to his son forever more. So I wanted Luke to imagine a more complex future with his father to match the more complex future he had already imagined with me.

Morally, Luke was very much of his generation. He was open-minded about most things political and social, and yes, probably sexual. His best friend lived with two women and he was fine with that. This much I knew.

But I also knew that he used the word "gay" to describe almost anything that he didn't like. The clothes I tried to buy him were either cool, or they were gay. Anything James suggested was deemed to be "gay", while anything Cliff said was (ironically) "*cool*". So though I wasn't counting on it by any means, I did need to know how Luke would react once forced to associate that word with his own father. I wasn't exactly *hoping* that Luke would turn against Cliff, but if it was going to happen, well, there couldn't have been a better moment for it.

The dark side of my personality – and I've come to accept that we all have one – rubbed its hands in glee as I imagined Luke running into my arms, as I imagined magnanimous Hannah saying, "There, there . . . Yes, I know it's a shock. He had me fooled too. But you'll get over it just as I have had to."

Cliff and I argued for almost half an hour, and whether Cliff came to agree with me, or whether he simply decided that I had him over a barrel, he eventually conceded defeat.

"OK, I'll tell him," he said wearily. "But let me choose the time and the place, OK? Let me tell him myself."

I agreed but insisted that I wanted it to happen soon.

"Luke's going to be here all this weekend," Cliff said. "So I'll tell him then."

I went to the bathroom, and by the time I got back, Luke

had returned with the pizzas. As he handed me the change, he asked, "So what did you need to talk to Dad about?"

He was standing next to Cliff, and they were both glaring at me. He looked somehow protective of his father, and in my over-sensitive state, that rankled.

"Nothing," I said, even though it cost me to do so. "It was nothing."

"It can't have been *nothing*," Luke said.

And though I had agreed with Cliff that he should be the one to tell Luke, and despite my promise that I would not say a word, I heard myself say, "Luke. Your father has something to tell you."

Cliff's mouth fell open. I'm not sure if I had ever actually seen that happen before, but it truly did. I could see his fillings. *There's no going back now*, I thought, with a sorry mixture of glee and dismay.

"Dad?" Luke prompted, turning from me to his father.

"That's unfair, Hannah," Cliff whispered. "That's not what we agreed."

"Please, let's just get this out of the way," I said.

"Not like this."

"Dad?" Luke said again.

"Just tell him, Cliff."

"Tell me what?"

"Jesus, you're a . . ." Cliff told me, and I guessed that the missing word was "bitch", and I thought that I probably deserved it.

"Your dad has something to tell you," I said. "About why we split up."

"We split up because you wanted to be with James," Cliff muttered, his top lip curling.

"Yes, that's part of it. I'm happy to take part of the blame. But I'm no longer prepared to take all of it. Because that's not the whole story, is it, Cliff?"

"Well it kind of is," Cliff said, disingenuously. "We actually did split up because you went off with James."

"And because you didn't really want to be with a woman anymore, did you Cliff?"

"Hannah . . . in god's name," Cliff said. "This isn't right. We shouldn't be doing this like this. Not in front of Luke."

"He has a right to know."

"Please, Hannah?" Cliff begged. He looked almost in tears, and if it had been possible to undo the beginning of this conversation, I would have done so, because I saw how brutal I was being and hated myself for it. But it was too late.

"I'm sorry. But it's happening now. So let's just deal with it, OK?" I said.

"Mum! Dad!" Luke shouted. "I know, OK?"

Cliff and I frowned at each other, then turned to Luke.

"I know," he said again.

"What do you know?"

"That Dad has a boyfriend," Luke said.

"You have a *boyfriend*?" I asked Cliff, astonished.

"No. I don't."

"He's really nice," Luke continued. "And his name's Rod."

"Rob," Cliff corrected before raising his fingertips to the bridge of his nose.

"And you've met him? You've met this Rob?"

Luke nodded. "He's a tree doctor."

"Surgeon," Cliff said. "He's a tree *surgeon*. But he's not my boyfriend, Luke. He's just a friend."

I turned on Cliff now, with genuine outrage. "Well you kept that one quiet. Don't you think that this is something I should know about?" I asked.

"What?" He sounded genuinely confused.

"If Luke's hanging out with your new 'boyfriend' . . ." I said, making the quotes with my fingers.

"They haven't been *'hanging out'*," Cliff said, aping my quotes. "They haven't even met."

"Well Luke says they have."

"Yes, well, Luke's lying."

"Dad!" Luke whined.

"That's not fair," I said, noting this first breach in their solidarity. "I think Luke's telling the truth and you know it. So blaming him because you're too ashamed to admit the truth is grossly unfair."

"I'm not ashamed of anything. How dare you!"

"Well then . . ."

"OK. Whatever. Luke's telling the truth," Cliff said, sounding exhausted.

"And has anyone thought to ask Luke how he *feels* about that?" I asked.

"Oh for fuck's sake," Cliff said.

"Don't swear, Cliff. Please. So, Luke. How *do* you feel about that?" I asked.

Luke frowned. "About what?"

"About your father. Wanting to be with a man?"

Cliff gasped, then opened his mouth to speak, and then closed it again.

Luke creased his brow. "God, Mum!" he said. "He's just *gay*. It's not a crime. It's not, like . . . the middle ages anymore or anything!"

225

And that was when I knew that I had definitely lost this battle.

Faced with another united front, I had no idea how to respond, and after a few speechless seconds, I muttered "You two are impossible," gathered my things and in sheer embarrassment I walked out, slamming the door on it all.

When I got home, I found James packing his suitcase in the bedroom. He looked up at me, said, "That didn't go well, I take it?" and then, as I folded into tears, dropped the socks he was holding and wrapped me in his arms.

His sympathy towards me lasted precisely as long as my sobs did, because as soon as I was able to explain that the tears were born not of Cliff's reaction to the divorce papers, but of the fallout from my own lack of self-control, he too turned against me. "Bloody hell, Hannah!" he exclaimed, releasing me and stepping backwards. "You just blurted it out? Jesus! Think about the boy a little, won't you?"

The next morning, I was driving a still-vaguely-frosty James to Heathrow when Cliff phoned. I didn't listen to the message until I got home.

I entered the silent house and slumped onto the sofa then hit the voicemail button on my phone: "Hannah, it's Cliff," the message ran. "Luke says he wants to stay here for the week. He actually says he hates you, so well done on that front. I can't say I blame him. That was a despicable trick you played last night."

I sighed and laid the phone down beside me, and stared at my reflection, alone, in the television. If I had had any tears left, I might have cried some more, but I just felt washed out and exhausted, unloved and yes, ashamed.

I phoned Luke twice during the week but he didn't take my calls so I left messages telling him that I was sorry for how things had gone, and that I had just wanted him to know all the facts so that he could make adult decisions.

Eventually, a full eight days later, unable to stand it any longer, I went to the school gates to meet him. Luke was walking diagonally across the playground with Billy when he spotted me. Shockingly, he pretended not to have seen me and diverted, with Billy, towards the side gate.

I ran along the street to catch up with them and after an initial bout of speed walking, Luke said something to Billy and they separated, Luke slowing down to allow me to catch up.

"Luke!" I said. I was out of breath.

He turned to face me. "I'm going to Billy's," he said, icily. "Dad's picking me up later."

"Please come back with me tonight. We can call your dad and let him know. We need to talk, Luke."

"Only we don't," he said.

"I—"

"I hate you," Luke said, interrupting me.

"You don't mean that. I know you don't."

Luke nodded exaggeratedly. "I do. I wish you'd just go to Australia and stop ruining everyone's lives."

"Luke!" I protested, hesitating between anger and a sudden desire to cry.

Luke looked down at his feet, shook his head slowly in apparent disgust, and then turned and ran to catch up with his friend.

As other kids streamed around me, I watched my son walking away until he reached the brow of the hill. When I heard him laughingly say a sentence containing the word,

"Crazy," I thought, *You know what, he's right. This is crazy. This is all, absolutely crazy.*

I dried my eyes and strode back to the car.

The very next morning, the postman rang the bell and, in exchange for my signature, handed me an ominous-looking envelope bearing the moniker *Jeremy Brown. Solicitor.* Eyeing the envelope, I made myself a coffee, then sat down at the kitchen table to examine the contents.

Inside were almost thirty sheets of paper. A quick scan revealed that they comprised the divorce forms, a *Statement of Child Arrangements* and a legal contract regarding the house. The fact that Cliff had hired a professional for all of this made me suspicious. I remembered only too well my meeting with Steven Bower-Reddington.

The covering letter was clearly designed to put my mind at ease. In it Jeremy Brown explained that he had been hired by my husband to represent both of us in a sprit of uncompromising fairness, for the simple reason that despite the best intentions, without professional guidance, divorces could become messy.

He explained that because some grounds had to be cited for the divorce, Cliff was filing on grounds of adultery. This, he said, would enable us to forgo the usual two-year separation period. He wanted to draw my attention to the fact that the child arrangements form, though acknowledging my desire to leave the country and according full parental responsibility in my absence to Cliff, explicitly ensured maintenance of equal parental rights over Luke at any time during which I was present in the United Kingdom, and at any time during which Luke, of his own accord, chose to visit me in Australia.

Finally he explained that although the contract regarding the house contained a blank percentage regarding the proceeds from the sale I would receive, he strongly advised both Cliff and me to agree to the standard fifty-fifty split so that *visible fairness* could be seen to have been upheld by both parties in all dealings.

The letter continued: *As emptying, listing and selling the property at the current time would appear to be a lengthy process, your husband strongly suggests that the house be "dust-sheeted" and simply maintained, in stasis by himself until such a time as you have decided definitively on your future whereabouts and until such a time as the housing market has (hopefully) recovered. Your husband is prepared to assume all maintenance costs and relevant taxes in the meantime, and this would have the advantage of enabling you to expedite your relocation plans, which, I gather, are somewhat urgent.*

Reassuring letter notwithstanding, I read through every horrible line of legalese in that paperwork, but as the letter had claimed, everything did seem to have been drafted with the utmost fairness. Other than the *fault* for the divorce being attributed to Yours Truly, I really couldn't find a single issue with it, and even that, once I phoned Brown (and then the Citizen's Advice Bureau to check) came to seem, if not fair exactly, then necessary at least.

Finally, with a deep sigh, I settled down to do what I had been meaning to do for days. I phoned Cliff to apologise, an apology he accepted magnanimously.

We discussed the paperwork, and Cliff reiterated that both Luke and he thought it in everyone's best interest if I were to go and join James sooner rather than later, and that dust-sheeting the house in the meantime was the obvious option, at least until I was able to make a definitive statement about where I wanted to be. "If it goes on too long, I can always stick everything in storage and get some renters in," he said.

I asked him why he was being so damned reasonable, and he asked me if I had ever known him to be anything else.

"You mean other than when you told me that James was dead?"

"*Other* than the James thing," he said, with a laugh, and I thought, *Gosh. Are we supposed to laugh about that now?*

"And other than the fact that you—?"

"And other than my confusion about my sexuality," he said, interrupting me again to show that he was well aware of his faults.

I was forced to admit that with those two exceptions, Cliff had been a model of reason for as long as I had known him. Certainly his equanimity over the divorce settlement was something I couldn't fail to appreciate. "So what happens now?" I asked.

"You take your time, and when you're ready, you sign the paperwork and send it back to Brown," Cliff said.

"And then?"

"And then you book yourself a flight to Brisbane, I guess," he said, and I thought, *God. Can it really be that simple? Have we really reached that point?*

"I'll need to resign from the school and work out my notice period," I said.

"Yes. I suppose you will."

"How's Luke doing?" I asked. "I miss him so much."

"He's here," Cliff said. "He wants to talk to you too. So are we done?"

"Yes," I said. "Yes, I think we're done."

"Goodbye, Hannah," Cliff said, and with the paperwork before me, that goodbye felt shockingly final.

After some scratchy microphone-blocking noises and some distant mumbling that sounded a lot like encouragement, Luke came on the line. "Hi, Mum," he said.

"Hi, Luke."

"Are you OK?" he asked me.

"Yes. Yes, I'm fine, dear," I told him. "Look, I've apologised to your dad, but I want to apologise to you too. I behaved dreadfully the other day."

"It's OK, Mum," Luke said. "Everyone's stressed out at the moment."

"I miss you so much."

"Me too," Luke said, and my heart fluttered.

"You do?" I croaked.

"Of course," he said, then, "Can I come to yours this weekend? Would that be OK?"

"Yes . . ." I gasped.

"Can Billy stay too? On Saturday?"

"Yes. Of course he can," I said, tipping my head back to stop my tears from falling onto the *Statement of Child Arrangements*.

Late that night, I phoned James to explain all the details. Through crunching sounds from the breakfast cereal he was eating, he told me that he loved me, that he missed me, but that there was no rush for anything. "Take your time," he said. "Read everything carefully. Get legal advice if you have to. And then do what your heart tells you."

I slept fitfully, my dreams filled with impossible forms and scary lawyers, then awoke the next morning feeling as though I had spent the entire night discussing divorce arrangements

– feeling so exhausted with the subject that I couldn't summon a single coherent thought.

It was a breezy sunny day and I wasn't due at the school until the afternoon, so I took a long energetic walk into town in an attempt at clearing my head.

When I got back, the pile of paperwork was still there of course, staring up at me accusingly from the kitchen table, and in a sudden frenzy, I signed every single sheet of paper, stuffed the lot into the return envelope, licked the seal, hesitated, pulled it all out to remove the house sale authorisation, then resealed the envelope and, lest I might change my mind, literally jogged to the post box.

Back at the house, I looked up the dates for the coming summer break and then logged on to the Quantas website to book myself a return ticket to Brisbane, before savouring, over lunch, the knowledge that at least from the twentieth of June to the third of September, I knew what I would be doing and who I would be with, and that it would be far, far away from all of this.

Beyond that, I decided that I wouldn't, for now, even *try* to imagine what came next.

That Saturday morning over breakfast, I told Luke about my plans.

"You're not going to try to make me come with you again are you?" he asked in dismay.

I shook my head. "Absolutely not. That's all over."

"Yeah!" Luke mugged.

"I honestly think you'll want to come one day," I told him. "And I think when you do, you'll really like it. But in the meantime I'm not going to do any more pushing, OK?"

232

Luke nodded. "OK," he said. He looked unconvinced.

"That's a promise," I insisted.

"OK."

"But if you ever do fancy some time in the sun, you just let me know and I'll organise it, all right?"

Luke nodded again.

"So are we OK again?"

Luke looked confused.

"Are we friends again?" I asked.

"Oh, yeah," he said. "Of course."

Though I had managed to sound very business-like about it all, I was gagging with emotion, and the second he headed up to his bedroom I turned to look out at the garden and silently cried.

Cliff's offer to dust-sheet the house took away a surprising chunk of the stress associated with the numerous changes happening in my life. Whether he had come up with this idea for the sole purpose of getting rid of me more quickly or because it truly did, as he claimed, make financial sense, it certainly made everything far more digestible. Leaving the house, changing country, committing to James, deciding where my future would be, even leaving Luke – it all seemed far less dramatic once I could pretend that nothing had really been decided, once I could tell myself that it was all, if I so decided, nothing more than a nice long holiday.

In my heart of hearts I knew that this wasn't the case, so in a way I was pretending. The "holiday" fiction allowed me to remain in denial about what was really happening to my life, but sometimes denial is the best place you can be.

Despite my new holiday myth, I found myself watching

Luke with new fervour. It was as if, knowing that I wouldn't see him for over two months, I had developed tunnel vision in which his presence shimmered with uncanny intensity, to the point where I could see little else even though looking at him gave me a physical pain in my chest. Frequently Luke would catch me staring and ask, "What?" and I would reply with some platitude. "I was just looking at how tall you are now," I would say, or, "I was just thinking that we need to get you some new jeans." But I wasn't. I was trying to burn every detail – the very essence of him – into my mind's eye. And I was trying to imagine how long I could survive without him.

Once the divorce papers had been signed and my trip had been booked, things eased considerably between Cliff and myself. We were both explicitly moving on and that seemed to take the tension out of our relationship. By May, things were calm enough that we could actually exchange a few banal phrases beyond those required to organise Luke's trips back and forth.

One particular day, Cliff admitted that he wanted Luke to spend the Friday night at mine so that Rob could stay over, and that conversation felt like a milestone in our relationship. Being able to talk calmly to my ex-husband about his new boyfriend struck me as almost absurdly sophisticated and really something of an achievement on both of our parts.

"So is Rob becoming a permanent fixture in your life, Cliff?" I asked in my special fake-casual voice.

"I'm not sure," Cliff replied. "I hope so."

I suggested that if this was the case perhaps I could meet him, even if only briefly, and Cliff replied that, yes, maybe I could.

My relationship with Luke had also calmed down to the point where eventually I was able to ask him what *he* thought about Rob. This led to a stunning revelation – that Luke had never met Rob at all. Cliff had been right: Luke had been lying.

"Would you *like* to meet him?" I asked. "Or do you think it's better this way?"

Luke shrugged. "It's up to Dad, really, isn't it?" he said.

Partly out of sheer nosiness and partly because I suspected that the second I was out of the country Rob would move in with Cliff, I was keen to meet him myself. Oh, I didn't want some agonising sit-down dinner, but I did want to exchange a few phrases so that I could get a feel for the guy and at least have an opinion on whether or not he was someone I was happy for Luke to hang out with.

But though Cliff agreed *in principle* that this was a good idea, he seemed to do everything possible to make sure that it never actually happened. Rob was always kept out of sight of both Luke and myself, and I started to wonder why that was; I started to worry what might be wrong with the guy that Cliff should be so reluctant for anyone to see him. So, of course, I started to scheme as to how I could bump into him of my own accord.

TWELVE

Cliff

Even trying to *suggest* that Rob might meet anyone proved explosive. Initially, because she had requested it, I asked Rob if he would meet Hannah. Rob and I had been getting on well and ever since Luke had revealed his stunning tolerance for all things gay, a tolerance that left me feeling as proud as I ever have, I had been fantasising about integrating Rob into my broader life in a more satisfying manner for all concerned.

"No," Rob said simply, when asked.

"No?"

"*No.*"

"Why the hell not?"

"God, do I have to justify myself?"

"I'm not asking you to *justify* yourself," I said. "I just want to know why."

"Look, Cliff," Rob said. "You asked me if I would mind. You have my answer: Yes. I mind."

That conversation was followed by a shorter-than-usual visit (he left at eight-thirty rather than ten) and the withholding of all physical contact – a first. It was hardly encouraging, and so it took me two weeks and four further visits, not to mention repeated prompting from Hannah, before I dared revisit the subject.

This time I was sharp enough to wait until Rob was *leaving* before I tackled him – I wasn't going to forgo my dose of intimacy this time around. "Rob," I said. "I know you said 'no' already, but I was wondering if you'd reconsider meeting Hannah. Just for a coffee."

"Sure," Rob said. He was pulling on his coat.

"Oh. Really?" I replied, disconcerted.

"Sure. I'll *reconsider*," he said. He squinted at the ceiling for a moment. "There, done. I've reconsidered. The answer is still 'no'."

I pulled a face.

"Cliff. I'm married. You know this. I have kids, I have—"

"Me too," I interrupted. "And Luke will be living here come June. So it would just be easier if you would spend five minutes meeting him and his mother to put everyone at ease. That's all I'm asking."

"Now, you want me to meet them *both*?" Rob asked, pulling on his lumberjack hat – it was raining outside.

"Ideally, yes," I said, annoyed, but despite myself thinking how cool he looked in the hat.

"There's no way, Cliff," Rob said, pulling his keys from his pocket and heading for the door. "So drop it."

"So what happens in June, Rob?" I asked. "What happens once Luke's here?"

Rob paused at the front door just long enough to deliver his parting shot: "Who says we'll even be together by then?"

So I was worried. Rob had been coming to my flat twice or three times a week for almost three months and though his *other life* as we referred to it, remained strictly off limits, we had spent enough time together to know that, fundamentally, we got on well. In fact, we got on brilliantly – we agreed on

237

politics (both centre-left), we liked similar foods, we enjoyed the same films, appreciated each other's music collections, fitted together perfectly in bed and best of all – and most surprisingly for me – were having lots of good sex.

Sex had always been a complicated subject for me, and my fifteen years with Hannah had done nothing to ease that. Rob's attitude was that sex – which he generally referred to as *a quickie* – was as unworthy of concern as any other activity. Whether Rob had engineered his belief systems to justify cheating on his wife, or whether he was just built that way and the cheating naturally followed, this down-to-earth attitude was exactly what I needed. It neutralised a lot of the guilt I felt myself around the subject. Seducing someone (particularly a man), or allowing myself to be seduced, were both complicated for me, and yet responding to Rob's request for a quickie, or even sometimes a *quick quickie*, a request presented with all the nonchalance of a request for a coffee refill, enabled me, somehow, to relax about the subject. Gone too was any requirement for performance. If one of us couldn't get it up, or one of us couldn't come – and we all know that these things happen – in Rob's book, it was as noteworthy as leaving that cup of coffee to go cold; it simply didn't matter. After trying to perform for Hannah all these years, as much to reassure myself as her, that was a major relief.

In many ways, Rob's grounded nature reminded me of James, and I wondered if there wasn't something terrifyingly Freudian lurking in those particular depths. But the implications of that were so unsettling that I decided early on simply never to go there, and rather successfully blocked any thoughts on the subject from my mind. It was the only aspect of my new life that I never discussed with Jenny either, the fact of which probably speaks reams.

Rob cancelled his next visit. He claimed it was because he needed, bizarrely, to cut down someone's Leylandii after dark, but I suspected that he was teaching me a lesson for having brought up the subject of Hannah and Luke again, so I gave my family reunion project up as a bad job. If Rob would not meet Luke then there was no reason for him to meet Hannah anyway, I reasoned. One five-day period without him was enough to remind me that what mattered here was not that our relationship fit some external model of normality, but that it quite simply survived. I would just have to organise regular evening activities for Luke so that Rob and I could continue our "relationship", within the constrained space that Rob allowed.

Three weeks from the end of term, Hannah phoned me at work. She was in London renewing her passport and had received a call from Luke's school. He had, they shockingly claimed, attacked another boy. One of us needed to go in, and that particular day, this meant me.

By the time I got to the school, the victim of Luke's aggression had been shipped off to Accident and Emergency, where he was reportedly receiving stitches to his eyebrow. Luke and Billy, who was also involved, were sitting on a bench outside the headmistress' office looking muddy and sheepish.

"She's not there," Luke said the second I arrived. "She said she'll be back in five minutes."

I sat down on a chair opposite and looked at the two boys. "So what happened?" I asked.

Luke shrugged.

"A shrug won't cut it this time," I said.

Luke shrugged again anyway.

"Do you have any idea how much trouble you could be in?" I asked. "You need to tell me your side of the story before she gets here."

Luke glanced at Billy and I saw him shake his head almost imperceptibly.

"He was giving Billy a hard time," Luke said.

I looked at Billy. He had mud all up his left side and his collar was ripped. He reminded me of myself during my own school days. "Have they phoned your parents?" I asked.

"They're both working," Billy said.

"What was he hassling you about?"

Billy shrugged. "Nothing."

At that moment, the headmistress appeared. She was a stern-looking woman in the Margaret Thatcher mould, who I had always found to be firm but fair in past dealings. Her name was Mrs Slocombe, which always supplied a brief pique of amusement when we met. I presumed that, luckily for her, most modern kids knew nothing of *Are You Being Served?*, nor of Mrs Slocombe's endless problems with her pussy. I wondered if Luke was old enough yet to share the joke with.

"Mr Parker!" she said, opening her door and ushering me in.

"Mrs Slocombe," I said, stifling a smirk.

"So, as I'm sure you have gathered, this is a rather delicate affair," she said as soon as the door was closed. "Unfortunately, the boy Luke hit, Karim, is claiming that it was a racially-motivated incident, which puts us all in a rather difficult position."

I frowned at the preposterous nature of the accusation. "I really rather doubt that," I said. "Luke doesn't have a racist bone in his body."

"Well neither Luke nor Billy have provided any other explanation, so I'm afraid that we only have Karim's word to go on. Now we haven't got the police involved yet because, frankly, knowing Karim's parents, they won't be keen to make a fuss, but unless we can get to the bottom of what actually happened, it may still be the best option."

"The police?!" I exclaimed.

"A boy has been injured," Mrs Slocombe said with a shrug. "Action may need to be seen to be taken."

"OK, well we had better get Luke in," I declared. "Maybe he'll talk to me." Upon which Mrs Slocombe shouted Luke's name in an astonishingly loud voice that made me physically jump.

Once he was seated beside me, I told him, "So, things are getting serious here, Luke. You need to tell us what happened. Because Karim is saying you were being racist."

"Racist?" Luke said. "No way."

"Did you call him Osama Bin Laden?" Mrs Slocombe asked.

Luke shrugged and stared at his feet. "He called Billy worse."

"What did he call Billy?" I asked.

"It doesn't matter."

"Did you call him Osama because he's Arab?" I asked.

"No, I . . . It doesn't matter."

"Luke. You're not helping yourself here," I said. "Once accusations of racism are made then things are out of hand. You need to tell us what happened."

"He wrote all over Billy's books," Luke said.

"What did he write?"

"Just stuff."

It was like extracting blood from a stone, but by interrogating Luke and then Billy and then the two together, and by forcing poor Billy to empty his schoolbag, we were able to discover that Karim had crossed out Billy's name on all of his schoolbooks and written "Ellen" instead.

"Why Ellen?" the headmistress asked.

Both Billy and Luke stared at the floor.

I sent the boys back outside so that I could speak to the headmistress privately.

"Well?" she asked, once the door had closed again.

"I think I know what this is about," I said.

"Good. Then please share. I really want to get to the bottom of this."

"Billy's mother lives with her partner. A woman."

"Yes. I'm aware of that."

"So I think we can be pretty sure Karim was taking the mickey out of Billy because of his mothers."

"Because of his mother's . . . ?"

"I'm sorry?"

"Because of his mother's what?"

"Oh. No. Because of his *mothers*. As in the plural of mother. Ellen is an American chat-show host, she's a lesbian, so, his calling Billy 'Ellen' will be a reference to that."

"Ah. Yes, I see."

"You've seen Billy's clothes, right?" I asked.

The headmistress nodded.

"So you can see that he was being bullied."

"I can't really make that deduction, no," she said. "And unless we get the whole story, I think getting the police in may still be the best option. They have a tendency to get to the bottom of these things."

242

I had been casually flicking through Billy's geography exercise book as I spoke to her, and now I had reached the end, I flicked it closed, revealing what looked, initially, like a game of hangman on the back cover. On closer inspection though, the hanging man had glasses and a *Tintin* quiff like Billy's. Beneath it, the completed letters of the "game" read, "Sharia Law: Hang The Queers."

"Ah," I said, turning the exercise book so that it faced Mrs Slocombe. "And what about that?"

"Oh dear," she said with a sigh.

"Indeed. How *does* homophobia stack up against racism in the great league table of modern wrongs?" I asked.

She leaned towards me to study the picture, then sat back in her chair, pursed her lips and said a prolonged, "*Humm.*"

After ascertaining that Karim had indeed been defacing Billy's books with death-sentence artwork, Mrs Slocombe and I resumed our discussion. "Between you and me, I don't think any of this would have happened if Billy's mother had kept her private life private."

"Really?" I said, feeling a swell of outrage rising.

"Oh, don't get me wrong. I'm all for live and let live. But kids will be kids, and at this age they're all homophobic. Billy was bound to be hassled about it once it became known."

"And that's OK, is it?"

"Not at all. I'm not condoning it. No, of course not. I'm just saying that it's a fact of life."

"And racism, then? Is that not a fact of life?"

"Well we do everything we possibly can to combat racism. I'm sure you're aware of some of our actions."

I nodded. I could feel heat rising in my cheeks. For the first

243

time in my life, I felt the urge to become militant. I wanted to say, "So gay parents should just keep it a secret? Gay partners should be banned from picking their kids up at school so that everyone can just pretend that we don't exist?" But I knew that Luke would hate me for that. He had already intimated that both he and Billy agreed that Billy's mother should have been more discreet about her living arrangements.

Instead I asked, "So what do you do at the school to combat homophobia?"

Mrs Slocombe frowned at me. "I'm sorry?"

"You say you do everything you can to combat racism."

"Yes. We have a number of programs that fight—"

"So what do you do to combat *homophobia*?" I asked.

"Well, it's not currently part of the curriculum," she said.

"So, nothing at all?"

"No. No, we don't specifically have, um, a policy on that."

"Might that not explain why the kids *all* seem to be so homophobic?"

"Yes, all right," she said. "Yes, I get your point. We should probably look into that."

As I drove Billy home that night, he begged me not to mention what had happened to Brenda or Sue. We came across Brenda carrying a huge bag of clothes and gave her a lift for the final half a mile. She seemed far more concerned at the state of Billy's uniform than at what might have occurred. "I've just *been* to the launderette," she told him, fingering his blazer. "I'll have to hand wash that now. As if I don't have enough to do." Turning to me, she added, "You come out of a day of slog, spend two hours in the launderette and then have to go home and do it all again. Honestly! Kids!"

It was fair enough, and I could see her point, but I couldn't help but wince at the memories of my own mother slapping me because someone else had dragged me through the mud, and I admired Billy for not revealing how this had all come about.

I realised the multiple stresses upon the boy, caught between taking flak at school because he was being raised by two women, yet hiding those stresses from the women in question to avoid making them feel guilty for his troubles. In that moment, I came to like Billy a lot, and I decided that Luke had a friend worth defending.

A week later Hannah and I were summoned to the school once again to meet Karim and his parents. Mister and Mrs Khoury were mortified by their son's behaviour, that much was clear.

"What on Earth has got into the boy?" Mrs Khoury declared. "We're not even Muslim."

"We left Persia to get away from all of that sharia silliness," her husband remarked, holding his son's drawing in one trembling hand.

Karim, his brow beautifully stitched, stared at his feet until the criticism moved onto Luke. When Hannah asked him whether he thought that punching Karim had been the right solution to this particular problem, Luke, perfectly coached by me, declared that, *No, violence was never the answer*, before apologising separately to both Karim and his parents.

"He's a good boy," Mister Khoury told Hannah. "You've brought him up well. That much is clear."

On the way home, the moral dilemma of the situation was clearly playing on Luke's mind. "Dad?" he asked. "I know I *had* to say sorry and everything. But it wasn't *really* wrong to punch Karim, was it?"

I glanced at his puzzled face, then back at the road. I thought about my own father and the fact that the only time he had ever showed me any respect was when I had beaten another boy senseless. I would not become my father. "You could have just told a member of staff," I offered instead. "Don't you think that might have been easier?"

"But I did," Luke said. "Billy did too. But it didn't make any difference. Karim wasn't going to stop punching Billy because a *teacher* told him to. It just made it worse."

"Yes, I understand that," I said. "But did splitting Karim's eyebrow actually stop him?"

Luke nodded energetically. "Well *yeah!*" he said. "Of course it did. He wouldn't dare touch him again."

"Then I don't know," I admitted.

"With people like Karim, whacking them one is the only thing that works," Luke said. "You can't just let someone beat your best friend up, can you?"

I suspected from the bullies I had come across in my own childhood that Luke was probably right, and I felt surprisingly proud of him for standing up for his friend, and relieved that he was capable of landing a blow on a big guy like Karim and coming out on top. But I knew if I sanctioned violence as a solution, it would, at some point, come back to bite me, and again, my father's memory lingered over me like a cloud so I simply said, "Hum," winked at my son, and left the question hanging there.

Amazingly, a few weeks later, I came home from work to find Luke, Billy *and* Karim playing on the Xbox.

I put down my briefcase and removed my tie, then headed to the corner of the room so that the boys could see me.

"Hello," I said, shouting over the noise of the racing game they were playing. "Hi, Karim," I added. "How's the eye?"

They were so absorbed by the game they barely looked up.

"Luke. May I have a word?" I asked.

"I'll just finish this level," he said, "then we can pause it."

I went through to the bedroom to change and was just pulling on a T-shirt when Luke put his head around the door. "Is it about Karim?" he asked.

I nodded, beckoning him in. "Yes," I said once he had closed the door behind him. "I thought we had an agreement that you would ask before bringing any new friends home."

"Yeah, but you said anyone you don't know," Luke said.

"Exactly."

"But you *know* Karim."

I laughed. "I don't think meeting someone in the headmaster's office because you've whacked him in the face for being a homophobic bully really counts as meeting him, do you?"

Luke frowned but nodded. "Sorry," he said. "Do we need to go out then?"

I sighed and put my suit in the closet. "First explain what's going on here," I said. "Are you two friends now?"

Luke shrugged. "Kind of."

"He's not pushing Billy around anymore?"

Luke shook his head.

"He's not being homophobic about Billy's parents?"

"No. He was just being a dick. He didn't mean it."

"Does he go round to Billy's house?"

Another shake of the head. "No one goes round Billy's except me."

"Because?"

"Because Billy's embarrassed I s'pose."

247

"Right. Well that's a shame."

"It's how it is," Luke said. "Billy likes Sue and everything, but . . ."

I nodded. "Sure. I understand."

"And we can't go to Karim's . . ."

"Why?"

"They have a no friends rule."

"Do they?"

Luke nodded. "Their flat's too small or something. So we *had* to come here."

"Well, you just need to ask next time, OK?"

"OK," Luke said, then, "They got a washing machine."

"Who did?" I asked, even though I knew full well.

"Brenda and Sue," Luke replied.

"That's good."

"They didn't order it. It just came."

"Really?"

"Yeah. Brenda thinks it was a mistake," Luke said. "But I think it was you."

"Me?"

"Yeah. It was you that bought it."

"Me *who* bought it," I corrected. "But, no, it wasn't me."

"I *so* know it was," Luke said, grinning. "It came from that warehouse place you always use. Discount electricals or something."

"Well I can assure you that it wasn't me."

"Yeah, right," Luke said, still grinning and raising one eyebrow.

The gesture was so adult I couldn't help but grin.

"Ha! I knew it," Luke said, taking the smile as an admission of guilt.

248

"Well don't tell them. Not ever. OK? Not even Billy."

Luke nodded vaguely. "Why?"

"Because if you do something for someone, that's nice. But if you tell them about it it becomes something different, OK?"

"Because they might think they owe you something?"

"Exactly."

"OK. I get that. So can Karim stay?"

"Stay?"

"Till dinner, I mean. He has to go by seven anyway."

"Sure," I said. "But next time . . ."

"Ask," Luke said, completing the phrase.

"And do you think you could go to your mum's or Billy's on Friday night?" I asked. "Maybe stay over?"

"Sure. I'll stay at Billy's. Is Rob coming?"

I nodded.

"I thought I was gonna meet him properly."

"You will at some point, but not this time, OK?"

"Luke!" Billy was calling him back to the game from the lounge.

"Get back to your screen," I said. "But after dinner, it's switch-off time, OK?"

THIRTEEN

Hannah

A few weeks later, I asked Luke if he had met Rob yet.

"Nope," was his simple reply, but this time – a sign of our thawing relationship – he added, "Dad doesn't seem that into anyone meeting him. Billy reckons he must be weird or have a stupid voice or something."

As I was laughing at this, I realised that I could enrol Luke in my plan. "If you told me the next time he was going to be there," I suggested, "then maybe I could drop in and surprise them. See how funny his voice really is."

"Dad wouldn't like that," Luke said, looking doubtful.

"No, but at least it would be done. I reckon once that has happened, we'd all be able to meet up in a civilised way instead of all this skulking around. What do you think?"

Luke wrinkled his nose, looking concerned but also vaguely intrigued by the idea. "He's there on Friday actually," he said. "Dad asked me to stay over at Billy's."

"Really?"

Luke nodded. "But you didn't hear it from me, right? And you have to tell me what he's like, OK?"

I parked my car at the far end of the little street that led to the car park. I was far enough away to be out of sight of the apartment, yet close enough to spot Rob's van when it arrived at seven p.m.

I left my car and moved a little closer where, from behind a tree, I watched as the man I presumed to be my husband's new boyfriend, climbed out. The whole thing somehow became real at the sight of him. It was a shock.

I was surprised at his appearance. It's stupid of me, I know, but I somehow expected him to look *gayer*. This bearded, check-shirted gardener couldn't have looked less like any of the stereotypes I had managed to conjure up in my mind's eye. He was young and fit and masculine, and, I hate to admit it, surprisingly attractive.

I waited a few minutes before I followed on – just long enough for Rob to have reached the apartment but not long enough for him and Cliff to have jumped into bed, I hoped. A woman was leaving the building, so I timed my strides and just managed to grab the front door before it closed, enabling me to reach Cliff's landing without being buzzed in.

I knocked on the door and from behind it heard Cliff's voice say brightly, "If it is, then it's the fastest pizza I ever ordered."

He yanked the door open, then, at the sight of me, pushed it closed again so that I could see no more than his face through the gap. "Hannah!" he exclaimed.

"Hi, Cliff," I said. "May I come in?"

"I . . . I'm sorry," he spluttered, "but no, it's not convenient."

"Is Rob here?"

"*Rob?* No," he said unconvincingly, moving his foot to block the door even as I reached out to push it further open.

"Then why can't I come in?"

"As I said, it's not convenient," Cliff said. "Anyway, what's this about? Why are you here?"

"I need to meet him, Cliff," I said. "Before I go, I need to see what he's like. You said that you understood that. And I'm going in a few weeks."

"But Rob's not here," Cliff said again.

"Cliff!" I laughed. "Stop lying. I just saw him come in. Let's just get this over with. How bad can it be?"

"You're impossible, Hannah!" Cliff said, sounding genuinely angry now. "Now please, just . . . ?"

"Cli—" I started to protest, but he surprised me by gently knocking my shoe from the gap with his own foot and slamming the door in my face.

I knocked on the door for a minute and even tried Cliff's mobile and landline, but he wasn't giving in so, disappointed at my failed plan and wishing I had simply accosted Rob in the car park instead, I gave up and headed back downstairs.

As I reached the corner of the building and Rob's van came into view, I saw that he was there, fumbling with his keys, then unlocking the door. I realised that he must have used the fire escape.

As he started the engine, I ran towards the van, calling out, "Rob! Rob! Stop! This is ridiculous! I only want to meet you!" But the van was already screeching away.

I glanced up at Cliff's windows and saw him watching all of this from above, shaking his head dolefully and felt, once again, embarrassed by my own behaviour.

I shrugged exaggeratedly up at him and mouthed, "What?!"

Then shaking my own head, I crossed the car park and headed up the street to my Polo.

I pretty much gave up on meeting Rob after that. Logic allowed me to conclude that if he was that afraid of being spotted, then Luke was unlikely to meet him either, and therefore my parental responsibility to vet him was a moot point. Plus, of course, I felt too embarrassed to bring the subject up again; though I didn't admit it to myself at the time, I think that I had also sensed, at the moment I spotted him, how challenging it might be to actually meet my husband's new partner. I had realised that it was, perhaps, better left alone.

Finally, if truth be told, I was too busy with other things to continue giving it that much thought. Because I was leaving my job at the school, I had been given the extra responsibility of explaining to my replacement, Deirdre, how everything worked. This included showing her how to use my filing system, which, over the years, had become organic to say the least. So I had to reorganise all of the files even before I could begin to hand them over. This involved late nights at the school, and even a couple of trips in during my days off.

At home I fought a constant battle with myself over what to take, what to store and what to throw away. Like some obsessive TV hoarder, the throwing away proved most challenging of all. What to do, for example, with an elephant-shaped "piggy" bank Cliff had given me? It had, all those years ago, contained my engagement ring, and had been so wildly inappropriate that I had found it cute and amusing for as long as we had remained together. But I could hardly ship the damned thing to Australia; neither, it seemed, could I throw it out, as every time I tried, I quickly fished it back out of the refuse sack again. Leaving it behind in the house would have seemed the obvious answer, but the thought of Cliff wandering around the house and finding it was equally unbearable too. And so, for weeks, I binned and un-binned it, until finally, in a pique of frustration with myself, I ran outside and hurled it directly

253

into the bin man's refuse hopper. Once I got back, I felt elated with myself, as if I had managed some marvellous feat. And then within seconds I felt distraught at the loss.

My feelings towards Luke amplified day by day during those final weeks and I did everything I possibly could to make sure not only that we spent time together, but that it was good, enjoyable time, and what's more, good, enjoyable time recorded on camera for posterity. I bought a new point-and-shoot digital camera (I had never been able to get the old one to take a decent picture) and took as many photos of the two of us as I could. I wanted his memories, once I left, to be not of the emotionally unstable, hysterical character I had recently been drifting towards, but of a wonderful, loving mother a son might feasibly want to visit.

And then, on the first of June, I flipped over the kitchen calendar, and there it was, staring me in the face. The twentieth of June. Less than three weeks to go!

From that moment onwards the preparations went into overdrive and my feelings for Luke became so fierce that despite all the activity preparing for departure, I regularly awoke thinking, *No, it's impossible. I simply can't do it.* On three separate occasions, I dropped Luke off at the school gates and because I couldn't help but picture that final goodbye on the twentieth, I collapsed, as soon as I reached the car, into floods of tears.

But each time my willpower began to fade, I would have a conversation with James and remember the light in Brisbane, or the sensation of his arms around me, or the joy of lying beneath him, and would think, *No. I deserve this. I can't possibly turn back now. I have to be brave.*

The final week was the worst. I had stopped working, and

the packing and cleaning were done. The only tasks that remained were to drop dust sheets over the furniture and switch off the water and electricity – a five-minute list.

With nothing to occupy myself, the only thing left to do was ponder my impending separation from my son, and this wreaked such havoc with my mind that I suspected that I really might not leave when the time came. My fiction that this was a temporary trip had, because of the scope of my preparations, become untenable. Instead, I felt as if I were preparing my part in a farce, preparing for something that clearly could never happen.

Three days before my departure, I handed Luke his breakfast, and at the thought of never doing it again, burst, yet again, into tears. It was the third batch of tears Luke had witnessed in twenty-four hours, and it proved to be too much for the boy.

He looked up at me, watery-eyed himself, and said, "Mum. I know you're upset, but this is all really weirding me out. I know you're going on Saturday and everything, but would you mind if I just stayed at Dad's from now on?"

I couldn't hold it together, and my emotional crises were ruining my strategy of shaping Luke's final memories, so I dried my eyes, forced a smile, nodded and drove him to Cliff's.

My sister Jill was worried and phoned me constantly, but because her gentle *how-are-yous* were enough to provoke fresh floods of tears which scared her, while doing nothing for me, I started to filter even her calls.

And so it came to pass that the final three days were spent alone, without my son, in the so-clean-it-felt-like-a-morgue house. I sat and stared at the muted TV, constantly on because I needed the company to distract me from what I was about to do, constantly muted because that very company interfered with my ability to think about the *gravity* of what I was about to do.

The night before I was due to leave, I became overwhelmed again by a sense that the entire idea had been stupid, that it was the worst, most selfish, idiotic idea I had ever entertained – that it was no less than madness.

I waited until it was late enough to be morning in Brisbane and then phoned James to tell him that it was all over, to tell him that I couldn't come, that it had all been a terrible, terrible mistake.

Having just woken, his voice was sleepy and sweet, and it reminded me of how safe and happy I felt when I woke up next to him. He asked me how I was, and because I was unable momentarily to reply, he continued, telling me that he had been looking at trips we might make for my birthday in July. Did I want to drive to Byron Bay or go sailing on The Great Barrier Reef? he wanted to know.

And I heard myself croak, "The Great Barrier Reef. Yes, take me there."

The next morning, I woke up early and, feeling like a zombie, I walked around the house completing the final tasks on my list. Sofas dust-sheeted: tick. Refrigerator defrosted and unplugged: tick. Bed stripped, toiletries packed, water turned off. Tick.

My sister came to pick me up at eleven, and found me numbly staring at the muted television screen.

"Are you OK?" Jill asked.

"Tell me I'm doing the right thing here," I said.

"Of course you are!" she enthused, sitting on the sofa beside me and taking my hand. She was tanned and healthy-looking from her recent trip to France, and the contrast between the two of us couldn't have been more marked. "You have to take chances in life," she said. "And the best thing is that if you don't like what you've chosen, you simply go back to whatever your life was before."

I thought about pointing out that my life, as before, was no longer really an option, but restrained myself. I knew what she was trying to say.

We loaded my two suitcases into the car – the two chests had been shipped a week before – and drove to Cliff's.

Prompted by a call to his mobile, Cliff and Luke came to the kerbside to meet us – we were running late.

I got out and Cliff and I hugged rigidly. "Have a great trip, Hannah," he said. "Enjoy Australia. And say, 'hi' to James for me." He sounded genuine enough.

It wasn't until Cliff had gone back inside the building that Luke, who had been lurking in the shadows, stepped forward. "Hello, Luke," I said, my voice already trembling.

"Dad says I should tell you what I really think," Luke said. "He says it's really important that I tell you."

I looked at my son through tearing eyes and remembered every step of his life, from the first moment when the nurse had handed him to me to the present moment, and the pain in my heart was such that I wondered if I could remain standing. People say that when you die, your whole life flashes before you, and I wondered now what these churning images of Luke's life meant. "It's probably best," I croaked – I could barely speak.

"I love you loads, Mum," Luke said, his eyes wet too. "And I'm gonna miss you like crazy."

Tears were rolling down my cheeks. I opened my mouth to speak but nothing came out. Instead, I opened my arms and stepped towards him. "Me too, Luke," I said as I wrapped my arms around him, thinking, madly, *My flesh! My flesh!* "You have no idea how much I'm going to miss you," I said.

"That's not all," Luke said ominously. "There's another thing I want to tell you."

I pushed him away just far enough to be able to stare into his watery blue eyes – in tears so like mine.

"I really want you to be happy, Mum," Luke said, his voice cracking. "Dad said it was time for you to be happy now, and that's exactly the same as what I think."

I collapsed against him. "How did you get to be so amazing?" I sobbed, pulling him tight and nuzzling his hair. "How?"

"I think I got that from you and Dad," Luke sniffed.

Eventually we separated. Jill was fidgeting from one foot to the other at the corner of my vision, and I was aware that we were running out of time. "I'll be back," I told him. "I'll be back in September, even if it's just for a visit, you know that, right?"

Luke wiped his nose on his sleeve and nodded.

"I'm so sorry, Luke," I said. "It was never meant to be like this."

"It's OK," he said, calmer now, then, amazingly, "Shit happens."

I laughed through tears. "Shit happens?" I repeated, resisting the urge to tell him off.

Luke shrugged.

"Han', we really have to go now," Jill said, checking the time on her phone.

"I know. I'll call you when we get there, OK?" I said to Luke.

He nodded again, screwed his face up against a fresh round of tears, then turned and, waving over his shoulder, ran back inside.

Jill took my arm and tried to pull me towards the car. "Come on, Sis," she said. "We have to go."

"I can't do this, Jill," I replied, and it really felt in that moment as if it was an impossibility. There seemed to be no way to separate my body, so dramatically, so geographically, from Luke.

"You *can*!" Jill said.

"I really don't think . . ."

"You can!" She laughed nervously, now pushing me towards the open car door. "It's just a flight. You'll be back in September. It's just a holiday, for god's sake. Now get in!"

I let Jill push me into the car, and I let her buckle me in. With my head twisted back in the hope of catching a final glimpse of my child, now almost a man, I let her drive me away.

But it didn't feel like a holiday at all. It felt as if I was heading to a funeral. Perhaps, even, my own.

Somehow, Jill got me into the airport terminal.

Repeating the Zen-like mantra that nothing was permanent, that I could always come back, that if I didn't leave I would never forgive myself, she led me to the check-in desk and watched with me as my bags trundled away on the conveyor belt. "There's no changing your mind now," she said.

During the ten-minute queue for security, she chatted constantly with forced joviality, saying things like, "I hope you end up staying there. Aïsha wants an Ozzie Christmas," and "I bet James takes you somewhere nice for a break the second you arrive."

But I wasn't really listening, and I wasn't really thinking about anything else instead. I just felt numb.

When finally we had to separate, Jill hugged me and said, "You know what Luke said? About you being happy? He was so right, you know."

I smiled meekly – it was all that I could manage.

"Now go," Jill said, pushing me towards the arch of the metal detector. "Go and be happy. And phone me in twenty-four hours, when you arrive. No! Phone me in twenty-five, once you've had a shag."

On the first plane, I thought about Luke and only about Luke. Again, I ran every detail I could remember through my mind's eye, torturing myself again with his birth, with the first time he called me "Mum", with his first day at school. I analysed every word he had said that morning searching for hidden meanings. He would miss me like "crazy", he had said, but was I making him actually crazy by leaving? Would we all end up in therapy because of my selfishness? I certainly felt as if I were on the verge of insanity.

I remembered Luke's first split lip, I remembered nursing him through chickenpox, I remembered the look of pride on Cliff's face the first time he managed to ride his pushbike without stabilisers, and with each thought I shed a few more tears.

I asked the hostess for more tissues, and the guy beside me, a less good-looking version of Bruce Willis, visibly edged away from me in his seat, and who could blame him?

After we had swapped planes in Dubai, my new female neighbour said, "Still, halfway there now!" And at that precise moment, something within me switched, and a huge surge of love for James, of excitement about the new life ahead of me, swept through me, energising every cell. It was as if I had completely forgotten why I was doing any of this, and now those thoughts were back, I was swamped with them. How fickle are our emotions? Perhaps it was simply a self-defence mechanism coming into play; perhaps that level of intensity of suffering – for suffering it was – is quite simply unsustainable.

Whatever the explanation, once that halfway point was behind us, I started to think less about Luke and more about James, remembering the sensation of him holding me, kissing me, lying on top of me – sliding, even, inside me. And as the pain faded and was replaced by love and joy and yes, arousal, I let myself purposely revel in those thoughts of him, of the farm, of Brisbane, of my new start.

"You look like you're happy to be going home," my neighbour said, and I realised that I had been staring out of the window and grinning. "Actually England's home," I told her. "Or it used to be, anyway."

After the final flight change in Sydney, I arrived in Brisbane feeling even worse than I had the first time around, and dragging myself through customs and passport control felt like a test of the limits of physical endurance. But then I stepped out into the airport lounge and James looked up and saw me, his expression shifting from one of utter boredom – the flight was almost three hours late – to one of downright adulation, and I couldn't help but beam back at him.

The path from where I was to where James was standing was too much to bear, so I abandoned my suitcases and ducked under the rail so that I could run into his arms. He was wearing a big sheepskin jacket and it felt like being enfolded within the arms of a vast teddy bear.

"I thought you'd never make it," he said.

"Me neither."

James gave me a peck, then went to retrieve the suitcases. When he returned, I asked, "A peck? Is that all?"

"Nope," James said. "Not at all. But not here. Come outside and see the day. It's a beaut'."

We wheeled my cases out of the airport, and I gasped at the blueness of the sky, at the stunning clarity of the light, at the freshness of the winter air, and felt the veil of depression that I had been living under for the last few months lifting already.

"Hang on there, girl," James said, and I realised that he had paused and that I had been striding ahead. I turned back to face him and smiled quizzically. He looked suddenly glassy-eyed and pale. "I've got something to say," he continued.

My grin faded a little. He looked deadly serious.

"I need to say that ... Well ... that you're single now," James said, and my heart began to plummet like a lift with a broken cable.

"Your divorce, I mean," James said, frowning as he read my expression. "It's all finalised, right?"

I grimaced in nervous relief. "Oh, yes. Yes, that's all done and dusted."

"So I ..."

"Yes?"

"Sorry but this is hard."

"What?"

James slid his hand to his pocket and pulled out a small box, and I instantly knew what was coming next.

"Will you ... ? Look ..." James stammered.

"Yes?"

262

"Look ... I ... Um ... OK. What I'm trying to say is, will you bloody marry me, Hannah?" he finally said.

It crossed my mind that this was unreasonably soon, and that I was unreasonably tired. It crossed my mind that I had sworn never to marry again. And it crossed my mind that this was the exact welcome I had been hoping for, nay, dreaming of.

"Yes, James," I said, stepping towards him. "Yes, of course, I'll bloody marry you."

FOURTEEN

Cliff

Hannah's final act before leaving was to unconsciously bust up my relationship with Rob. At least, I hope it was unconscious.

After repeated attempts at getting him to meet either Hannah or Luke, or both, I had given up and consigned the subject to the drawer of pragmatically-abandoned ideals. It had been plain to see how the idea terrified Rob, and I had realised that I was close to losing him over it. So without further discussion, I dropped the subject.

Hannah, as ever incapable of accepting anyone's point of view but her own, launched a surprise attack one Friday.

Rob had just arrived and – because he was muddy and sweaty from his working day – was in the process of stripping ready to take a shower.

By the time I had got rid of Hannah – or rather, given up trying to get rid of her and slammed the door in her face – Rob had vanished down the fire escape.

I watched in dismay from the balcony as he started his van and drove away, Hannah absurdly running behind him creating a cringe-worthy scene. From shy, closeted Rob's point of view, this was, I knew, the worst possible outcome.

I phoned Rob's mobile immediately, but he didn't answer. This was normal; he was driving. But when I phoned him again half an hour later, then once again that evening and *still* got no reply, I began to suspect the worst.

Over the following few days I left increasingly desperate messages, but things didn't improve: Rob's phone went from ringing lonely followed by voicemail, to voicemail direct – he had switched it off.

The following Tuesday I waited nervously for him to come to the house as planned, but long before the usual seven p.m. arrival time, I sensed that it was over.

Just in case he was checking his phone from time to time, I left further messages. I begged him to phone me. I promised him that I had known nothing of Hannah's visit. I told him that I missed him. I asked that, out of respect, if he was leaving me that he should at least tell me so. And finally I told him what I had never once said because until then, I hadn't realised it: that I was in love with him.

I hunted for his business on the internet and found, in addition to the defunct phone number, an e-mail address, to which I sent a long, eloquent, heartbreaking message. When he failed to reply even to this, I realised that I had reached the limits of what self-respect would allow. If he was a hard enough man to ignore *that* message, then he was too hard a man for me. He could, I muttered furiously, go fuck himself.

My final e-mail to Rob coincided almost exactly with Hannah's departure for Australia, another surprisingly traumatic event for me. If it hadn't been for Luke I think I might have had a meltdown, but following Hannah's departure, I was only too aware that the last thing Luke needed was his father falling apart. I forced myself to grin, get up and make breakfast every morning. And I held it together – just about.

At the beginning of July, Luke asked if he could bring a new friend home. Her name was Lisa and she was a pretty, quiet thirteen-year-old.

I asked Luke if she was his girlfriend and he answered, "Kind of." They had been together for a while, he said, but he hadn't said anything before because he hadn't wanted Hannah to know. That made me feel pretty special.

When I asked him if we needed to talk about the birds and the bees, Luke groaned. "Dad! I'm twelve!"

"Meaning?"

"Meaning that, A) I know all about the birds and the bees, and B) that I'm too young to do anything about it."

I laughed. "OK then!"

"The age of consent is sixteen, Dad. You can go to prison for years for doing stuff at my age!"

"Fair enough," I said, pulling a face. Even *I* hadn't known that.

Along with Billy and Karim, Lisa – another keen gamer – became an almost constant fixture around the flat that summer, and it was just as well. A house full of noisy teenagers couldn't fill the vacuum that Rob's disappearance had left in my life, but it certainly kept me busy.

Once, I caught Luke staring into the middle distance, and asked him if everything was OK. "Just thinking about Mum," he said. "It's funny that it's night-time there. It's weird. I suppose she's asleep." But other than that one incident, and the few quiet moments he would spend after each daily phone call from her, there seemed to be little evidence that he was suffering. He was twelve and he was living in the centre of town in a cool flat. He had a faithful best mate, a girlfriend and both an Xbox 360 and a PlayStation. He seemed pretty happy with his lot.

Once the term began again, Luke started spending occasional evenings at school, and to plug the gap I logged onto some dating sites again. But my heart wasn't really in it anymore. None of the guys I spoke to ever seemed as clever, or cute, or sane, or indeed, as mysterious as Rob, and without exception, I couldn't even motivate myself to go and meet them. I felt that I had somehow missed out on my destiny. I still vaguely believed that Rob would drop, once again, from a tree in front of me.

One Sunday, the day after Hannah had informed us that her September return trip would be no more than a one week visit to tie up loose ends, Luke asked me while I was cooking dinner if I missed her.

To avoid thinking too deeply about the question, I laughingly told him that I missed her lemon meringue pie, and the next evening when I got home from work, I found that Luke, Billy and Lisa had jointly cooked me one.

The kitchen looked like a bomb had hit it, and though the pastry was uncooked and the meringue was the texture of an omelette, I had tears in my eyes as I carved out four slices, because they were slices not of dodgy pie, but of love, offered to me by my son, and it hit me then how close I had come to losing him; it struck me in that moment that, wife or no wife, partner or no partner, the fact that Luke had wanted unveeringly to stay by my side made me the proudest, luckiest man on the planet. "You're amazing, Luke," I croaked. "You're the best son anyone could have."

THE END (ALMOST)

267

POSTSCRIPT: CLIFF

By October, Hannah had been back, shipped her remaining possessions to Australia, tied up all of her loose ends, and once again tearfully departed. Our old house had been put on the market because despite the fall in house prices, we both just wanted to get rid of it. Hannah needed the money, and I needed the mental space that the house was still occupying.

One night, I got home from work and found Luke not, as expected, playing video games with Billy, nor watching TV with Lisa, but lying in the dark in his bedroom. I switched on the light and Luke looked up at me glumly. It was immediately obvious that something was wrong, and I assumed that the Hannah crisis which I had long been expecting had finally arrived.

I sat on the end of his bed and jiggled his socked foot. "What's up, Champ?" I asked.

Luke sighed.

"No Billy tonight?"

"He's gone to the cinema with Sue."

"And Lisa?"

Luke raised an eyebrow. "With Greg, I expect."

"Greg?"

"Her new boyfriend. A sixth former. He's got a car."

"Ah," I said. "Hence the long face."

"Hence the long face," Luke repeated.

"Anything I can do to cheer you up?"

Luke shook his head.

"You'll get over her, you know," I told him. "I know it doesn't feel like that now, but you will."

"Well, *yeah*!" Luke said. "Of *course* I will."

Once dinner was served, I called him to the table. He slouched from his room and then slumped opposite me before proceeding to prod his dinner with a fork. "Omelette? Again?" he said.

"There's nothing else in. I'll go shopping tomorrow," I promised.

"We had omelette last night. And the night before."

"No, we had that salmon thing last night."

"Well we still have omelette almost every night."

"Luke!" I said. "Just eat it or don't eat it. I don't care."

"Sorry," he said, sitting up and beginning to eat.

"You're allowed to be a bit grumpy tonight," I said softly. "But don't push your luck."

"Sure. Sorry."

"Are you upset about Lisa?"

Luke shrugged, then frowned and said, "Maybe." Then, unexpectedly, he asked, "What happened to Rob?"

I looked up at him in surprise. "I . . . I don't know really. He sort of vanished."

"He *vanished*?"

"Yes. He went off and never came back."

"You must have called him."

"I did. But his number changed."

"Lisa stopped answering too," Luke said. "That's how I knew something was wrong."

"That's nasty," I commented.

269

I went round to see her," Luke went on. "But she wouldn't see me. Greg was there."

"Yuck. What did you say?"

"Nothing. I just came home. Did you ever go see Rob?"

"No. I never even knew where he lived."

"Wrecclesham," Luke said.

I swallowed hard and blinked at him. "I'm sorry?"

"They live on that Wrecclesham estate."

"How can *you* know where Rob lives?" I asked, my heart beginning to race.

"How can you *not* know?" Luke asked.

"Well he never told me, for one. Really? Do you *really* know where he lives?"

Luke nodded. "He's Tracey Ben's dad, isn't he. They live next door to that academy school."

"Weydon?"

"Yeah."

"But how do you know Tracey Ben?"

"She used to be friends with Lisa," Luke said. "She used to have really wicked parties round there, but I think they fell out over some stupid shoes or something."

The next evening after work I drove to Weydon school, and after less than five minutes of searching in ever-increasing circles, I spotted Rob's van parked on a driveway. I added his new number – written on the van – to my phone, but then returned home without calling. I wanted to speak to him face to face.

The next morning I got up early and drove to Rob's. I watched from the end of the close until, at eight, Rob left his house. From a distance, my heart thumping, I tailed him to a golf club in Alresford. I watched him park up, unload his ladder, strap himself into a harness and begin to climb a tree before I approached him. I didn't want him to be able to run away too easily.

"Rob!" I called. He paused, turned to look down at me, then said quite calmly, pleasantly almost, "Cliff! What on Earth are you doing here?"

"Hoping to talk to you," I replied.

Rob climbed back down and invited me to sit in the van – it was starting to spot with rain.

He was as beautiful as ever, and his proximity within the van was hard to bear. Despite everything that had happened, all I really wanted was to kiss him again.

"So what brings you here?" he asked.

I explained that Luke had revealed his whereabouts and that I had tailed him.

"Very cloak-and-dagger," Rob said. "I'm impressed."

"So what happened, Rob?" I asked.

He shrugged. "I was freaked when your ex turned up. And when you kept calling, I lost the plot and threw my phone in a pond."

"Why?"

"Stupidity?" Rob said. "It cost me over three hundred quid to replace it."

"But you know were I live," I said. "You could have come round."

"I'm sorry, Cliff," Rob said. "But I realised we were getting too close."

"Too close? How could we be *too close*?"

"Someone was gonna find out sooner or later. I couldn't risk it. And if Luke knows Tracey, well . . . I wasn't far wrong, was I? He didn't tell her, did he? About us?"

271

I shook my head. "He's a model of discretion."

"I missed you though," Rob said.

"Really?"

"Loads. Did you miss me?" he asked, reaching out to stroke my arm.

I laughed sourly. "You have no idea," I said.

"Maybe we could have another bash," Rob said. "I have more free time now, so . . ."

"Another bash?"

Rob grinned at me cheekily.

"Why do you have more free time?"

"Anne left me," he said. "She went off with some arsehole from down the road."

"Really?"

"Really!"

"What happened? Did she find out?"

"Nope," Rob said. "That's the best bit. She just fucked off one day. So I didn't even have to tell her."

Though we started seeing each other again on the same Tuesday and Thursday nights as before, and though it was in every way as pleasant an experience, I refused to let myself fold into the relationship this time around. Rob had proven that whatever was given could be taken away without notice, and as he remained as closeted as ever – he still refused to meet Luke – I protected myself by remaining wary, by staying detached.

Only once did I broach the subject of Rob's lack of honesty with his kids, asking him if he didn't feel that it was spoiling their relationship, inhibiting their ability to be close to him.

"From a bloke who spent the last fifteen years lying to everyone about everything, that's a bit rich," was Rob's reply, and I couldn't really argue with that.

Luke fell out with his friend Billy over Christmas, and then made up again in March. Karim moved away to Birmingham. Brenda, Billy's mum, split up with Sue, her partner, got back, amazingly, with Billy's dad, and then after less than a month went back to Sue again. Billy camped at ours throughout. Come springtime, Luke got back with Lisa then split up all over again. He dated Petra, then Kelly, then Petra again, and then a new dark-haired beauty called Laura, who bit her nails so much that her fingers bled.

Hannah came and went, bringing gifts of Macadamia nuts and jars of Vegemite that no one ate, telling farm stories and occasionally even going up at the end of her sentences like a true Australian. She was still trying to tempt Luke out there for visits, and he still wasn't going for the bait.

Our old house sold, and the partnership I worked in was bought out by a big London firm; my boss was promptly fired and I was promoted to managing director.

The seasons came and went, and the trees sprouted green, then turned to amber, and as Luke's girlfriends came and went, and as everything around me changed incessantly, only two things remained constant: my relationship with my son, and the clockwork regularity of Rob's visits.

I had almost started to relax into the rhythm of our relationship, almost managed to suspend my disbelief, when one day, a week before Luke's fourteenth birthday, I glanced at the clock and said to Rob, "You had better be going. Luke will be back at eight."

Rob shot me a strange, almost defiant glance, pulled a

cushion to his chest and settled into the sofa. "I think I'll stay tonight, if that's OK," he said.

"But Luke gets back in half an hour," I explained, frowning, thinking that he had somehow misunderstood me.

"Yeah," Rob murmured without averting his gaze from the TV screen. He fidgeted then slumped even further into the settee. "You said."

I watched him pretending to be engrossed in the television for a moment, then smiled vaguely and said, "Oh, OK then."

"That's OK, right?" Rob asked, half-glancing at me. "You don't mind?"

"No," I said, slipping into a wry grin. "No, I don't mind at all."

"Good," Rob said, then, "So what's for tea?"

POSTSCRIPT: HANNAH

I spent most of my summer break cooking and cleaning and fixing up the farm house. I sanded down doors and repainted walls; I stuck back fallen bath tiles and made vast pots of stew for the men.

I was missing Luke like crazy, but keeping busy helped, so I turned into a whirlwind of domestic efficiency. Every morning I would phone him, and after a few weeks this actually started to ease my pain rather than exacerbate it.

For my birthday, James drove us to Cairns, a funny, two-storey kind of a town surrounded by rainforests and vast golden beaches, all of which seemed unusable for one reason or another. Some had salties (saltwater crocodiles) and others scorpions or snakes or jellyfish. "I know, it's a jungle out there," James joked when I complained.

We smothered ourselves with mosquito cream and marvelled at the views. We wandered along the seafront and browsed the ubiquitous opal jewellery in every shop.

On the final day we took a three-hour sailing trip out to the Great Barrier Reef where, with nothing more than a mask and snorkel, I saw the most beautiful fish I have ever seen in any TV documentary. It was like swimming in a fish tank.

Afterwards, the crew cooked us all fresh fish and served it as we soared back over the waves towards Cairns, the sea spray lashing my face and salting my food. I had never felt so alive.

By the end of summer everything had become clear to me. I liked my life on the farm, and I loved James more than ever. I had fallen in love with Australia too.

I missed Luke so much that at times it was almost unbearable, but it was a pain I was learning, through force of circumstance, to live with. He seemed happy and contented living with Cliff, even, I suspected, happier and more settled than before I left. Being forced to alternate between the two of us had been difficult for him, I now realised. So yes, it was painful, but for my new life, for James, for Cliff and yes, for Luke too, that pain was a sacrifice I felt that I had to bear.

When I got back to Surrey that September, the divorce decree was waiting for me on the doormat. I had dinner with Cliff, Luke and Jill in a swanky Italian restaurant, and we managed to enjoy ourselves, even managed to laugh, if a little wryly, about our disastrous holiday in France.

I spent a final week closing bank accounts, changing forwarding addresses and preparing a final packing case of belongings to ship to Australia before another heartbreaking departure. Only this time, I had no doubts. This time Jill didn't need to push me into the car.

When I got back to Brisbane with my divorce papers, James immediately asked me again if I would marry him and this we discreetly did at the Brisbane Registry not two weeks later. We asked a single person, James' employee Giovanni, to be present as witness. Both of us had been married before, and neither of us wanted to make a fuss. The simplicity of the ceremony didn't stop it being one of the most beautiful days of my life.

My life in Brissie, as I now called it, was full of new experiences, which, though unexciting to some, seemed wonderful to me. I got a part-time secretarial job with a local fruit wholesaler, helping with his accounts, and I worked around the farm whenever I could. I became an Indigenous Community Volunteer and ended up helping out at a women's resource centre, fundraising and even giving sewing classes to Aboriginal women. If I couldn't undo the harm that had been done by my ancestors, I could at least try to ease their pain; I could at least resist becoming yet another white person who "didn't think much" about indigenous Australians.

I watched James birth cows and hand rear a rejected calf. I worked, stickily, alongside the men when the mango harvest came around and smothered myself with insect lotion in the evenings so that I could sit outside and read. Life was busy and physically exhausting, but full of cuddles and laughter and sex, and with every day that passed, I felt surer that I had made the right decision.

The human brain isn't, I think, that good at capturing change. We're unable to sense ourselves getting older, so we notice it in steps, when birthdays hit multiples of ten, or when we're suddenly too old for a young person's railcard or when a young girl in a nightclub is suddenly shocked that we are still able, at our great age, to dance.

Equally, we don't necessarily notice when we're demolishing and rebuilding our lives. It all seems like chaos and mayhem as everything is pulled apart, and then like a series of tiny, exhausting steps as something new is built.

One day I received a postcard from Luke addressed to myself and James at the farm, telling me excitedly that he had finally met Rob, Cliff's partner, and that he was "very cool". Seeing my name there associated with James and the farm and Australia in my fourteen-year-old son's hand made me realise that I had made it. Step by step, I had built a whole new life for myself. Those steps had involved pain and sacrifice and joy, but everything was now as it should be for everyone concerned. All seemed right with the world with one exception.

Though missing Luke got easier with time, and sometimes his absence no longer hurt at all, on other days I would see a child who looked like him or catch the tail end of *The Simpsons* and remember watching it with him, and the distress would intensify and, again, feel crippling – like an actual hole through my heart.

At such times, I did my best to force a smile and carry on. I threw myself at farm tasks and cooked two-gallon pots of stew for the men. But if we hadn't found a better solution, I think something within me would have died. I don't think I could ever have been whole again without my son in my life.

Luckily, as a result of persistent coaxing and a constant stream of luscious photos sent to Luke's e-mail address, he eventually, after two years, capitulated and agreed to come out for a visit.

I involved everyone in my plan to ensure that he would want to return, and in the three weeks he stayed, he drove tractors with Giovanni, went horse riding with Charlie, climbed the Glasshouse Mountains with me, learned to ride a motorbike around the farm, and went wind surfing with James.

By the time the holidays came to an end, I thought, looking at his sun-tanned face and his relaxed smile, that we had cracked it. With Luke being an adolescent, I couldn't, of course, be one hundred per cent sure.

Right now, here I am, standing in Brisbane Airport, and sure enough, here he is, my flesh, my blood – my Luke – coming through passport control and pointing me out to his new girlfriend, Charlotte, at his side.

A visit from time to time isn't *enough*, of course, but it's so, *so* much that I can barely stand the emotion. I squint at Luke through blurry tears of joy, and James, beside me, says, "There he is!" and squeezes my hand, and I know, finally, once and for all, that everything is as good as it can be.

"Mum!" Luke shouts, and I cry and smile and wave.

"Hello, son," I say.

Other fiction titles from Black & White Publishing

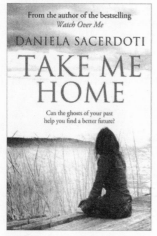

From the author of the bestselling
Watch Over Me

DANIELA SACERDOTI

TAKE ME
HOME

Can the ghosts of your past
help you find a better future?

Take Me Home
Daniela Sacerdoti
RRP £7.99 – 978 1 84502 746 9

Heartbreaking and uplifting, *Take Me Home* is a beautiful story of love, loss and never forgetting who you really are.

Inary Monteith's life is at a crossroads. After a stolen night with her close friend Alex, she's just broken his heart by telling him it was all a terrible mistake. Then she has to rush home from London to the Scottish Highlands when her little sister's illness suddenly worsens – and in returning she must confront the painful memories she has been trying so hard to escape.

Back home, things become more complicated than she could ever have imagined. There's her sister's illness, her hostile brother, a smug ex she never wants to see again and her conflicted feelings about Alex in London and a handsome American she meets in Glen Avich. On top of that, she mysteriously loses her voice but regains a strange gift from her childhood – a sixth sense that runs in her family. And when a voice from the past keeps repeating, 'Take me home', she discovers a mystery that she knows she must unlock to set herself free.

Take Me Home is a beautiful story of love, loss, discovering one's true abilities and, above all, never forgetting who you really are.

www.blackandwhitepublishing.com

Watch Over Me
Daniela Sacerdoti
RRP £7.99 – 978 1 84502 528 1

Eilidh Lawson's life has hit crisis point. Years of failed fertility treatments, a cheating husband and an oppressive family have pushed her to the limit. Desperate for relief, Eilidh seeks solace in the only place she's ever felt at home – a small village in the Scottish Highlands. There, Eilidh slowly begins to mend her broken heart but soon learns she is not the only one in the village struggling to recover from a painful past.

Jamie McAnena, Eilidh's childhood friend, is trying to raise his daughter Maisie alone. After Maisie's mother left to pursue a career in London and Jamie's own mother, Elizabeth, passed away, he has resigned himself to being a family of two.

But sometimes there is more to a story than meets the eye. Despite their reluctance, curious circumstances keep bringing Jamie and Eilidh together. For even when it seems all is lost, help can come from the most surprising places.

An ethereal and beautifully written debut novel, *Watch Over Me* is a poignant story about letting go and moving on – with a little bit of help from beyond the grave.

www.blackandwhitepublishing.com

"Soulful and stunningly written, this reads like a future classic."
LISA JEWELL

His Father's Son
Tony Black
RRP £11.99 – 978 1 84502 636 3

Australia is the Lucky Country, and Joey Driscol knows it. It's a far cry from his native Ireland, but he believes this is the place he and his wife can make a new life and forget the troubles of the past. And for a time, they do just that. There's a good life, a new house, regular work and, in time, they welcome their new son Marti into the world.

But as the years pass, this new life thousands of miles from the Old Country comes under threat. Joey's wife has been struggling with demons of her own, their marriage is on the rocks and suddenly, Joey's wife disappears and takes Marti with her. Joey is beside himself, with no clues about where they are, with both his childhood sweetheart and his son – his pride and joy – now missing.

Then, when Joey gets word that his wife and son have returned to Ireland, he knows that he'll now have to do the same if he ever wants to see his son again. And he also knows that he'll finally have to confront the ghosts of his past that he's been running from for years.

His Father's Son is a touching and beautiful story of a family struggling to come to terms with their past, their present and an uncertain future.

www.blackandwhitepublishing.com